To Tempt
a Viscount

by

Naomi Boom

To Tempt a Viscount

Cover Art by *RJ Morris*

The Wild Rose Press, Inc.
PO Box 708
Adams Basin, NY 14410-0708
Visit us at www.thewildrosepress.com

Publishing History
First Tea Rose Edition, 2017
Print ISBN 978-1-5092-1174-6
Digital ISBN 978-1-5092-1175-3

Published in the United States of America

"Are you sure you are a gentleman?"

Laura asked derisively. She immediately regretted her impulsive retort. He was just too near to her for her mind to perform rationally, otherwise she was sure she would have behaved herself.

One eyebrow lifted in question as he grinned wickedly. "Are you asking me not to conduct myself as a gentleman?"

His dark smile and wicked words made Laura pause as she stared at his lips, so near to her own. Her stomach was in knots, and she did not know if she should slap him or kiss him. She had never been kissed, but right now, she wanted his lips on hers more than anything. In Laura's heart of hearts, she wished, just a little bit, that he would not behave as a gentleman. She could not form words, however, and only managed to shake her head slightly as common sense prevailed.

"In that case, my dear, I suggest you run along." His feet moved silently as he stepped away from her, but Laura could not budge until he growled, "Go, or we both shall regret what happens."

Dedication

Thank you to all who did not
laugh at my idea to write a novel.
Without your support,
this never could have happened.
And to my incredibly supportive husband:
Go Dawgs!

Chapter 1

Lady Laura Rosing sighed as she watched the landscape fly past. She was typically a perpetual optimist, but in this instance, her positive nature was waning from sheer exhaustion. She had been restricted to this small, uncomfortably bumpy cabin for the better part of the day and sincerely wanted out.

"I just know the maid forgot to pack my paints, and then what? How will I occupy my time?" a shrill voice asked from across the confined carriage.

And then there was *her*. Laura's cousin, Miss Eleanor Ashford. Eleanor happened to preside as both Laura's best and worst friend and right now, was annoying Laura to her limits.

Laura spoke in neutral tones, despite her ever-increasing irritation with Eleanor. One simply could not travel with her for this long without some annoyance. "If there are no paints available, I am sure you can find something else to occupy your time once we reach Glendale."

"Such as?" Eleanor asked coolly. Her vivid blue eyes appeared glacial as she eyed Laura with skepticism.

"Such as mingling with the guests." Eleanor was, after all, used to being the center of attention and, if Laura were to hazard a guess, loved it.

"No one can be expected to socialize all day,

especially if the other guests are not quite the thing."

Her cousin smoothed back her light blonde hair, even though it was already perfectly coiffed. Laura knew her own light brown hair looked tragic in comparison, but she also did not wish to bother repairing it when the bumps of the road would ensure it remained a mess.

When Laura did not respond to her comment, Eleanor brought her blue eyes back to Laura's own violet eyes and smirked. "You know, I daresay I practiced socializing with the riffraff just last season. What was his name again? You know the gentleman I speak of."

A spark ignited within Laura as she began to see red. She clenched her hands into little fists and inhaled slowly in an attempt to calm her temper. The gentleman was Lord Harding and had been the man Laura thought she would one day marry. But that was before he met Eleanor, who promptly stole him away from Laura and then discarded him when she grew bored of his attentions.

Laura smiled blandly after she successfully reined in her temper. "I am afraid I cannot recall."

"Of course you can." Eleanor thoughtfully tapped her chin with a long, well-manicured fingernail. "If only I could remember…Oh! I know. His name is Lord Harding."

The interior of the already small carriage was suddenly much more imprisoning. Laura knew she should behave herself, but she could only be pushed so far. "You call him riffraff? Does your father not hold the same title as Lord Harding?"

An unusually cat-like shriek emitted from

Eleanor's lips, and Laura was positive she would pounce on Laura. Of course, neither of the girls was unladylike enough to engage in anything so uncouth, but sometimes Laura dearly wished to.

"Girls." A stern voice interrupted the tiff, which signaled Mrs. Westfield had awoken from her nap.

Eleanor's sour mien changed instantaneously as she regarded her aunt. Her lips turned upward into a charming smile. "Did you have a good rest, Aunt?"

Mrs. Westfield grumpily muttered, "Yes, until you two woke me up. What is the matter, girls?"

"I fear the maid neglected to pack my paints," Eleanor said with downcast eyes.

"You poor dear." Mrs. Westfield patted her hand sympathetically. "I am sure there will be paints at Glendale."

"That is precisely what I said," Laura piped in. "Or if all else fails, I could give a recommendation on worthwhile reading materials." She especially enjoyed reading novels deemed romantic drivel and occasionally read more appropriate material for ladies her age. Her current interest was ancient Egypt, but any ancient civilization piqued her imagination.

Eleanor snuck a glare at Laura, and Laura responded with a cheery smile. Laura had gotten the last word in before Mrs. Westfield awoke and was now in a generous mood.

Just then, the carriage hit a bump, and Laura could not help the words that issued forth. "Bloody hell." Covering her mouth, she grimaced. She was not supposed to know such words, but she liked to read, and certain things were unavoidable in the good books.

"Laura!" Mrs. Westfield said, aghast.

"Forgive me, Mrs. Westfield. I do not know what overcame me."

Mrs. Westfield simply shook her head in exasperation and closed her eyes.

"It appears riffraff can be found in all classes," Eleanor whispered as she smiled a gloating smile.

Even though Eleanor's father held the title of baron while Laura's held the superior title of earl, Eleanor always knew how to make Laura feel inferior. Laura could either continue the fight or ignore Eleanor by looking out the window. Laura chose to give her attention to the window and relaxed into the cushion behind her. After all, ignoring Eleanor was almost better than a witty rejoinder.

Reaching up to her temples, Laura tried to rub away the headache that was slowly developing. She had been stuck in this carriage for the greater part of the day and was ready to reach Glendale. She could view only so many trees before they all looked the same, so the window was not a good distraction.

Her gaze shifted to a large manor mostly obscured by the endless number of trees. They had finally reached their destination. The sun was sinking, but some of the gardens that surrounded the house were still visible as well as a brook, which wended its way behind the house. The colors of fall were on full display, but she would have to wait for daylight to truly appreciate their beauty.

"Finally," Mrs. Westfield said with a small smile. "I thought our trip would never end."

Laura did not speak but signaled her agreement with a tired smile. They had departed London that morning to attend a house party in the country. The

Songfeld house party was an exclusive event, and Laura should be excited about attending such a sought-after social gathering, but she could not seem to rise to that feeling. Truthfully, Laura would have preferred a solo visit to the country where she could relax with *uninterrupted* reading and riding.

The ladies were greeted by a pair of liveried footmen who helped them descend from the tiresome carriage. Laura regarded the manor, built in a charming Tudor style, which had possibly existed since the style was popular. The size of it, however, gave it an intimidating aura, which Laura hoped would not extend within.

A friendly-looking butler swung open the heavy oaken door and immediately led the ladies to their chambers. Laura sank on to her bed and pried the gloves from her hands. Her skin felt as if it were caked in dirt, but she was too tired to wash tonight. Instead, she closed her eyes in hope of warding away her headache and laid her head gently on the pillow. The yellow theme of her room was somewhat soothing, but nothing would work as well as a nap to take her pain away.

****

Laura stretched and sat up. Her nagging headache was no longer plaguing her. She had napped longer than expected, if the silence of the house and the light of the moon were any indication. Her gaze drifted about the room in search of water, which was still disappointingly absent. Her room was charmingly decorated but appeared to be lacking in refreshments, which a maid should have remedied long ago. Unfortunately, her own maid had likely been commandeered by Eleanor for the night. Eleanor had a frustrating tendency to forget that the maid they shared was shared between them.

As her eyes searched the room, she caught her reflection in the mirror and cringed at the sight. Her hair was a mess, and the grime from the road still soiled her travel garments. She ought to rectify her appearance immediately, but she could not undertake such a task without first procuring a drink.

Laura exited her room into the darkened hallway without making a sound. The other guests were likely sleeping, so she hurried silently on her way to the kitchens. Each light step she took brought her closer to the water that would soothe her parched throat, and she was confident she would find her way downstairs and back without meeting anyone on the way.

The kitchen was empty and almost identical to every other kitchen she had stepped foot in. She exhaled an unwittingly pent-up breath and snared some water and a chunk of bread from the bread box. Laura then began the short walk to her room. She had begun to ascend the stairs when she spied a room that looked suspiciously like a library.

A good book would be just the thing. She changed her course and surreptitiously stepped over to the inlaid bookshelves. She held her candle up to the array of tomes in an attempt to find a book that looked even remotely interesting. Her eyes settled on a volume of Shakespeare's work, *Hamlet*, and she procured it before she turned to leave the library. The soft tread of her feet abruptly stopped as a loud thump sounded from the hallway. The world seemed to freeze around her as Laura stood still, waiting silently in the darkness for the threat to pass.

A large, intimidating figure stood framed in the doorway. She feared the erratic thumps of her heart would betray her apprehension as the notorious Lord Farris stepped into the library. He had clearly just come in from the outdoors, as he was still attired in his greatcoat and perfectly polished Hessian boots. The smell of the frigid fall air and an enticing male scent of horses and cigars wafted to where Laura was standing. Her nostrils flared slightly as she caught the pleasant aroma, but aside from that one slight movement, she remained rooted in her place.

Lord Farris stood momentarily still in the door frame. His bold, dark eyebrows slanted across his face above dark and foreboding eyes, which currently assessed her. Laura had never been so nervous in her life or more annoyed that she was now alone with a renowned rake.

"Well, well, what do we have here?" he lazily drawled as his eyes took in her fully-clothed, albeit messy, figure. His appraising look changed to a charming smile. "Tell me your name, darling."

Laura stood transfixed as a smile transformed his face. The stirrings of an unfamiliar emotion began to build in her stomach, but she shook herself from her trance. She absolutely detested rakes. Not that she had met many, but she had seen Lord Farris at a ball once and had been ashamed for the multitudes of women who had swooned over him. Rakes held no allure for her, especially alone at night. "I will not," she finally said frigidly as she stepped toward the door. "Now, kindly remove yourself from my path so I may leave."

Lord Farris ignored her request and bowed elegantly. "Well, let me start off the introductions then.

I am Lord Farris." Somehow his demeanor managed to convey what an honor it was to meet him, all while acting as though he did not care.

Laura continued her approach until she was standing in front of him. Placing a hand firmly on her hip, she looked up at him and said haughtily, "I guess we are bypassing all rules of etiquette tonight."

He appeared to consider her words momentarily until a smirk appeared on his overly handsome face. "*All* rules?"

Blood rushed to Laura's face as she processed the meaning of his words. She had never been so insulted in her life. For once, she wished Eleanor was here. Her cousin would know just what to say to a cad such as Lord Farris.

Laura did not want to be the sort to crumble in the face of adversity, so she mustered her courage and said, "Hardly, my lord. A lady does not do such things."

He raised a skeptical eyebrow at her while his eyes skimmed her from head to foot. "A lady?"

She stiffened. Why was he questioning her status? She knew her appearance was somewhat lacking presently, but she was certainly a lady. Anger coursed through her, overtaking common sense and her tongue. "Yes, a lady. And this lady knows you are not as attractive as you think, so please remove yourself from my path."

Lord Farris's dark eyes bored into hers before he stepped predatorily closer to her. He gazed down at her with his dark, smoldering eyes and said, "You do not truly believe that. Judging by your dilated pupils and the blush on your skin, you find me incredibly attractive."

Laura scoffed and backed up a step. She needed room to breathe. "You would like that, wouldn't you?" She gulped nervously as his eyes narrowed, and he took a step closer to her. Naturally, she continued to reverse her step until her back hit the bookcase.

He smiled as he slowly removed the glass of water from her hand and set it on the bookcase. He then brought his hands to either side of her and leaned in until their faces were mere inches apart. "Yes, I would like that very much. Unfortunately, I am too much of a gentleman to act on our mutual attraction."

As he spoke, Laura could not seem to take her eyes away from his full lips, at least until his words sank in. Her eyes regained their focus as she realized he was standing much too near. This was precisely why she preferred normal gentlemen. They did not act strangely.

"Are you sure you are a gentleman?" Laura asked derisively. She immediately regretted her impulsive retort. He was just too near to her for her mind to perform rationally, otherwise she was sure she would have behaved herself.

One eyebrow lifted in question as he grinned wickedly. "Are you asking me not to conduct myself as a gentleman?"

His dark smile and wicked words made Laura pause as she stared at his lips, so near to her own. Her stomach was in knots, and she did not know if she should slap him or kiss him. She had never been kissed, but right now, she wanted his lips on hers more than anything. In Laura's heart of hearts, she wished, just a little bit, that he would not behave as a gentleman. She could not form words, however, and only managed to shake her head slightly as common sense prevailed.

"In that case, my dear, I suggest you run along." His feet moved silently as he stepped away from her, but Laura could not budge until he growled, "Go, or we both shall regret what happens."

Her feet grew wings as she flew out the door and down the dark hallway. As she rounded a corner, she realized she had left her water on the bookshelf, although her bread and book were still clutched in her other hand. No matter how strong her thirst, she would never return downstairs now. Not when he was there.

****

"Please tell me you found the brandy."

Lord Farris turned to acknowledge his best friend, Lord Maxon Collins, as he entered the library. "Of course I did. It is not a bad vintage, either."

"Thank heavens. This house party would be insufferable without extra fortitude."

"Indeed," Lord Farris said gravely. "Could you imagine dealing with the unmarried misses sober?"

A derisive snort filled the room, and Lord Collins shook his golden head as his blue eyes showed their horror. "Absolutely not, and if that were ever an expectation, I think I would prefer life as a hermit."

Normally, Lord Farris would agree, but his brief interlude with a mysterious woman this very night had overtaken his senses. Although the lady did not qualify as an unmarried miss, he had still been completely sober while dealing with her. Her attire had suggested she was a poor relation, acting as a companion to some benevolent lady, but somehow she had enchanted him more than any eligible miss ever could.

Her violet eyes and light chestnut hair had been inviting in a way that even his mistress could not compare to. He frowned as he thought of her curves. Her bottom had been well-rounded, but she was not as shapely as he normally preferred. For her, however, he did not think he minded. Unfortunately, the woman was beyond his reach. She served as a companion, which was basically a member of the servant class, and he would never prey on a woman who was not in a position to say no.

"Ahem."

Lord Farris's musings were interrupted, and he glanced irritably at Lord Collins. "Yes?"

"Did I interrupt something?"

He had no desire to betray his brief interlude with a woman who was basically a servant, and instead said with a grin, "Why, yes. I was just remembering the merry widow, Lady Robbins. These next two weeks without her will be arduous, indeed."

Lord Collins smiled mockingly. "Small wonder you did not procure an invitation for her. Two weeks is a long time, and I wonder how you will survive."

His brandy burned a trail down his throat as he took a long drink. "Joke all you want, but I am hardly the only one that wishes to enjoy her favors. I would not be surprised if she had found my replacement by the time I return to town."

"I am sure you have nothing to worry about." Both gentlemen were considered among the most handsome gentlemen of the *ton* and were certainly the tallest. Lord Collins sat down on one of the chairs next to the roaring fire and groaned. "Why do they have to make such dainty chairs? This is the study. They should leave such contraptions in the parlor for the women."

Lord Farris chuckled and pushed off from the wall

he had been leaning on. "That would be much too sensible. We gentlemen can just stand all the time." His eyes shifted to a similarly fragile-looking sofa, and he smirked. "Or maybe it is just the Songfelds' way of dissuading us from using the furniture for nefarious reasons." Now that he thought of it, he realized the mystery woman would have looked remarkably delicious sprawled on the sofa in a state of dishabille. He shook his head. Such thoughts would not do. She was too far beneath him and not in the literal way he would prefer.

The wind howled outside, as if it were offering its own foreboding message of the future. Neither gentleman heeded its warning. Rather they downed the remainder of their drinks and Lord Collins stood. Lord Collins patted Lord Farris on the back and said, "I am sure you hit the nail on the head. Why should they throw a house party and expect anyone to enjoy themselves?"

Chapter 2

The morning dawned bright and clear. The subtle chill of winter's approach prickled Laura's nose as she stepped outside in the cold autumn air. She looked forward to this time of year, even though winter was symbolically a time of death. She always viewed it as a warm and promising time when people gathered together against the cold.

She had dressed in her well-used riding habit, which Eleanor was perpetually trying to convince her to throw away. Laura had even caught Eleanor red-handed as she ordered the maid to burn it. Eleanor usually did not bother with Laura's style, but neither did Laura. She loved her dress, and she would keep it.

Eleanor herself owned a beautiful riding habit, one almost every other lady envied. Unfortunately, Laura did not find it practical. She tried to ride almost daily and could not imagine wearing a stylishly immobile riding habit. Her vigorous rides were a time when she could clear her mind and enjoy life free from any worries, after working out her problems on horseback. This morning's ride would be no different and would involve intense reflection on her newest problem—her confrontation with Lord Farris.

Laura scowled as chagrin overtook her. She had responded most disappointingly to the gentleman's rakish behavior. The excitement from his mere presence alone had left her enthralled. Then she had practically begged him to kiss her. She could only imagine what would have transpired if he had given in to their mutual attraction and her silent plea.

Her cheeks heated at the thought. To think a gentleman such as Lord Farris had found her attractive. He had even admitted his attraction for her, not that Laura cared. He was still a rake, and rakes were unacceptable. Now, if only her body actually agreed with that notion.

A groom prepared a spirited little mare and helped Laura mount. She was an expert rider and had spent her childhood with a carefully selected mare at her disposal. Even though she had spent her youth with Eleanor's family, her father had always ensured she had a horse at her disposal. As the daughter of an earl who loved horses, Laura had begun her infatuation with riding early.

"Let us get started then," Laura soothingly whispered to the mare. "How about we head over to that copse of trees over there?" She loosened her hold on the reins and allowed the mare to pick its pace. The mare broke into a smooth canter that sent a tingle of exhilaration down Laura's spine. The icy wind on her face and through her hair reminded her what freedom was. Nothing could ruin this magical moment, nothing.

"Whoa, there!" A commanding voice pealed out next to her as a hand shot out and grabbed her horse's bridle. Much to Laura's dismay, it was Lord Farris, and he was slowing her horse to a stop.

"What do you think you are doing?" Laura demanded.

Lord Farris quirked a stern eyebrow at Laura, while

firmly holding her horse's bridle. "Obviously, I am rescuing you." His tone suggested he was exasperated with her, although Laura could not comprehend why. He was the high-handed one here. "I saw your horse take off on you. I cannot imagine what possessed the groom to give you that mare. She is much too high-spirited for a lady such as yourself."

Laura could not believe her ears. Apparently, women were incapable of riding horses in Lord Farris's world. Disdain dripped from Laura's voice as she said, "My mare did not run away on me. I happen to excel at riding and had everything under control until you appeared to ruin my ride."

"I find it hard to believe you had everything under control, madam. I saw the mare take off and witnessed you shaking. Either your horse was out of control, or you were in need of medical attention. Whatever the case, I am now at your service." Lord Farris gave a smart little bow, somehow very elegantly from atop his horse.

He would bow perfectly from atop his horse, and even more infuriating, he looked perfectly put together. The wind was quite gusty, yet his hair remained completely unaffected.

He seemed so very in control of everything around him, and Laura wanted to change that. "I was enjoying myself immensely on my *very* controlled ride. That shaking you saw was simply a shiver of excitement. While I appreciate the effort on your part, in the future I ask that you leave me alone."

She was thoroughly fed up with the encounter, and Laura jerked the reins which caused Lord Farris to lose his hold on the bridle. His handsome demeanor remained stoic despite her set-down, which was no surprise to her as she was coming to realize the man had no heart. No one should be as handsome as this infuriating man. If only his personality matched his looks.

Lord Farris smiled patronizingly at her. "A mere thank you would suffice. No one will fault you for getting caught on a runaway mount."

With a cry of indignation, Laura breathed in a calming breath before realizing her argument was futile. He was not going to listen to a word she said. She gritted her teeth and said, "I suppose I can thank you, my lord."

He nodded and smiled charmingly. "In that case, I will accept my duty and accompany you for the rest of your ride. Just to ensure your horse does not run again."

Laura gripped the reins until her knuckles turned white in an attempt to remain calm. The typical gentleman would have no trouble believing her when she said she had everything under control. Why did this oaf have such a difficult time grasping the idea that she was capable? Continuing to ride with such a gentleman was not something Laura desired, and she tried to dissuade him with rational argument.

"I really do not think it wise to ride with you, my lord. We have no chaperone."

He appeared to consider her quietly for a moment, and then said plainly, "I cannot imagine anyone would care."

"What do you mean?" Laura asked, confused, and then rushed on to say, "Never mind. I shall be riding toward those trees, and you can ride anywhere else."

"You mean you do not yearn for my company?" he

asked, appearing unfazed by her dismissal.

"I think not. As I mentioned previously, we do not have a chaperone, and I will not be missing my ride."

Lord Farris exhaled slowly and then swept his hand out before him. "By all means, my dear, please get on with your ride then."

The horse seemed to sense Laura's desire to get as much space as possible between herself and Lord Farris and broke into a canter. She truly had the worst of luck, running into Lord Farris in the library and then out here on her ride. He may have thought he was doing her a favor, but that did not excuse his refusal to leave her now.

The tree line materialized before her, and Laura slowed her mare to a walk. The vast array of colors around her painted a picture of an idyllic fall day, and she almost failed to notice the sound of another horse beside her. She had not wanted to look back in fear that Lord Farris had not heeded her directive to leave but was not surprised to see he was still with her. Lord Farris could have his pick of willing women. Why force his attentions upon her in such a manner?

She continued to look out ahead of her as she said bluntly, "You know, if someone catches us together, it is your fault and not mine."

The sound of a dove met Laura's ears, and she sighed. Her morning ride could have been so perfect, but instead, she was with *him*. Her gaze drifted to his location, and she was surprised he had dismounted and now stood amongst the foliage. His darkly good looks were only heightened by the autumnal colors.

"Would you care to join me for a stroll?" he asked pleasantly.

Remaining seated firmly on her mount, Laura looked at him dubiously. "Are you feeling all right, my lord? No other explanation could exist for why you would think I want to walk rather than ride."

"Why don't you dismount and find out?" he asked cryptically as he leaned against a tree.

Laura remained seated on her horse and considered his actions. His behavior was unusual, but it might be due to having a fever. Either that, or this was just how rakes acted. If that was the case, why did so many women fall for them? He must be under the weather.

She dismounted and crossed over to his location as the scent of the dank, decaying earth greeted her. He smiled at her approach, and she brought a hand to his forehead. His temperature felt normal, although she was beginning to think she might be the fevered one. His presence made her temperature rise, which was completely different from the sensations she felt around other gentlemen.

"You appear well, my lord," she finally said.

His sudden grin caught her off-guard, and she could tell he was definitely laughing at her. Her eyes narrowed, and she asked with barely restrained anger, "I take it you are not worried about your health, my lord?"

"You mean you were serious about that?"

"Of course. You invited me down to ascertain whether you had a fever or not." Oh, how she hated rakes. Granted, some of her anger was toward herself. She should not enjoy his presence as much as she did. And she really, really did. In fact, the hand that had caressed his forehead even now tingled.

His grin broadened, and he laughed loudly.

Somehow, Laura got the impression he did not laugh often. "You are a breath of fresh air, darling. Now that I have you down here, we may as well walk a little."

No stump or rock large enough to help her mount was within sight, and she doubted he would help her back on to her horse. He evidently did not need her answer, either, as he pried the reins from her hand and tied the horses to a tree. He extended his arm as though they were in the loftiest of London ballrooms and asked, "Shall we?"

She stonily accepted his proffered arm, although what she had really wanted to do was march angrily away from him. A well-bred lady did not act so rudely, however, which was why she found herself strolling with Lord Farris in the forest.

"We could not have chosen a lovelier day for our outing, could we?" Lord Farris asked pleasantly as he led her beside a gully.

Laura bristled at his absurd question. No part of her had wanted to take this walk, especially with him. She eyed him suspiciously. He looked completely sane, but these things could be deceptive.

"You can relax, you know."

"What?" she asked sharply.

He stopped their leisurely stroll and turned her to face him. "You have been acting like a shrew for the entirety of our outing, even though I assured you last night I am too much of a gentleman to take advantage of you."

A sudden wind tore through the trees, which made Laura shudder from its chill. This day was slowly going from bad to worse, and once again, he had referred to their outing as if it was some planned rendezvous.

"Oh, do stop it already."

"Excuse me?" he asked darkly.

"I do not know what is the matter with you, but you hold some peculiar beliefs about today's events."

Suddenly, his brooding mien turned into a humorous one. He grinned and said mischievously, "See, the shrew has returned."

Unable to stop herself, Laura stomped her foot. Hard. "I am most certainly not a shrew. You just happen to vex me at every turn."

"Name one thing I have done to vex you."

She scowled. His adorable grin was still plastered to his face, but no one called her a shrew and got away with it. "You assumed I could not ride my horse properly. You did not listen when I told you I wished to ride alone. You made me go on this walk with you. And finally, last night, you made me forget my water in the library, and I was extremely thirsty."

The charming grin on his face transformed to a predatory one as his eyes narrowed on her face. "Now, what could I have possibly done to make you forget your water?"

Laura's pulse quickened, but instead of backing down, she placed her hands on her diminutive waist. "For being a self-proclaimed gentleman, you certainly point out a lot of things in a most ungentlemanly manner."

"Are you questioning my honor?" His face had transformed to a granite mask, and he looked far from amused.

"Every second that I am forced into this walk with you proves my very point, my lord."

"Allow me to remedy my error then." He bowed

mockingly, and then grabbed her arm to guide her to the horses. His hand was like steel as he escorted her, although he still showed consideration toward her by leading her around potential dangers rather than through them.

Laura's shock at his boorish behavior kept her from voicing her anger, even when he picked her up roughly and dumped her on the back of her mare. Her skirts were in a tangled heap, but she ignored them and sat her sidesaddle proudly.

He untied the reins, and Laura stuck her nose in the air haughtily as she regained control of her mount. "I should thank you to *not* grace me with your presence in the future." And then she could, hopefully, stay amongst people where sanity prevailed.

"I would be delighted to oblige you."

Laura rode as swiftly as her mare could carry her, but Lord Farris still managed to keep up on his stallion. Her nerves were strung taut, and she did not know how she would relieve the tension. Normally, she went riding to lessen stress, but that was impossible with Lord Farris at her side. Her return ride seemed to take much longer than when she had first begun, but eventually she could see the manor. The stables appeared, along with Eleanor and her male companion.

"Oh, there you are!" cried Eleanor in her sugary sing-song voice as they entered the courtyard. "I have been looking all over for you. Luckily, Lord Collins has aided me in my search, or I would have quite given up by now." Eleanor looked very pleased to be hanging off the arm of a belted earl. She was perfectly pieced together in a light green day dress that complemented her complexion. Unfortunately for Laura, Eleanor's dress only showcased how outdated her own riding habit was.

Lord Collins grinned at his friend and said, "Ah, Gavin. Let me introduce you to Miss Ashford. Miss Ashford, this is Lord Farris."

Eleanor curtsied prettily and said, "Well, of course I was able to guess who you are, my lord. Your many charms are well known." Eleanor then turned to Laura, arched a perfect eyebrow, and asked, "Tell me, however did you happen across Lord Farris? I had not realized you ever talked to gentlemen, much less went on clandestine rides with them." She turned back to Lord Farris and snidely informed him, "My cousin is terribly shy. More of a wallflower really, so unfortunately, she is not very popular." She added melodramatically on a sigh, "Sad, she is such a sweet girl and should have done so well."

Laura sat atop her horse and gritted her teeth. Her strongest wish at the moment was for Eleanor to simply stop talking. Eleanor's rude antics were not unexpected, but they still hurt, and there was nothing Laura could do at this point. If she gave a rebuttal, Laura would look catty, so it was best to simply shut her mouth.

Laura was not surprised Eleanor had already snared a gentleman, especially one of Lord Collins's caliber. He and Lord Farris were exactly the same, if rumors were to be believed, and Laura and Eleanor would be much wiser to avoid both of them.

Lord Farris stepped to Laura's side and helped her dismount. He turned back to Lord Collins and Miss Ashford and said kindly, "Miss Ashford, it really is nice of you to bring your cousin to the house party. Sometimes it is important to give small acts of charity to one's family. Country air is an uplifting boost to one's constitution, you know."

The sweet giggle that issued from Eleanor's mouth betrayed none of the venom that would soon follow. "Oh, what did I tell you! I warned you about that riding habit, but you never listen to me. He thinks you are my poor relation! I guess one cannot expect a little country mouse to truly blossom after only one season."

Never mind that Eleanor had also grown up in the country, and that Laura's father had piles more money than Eleanor's. She turned stoically to Lord Farris and said, "Actually, my father is the Earl of Krant. I had been waiting for my dear cousin to formally introduce us, but this will have to do." Upon uttering her father's name, Laura could have sworn she saw a muscle spasm on Lord Farris's face.

The twitch seemed to continue as he bowed stiffly and said, "Well then, let me apologize immediately for mistaking your situation. I should have known better than to make an assumption like that."

As far as apologies went, Laura was impressed with the one she had just received from Lord Farris, although she wondered if his apology was just for show. If his previous behavior was any indication, he would act as he wanted no matter what convention dictated.

"All is forgiven. My cousin is used to mistakes like that. I am sure no one even recalls what was said to offend." Eleanor beamed at all around her. Laura had been the one offended, yet Eleanor managed to turn the situation around to benefit her. "Shall we go in now? I believe luncheon will be served shortly."

****

Lord Farris and Lord Collins left the ladies in search of the promise of solitude in the library. The house party officially started today as the last of the guests had arrived late last night. For now, the library was empty, but who knew what the future held.

The sun shone through the windows of the library as Lord Collins and Lord Farris sat on the diminutive furniture. Gavin noted a small glass perched on a bookshelf and was reminded of the proprietor of the drink. The previous night was imprinted on his brain. He could not seem to push Lady Laura from his mind. If he had known she was an earl's daughter, would he have behaved any differently toward her?

He paused. He knew the answer was a resounding yes. He would have kissed her senseless against the bookcase, even if it made him a cad. The chemistry between them had been almost irresistible, especially when she had looked at him with her unusual-colored eyes. Those eyes would be his undoing. He just knew it.

"So, what do you think of Miss Ashford?"

Why was his friend asking him for his thoughts on some random maiden? "She seems fine." A banal response would do.

"Only fine?" Lord Collins asked indifferently as he looked out the window.

"It depends on what you are considering her for. For your bed? Just fine. For matrimony?" Gavin laughed. "Please, do not be absurd."

Lord Collins shot him a penetrating frown. "I am afraid I am leaning toward the latter option."

Gavin had been drinking plain, undoctored tea but, when his friend announced his decision, coughed. "Are you serious?"

"Very much," Lord Collins stated calmly. "I have been considering marriage for some time now, and Miss Ashford has an air about her. I think she was born to be my countess."

"And you have known this for how long?"

"For a little over an hour," Lord Collins stated seriously.

Gavin sat in his chair, dumbstruck. Lord Collins and he had sworn off marriage until a much later date, when they would be forced to marry to secure their lineage. Now was not that time. Besides, Miss Ashford hardly seemed the sort to compel a man to marry earlier than he had planned. She was undeniably pretty, but a pretty face could be bought cheaply.

"You do not honestly see yourself marrying the chit, do you?"

"It is too soon to tell, but I doubt I will find a better match in the future."

Gavin's scowl deepened, and Lord Collins said rationally, "You may be opposed, but I must have an heir. What better person to procreate with than Miss Ashford? I would enjoy bedding her, and she seems the intelligent sort."

"Hmm." He did everything with his friend, but now Lord Collins was considering leaving him for the shackles of matrimony. He could not countenance his best friend behaving so irrationally.

Before Gavin could say anything else, Lord Collins added, "I will be moving forward with my courtship, whether you approve or not. Naturally, I would appreciate your support."

"Fine," he stated abruptly. Apparently, the witch had him spellbound. Gavin did not understand his friend's sudden feelings for her, but he could support Maxon until he found a solid reason to dissuade his friend from courting her.

"Are you even listening?" Lord Collins asked in a bored tone as he inspected his jacket. He pulled a minuscule speck of lint from his otherwise pristine coat and tossed it aside.

Gavin was brought back to their discussion by Lord Collins's query. He was not sure what his friend was saying, but he could hazard a guess. "But of course. You were talking about Miss Ashford, again." He crossed his fingers and hoped his guess was correct.

Lord Collins took a sip of his tea and trained his gaze on Lord Farris. "I was saying you should continue to occupy her cousin's attention. Miss Ashford is fond of her and would not be willing to allow her cousin to sit idly by."

"You actually think that would be a problem for Lady Laura? She is quite lovely and is sure not to want for suitors." As far as Gavin could tell, Laura had much more to offer in looks and certainly personality. Plus, she was an earl's daughter. Pedigree did not get much better than that.

In fact, her pedigree should have been evident the very first moment he met her. Assuming she was a poor relation was one of the least intelligent things he had done lately, and he should be grateful with every fiber of his being that she had not been the sort to claim he had ruined her and demand marriage.

"We both heard Miss Ashford. Her cousin is quite the wallflower. Just do this for me, and I will owe you one." Lord Collins typically did not ask for favors, which dictated Gavin say yes. Besides, for an unmarried miss, she held an amusing spark that intrigued him.

"I will do my best. Just hope that their chaperone is as willing to oblige us."

"Well, that is the beauty of all this. The ladies only have one chaperone, and I doubt they will do everything together."

"Yes, but who do you imagine the chaperone will choose to follow?" Gavin sincerely hoped it would not be Laura.

****

"We really must get you changed before everyone assembles for lunch," Eleanor commanded Laura as they ascended the stairs. "I can help pick out your outfit, if you like."

"That sounds delightful." Laura winced guiltily at her sarcasm, although Eleanor always took her words at face value. The ladies entered the bedroom, and Eleanor crossed over to the wardrobe. She selected a dress blindly from the tidy row of gowns and threw it on the bed. "Now, you really must tell me all about your morning."

Anna, their maid, helped Laura to undress while giving her a pitying look. Anna and Laura tended to act as bulwarks to each other when dealing with Eleanor, especially when Eleanor was unhappy about something. When dealing with Eleanor, it always worked to redirect the conversation by focusing on Eleanor. Eleanor's favorite topic was Eleanor. "Lord Collins looked like he had a grand time with you this morning."

Eleanor's doll-like face lit up as she spoke of Lord Collins. "Oh, yes. He is quite the intriguing man. Not only did he remark several times on my beauty, but he was also very attentive when I was talking to him." She sighed dramatically. "He is a paragon."

Laura held back a laugh. Lord Collins was friends with Lord Farris, which meant Lord Collins was a rake and almost the exact opposite of a gentleman. His status as a bachelor was well known, and Laura could not quite determine why he had been with Eleanor that morning. "Do you think he is interested in marriage?"

"Of course. Men do not speak to me unless they are interested. We looked absolutely marvelous together, did we not?" Eleanor preened in the mirror and failed to notice when Laura selected a different dress from the wardrobe. Laura directed Anna silently to help her into it and hoped that Eleanor would not notice the change.

"Oh, absolutely. A more perfect pair could not exist."

Eleanor eyed her and said, "I do not need your sarcasm. We did look perfect for each other, not that you would know. Your eye for detail is clearly lacking." She tittered. "Can you believe Lord Farris mistook you for a poor relation?"

It amused Laura to no end that her cousin could not understand when she used sarcasm. This time, as usual, her cousin was confused. She had been serious. Eleanor's response, however, had dealt Laura a slight blow. If she did not require comfort while riding as much as she did, she likely would have thrown out her habit after the morning's ordeal. She had no desire for Lord Farris to be interested in her, but her pride dictated he at least could entertain the possibility.

A pin fell on the vanity as Laura began to unbind her hair. She did not want to admit how humiliating Lord Farris's misinterpretation of her situation was. It had stung, but now that she understood his actions, she realized he had acted so ungentlemanly purely due to her imagined station. She was curious to see how he would behave henceforth.

The last of her pins came loose, and her long, chestnut hair cascaded down her back. She massaged her scalp and said, "Well, I wish you the best of luck in pursuing Lord Collins, but I, for one, do not look fondly on rakes."

Eleanor giggled softly at her harsh tone. "I cannot imagine why. A successful rake must be charming and smooth with the ladies, just like the heroes in those dreadful novels you read."

They were nothing like the heroes in her books, not that Eleanor would know. Eleanor never read books. None of the heroes in her novels would have insulted her in the library or faked an illness to entice her from her horse amongst the trees. No, they were not similar in any way. "Just be careful with him. You should not trust a man you just met, especially one like him."

"I met him last season," Eleanor said flatly. "Besides, I am hardly going to allow myself to be compromised."

Laura nodded slowly. It was Eleanor's decision, and Laura knew her cousin would be fine, assuming Lord Collins's intentions were pure.

"Could you imagine if I were to actually marry Lord Collins? I would finally fulfil my dream of becoming a countess."

Laura had heard that particular aspiration since they were little girls. While Eleanor aspired for riches, Laura had been the one who fantasized about love. She would read romantic novels and poetry, dreaming of the perfect man who would sweep her off her feet. Eleanor, on the other hand, had dreamt of a titled gentleman who would keep her in diamonds and the latest fashions. The two held very different goals in marriage.

****

Lunch was a mellow affair served buffet style. Their hostess, Lady Songfeld, had greeted Eleanor and Laura warmly once lunch finished and explained the makeup of the party. "I tried to keep the gathering small this year. There are only twenty-one guests. Fortunately for you girls, there are five unmarried gentlemen and four unmarried ladies. I believe you are all acquainted with the members of the party, but if not, please let me know, and I will make the proper introductions."

Laura and Eleanor smiled pleasantly and agreed to do just that. The sound of idle chatter could be heard as they entered the throng of guests, none of whom Laura recognized until her eyes landed on Miss Allison Somers.

Allison rushed to Laura's side and beamed at her happily. "I am overjoyed to see you in attendance. I was a trifle worried I would only have Miss Cannis to visit with."

Laura's eyes searched the crowd until they landed on the lady in question. She was not well acquainted with Miss Cannis but could not help feeling sorry for the girl. Miss Cannis reportedly lacked a dowry and had very few connections in society. "I wonder how she managed to receive an invitation."

Allison lifted her fan to her face, which only allowed her brown eyes to remain visible as she whispered, "I believe she is related to Lady Songfeld."

"Aah," Laura replied, as she continued to assess

Miss Cannis. The girl was fairly pretty, but her nose left much to be desired. It was hard enough to find a husband when one had perfect features, but add in the lack of a dowry and it would be almost impossible.

A general hush descended on the crowd as Lord Collins and Lord Farris entered the room. Her eyes narrowed on Lord Farris, who was looking entirely too handsome, and Laura had to fight back the tide of emotion that overtook her. She was clearly still upset about his confusion on her status, but she also could not help how her body thrilled at his presence. In hindsight, it might have behooved her to introduce herself in the library, but he was still in the wrong here. Not her.

Miss Somers exclaimed excitedly, as she returned the fan to her side. "This is just turning out to be the most splendid party I have ever attended! Did you see who just walked in?" For once, Laura was glad Eleanor typically commanded everyone's attention, because Eleanor had promptly ensnared the gentlemen's focus when they sauntered in.

"Oh yes, are we not in luck?"

Allison nodded her head in enthusiastic agreement to Laura's question, and Laura wondered why no one ever seemed to understand her sarcasm.

Lady Songfeld clapped her hands together and began to address the assembled crowd. "Ladies and gentlemen, please give me your full attention for a few minutes. I will be posting an itinerary of the upcoming events in the foyer. Everyone please take a look, and if you have any suggestions feel free to voice them. Now, just so everyone does not swarm the itinerary at once, I will tell you a little about the upcoming festivities. Tonight, we will have a formal dinner with some music afterwards. The kitchens are always open if anyone is hungry, and all other amenities of the property are available to one and all. Thank you."

A smattering of applause greeted Lady Songfeld's announcement, and Laura relaxed with the promise of interesting events. These next two weeks would be very enjoyable indeed.

"So, Lady Laura, we meet again." Laura watched as Allison's eyes widened in shock, and Laura turned to find Lord Farris at her elbow.

"Why, Lord Farris, it appears you have learned how to correctly address me." Her words dripped of sarcasm, which allowed her irritation with the gentleman to diminish slightly.

"I am a very intelligent individual, Lady Laura, and pride myself on things of this nature." Lord Farris spoke these words almost directly into Laura's ear, which caused a smattering of goose bumps to rise up on her flesh as a shiver ran thrillingly down her spine. He then latched on to her elbow and began to direct her away from the guests.

She did her best to ignore the effect he had on her, but panic overtook her as they reached the doorway which led to unchaperoned areas. "Is your goal to marry me, my lord? Because if you continue to lead me away, in plain view of all assembled, you will have accomplished just that."

He shuddered dramatically and halted their procession just barely within view of the onlookers. "Of course not."

Laura would have preferred a response free from his reaction of fear and certainly could have done without his stern denial, but she more than willingly accepted his decision to stop their stroll. She held no secret desire to marry the man, but he did not have to act as though she repulsed him.

"Good. The feeling is mutual, then."

"Can you not relax a little, darling? I already apologized, and aside from mistaking your identity, have done nothing wrong."

She stared up at him in disbelief. How could anyone be so obtuse? "You have insulted me more times than I can count!"

He appeared unfazed by her declaration and asked, "Please, name one thing that was not in relation to your misunderstood station."

The conversation in the room had reached a normal volume again, but Laura could still feel several eyes on her. She paused for a few moments to consider his request and plastered a fake smile on her face to appease the onlookers. She did not need to start unnecessary gossip about her nonexistent relationship with Lord Farris. "For starters, my lord, you forced me to spend a night in dire need of water."

"Is that the best you can come up with?"

"Of course not!" She lowered her voice as she realized she had responded a trifle too excitedly. "You also forced me to walk with you, unchaperoned, when I had wanted to ride."

"And you also agreed to walk with me. You never raised a single objection."

His calmness incensed her further, but she supposed he had a point. She had assumed he would not help her to mount her mare and had acquiesced too easily. "Fine," Laura said petulantly. "But you apologized, and I never accepted."

Lord Farris ensnared her hand and began stroking it. Naturally, she kept her hand stiff, which she hoped he would understand as her message that she did not want to hold his hand in return. Unfortunately, he continued to stroke hers, which made Laura lose all rational thought. He must practice holding hands. How else could one explain the skill employed so easily? Focusing back to Lord Farris, she realized he was speaking. "And as you see, I am terribly sorry for any inconvenience I have placed on you. Will you please forgive me?"

This was the one moment Laura wished she had paid attention and, without thinking, blurted out, "I am sorry, Lord Farris, but would you please repeat what you said? I was not listening." Heat instantly spread across her face as she regretted her entreaty. She should have just accepted his apology. She did not need to actually hear the entirety of it.

"You. Were. Not. Listening?" He appeared affronted and startled, as if this was an unspeakable crime she had just committed. "Forget it. You do not deserve to receive my apology twice."

"What do you mean by that?" asked Laura a touch crossly.

"Well, maybe if you had been listening the first time, you would understand." He extended his arm and offered coldly, "Please, allow me to escort you back to your chaperone. I would hate to do anything unseemly."

With a nod from Laura, who was still a bit unsure if she should still be angry with him, he guided her to Mrs. Westfield. The rules on etiquette were very unclear in such a situation as this, and Laura was not sure if she should be apologizing to him now or if she was still justified in her anger. Etiquette aside, her heart continued to beat angrily, and she decided she would remain irritated.

Allison's abrupt approach allowed Laura's anger to dissipate, at least for now. Allison asked excitedly, "What was that about? How do you know Lord Farris?"

Laura really did not want to make a big deal out of knowing Lord Farris. She doubted she would have much interaction with him in the future and would consider him no further. She waved her hand and said dismissively, "It is nothing. I met him on my ride this morning."

"Well, I think it is just wonderful. Could you imagine if you were to be the one to tempt Lord Farris into marriage? I am so very excited. This could not be more wonderful." Allison sighed, and a dreamy expression registered in her eyes. Laura had to hold back the urge to laugh at her friend. Nothing about Lord Farris was wonderful, and truthfully, he was possibly the rudest gentleman in her acquaintance.

"We both know no one will ever tempt him into marriage. What a ridiculous notion."

"I do not know about that anymore. Have you seen how Lord Collins is with your cousin? He has likely changed his mind about matrimony, so I do not see why Lord Farris could not, also."

"That is debatable, although I am beginning to wonder. Just look at them together." Laura waved her hand toward Eleanor and Lord Collins, who were currently engaged in conversation. Eleanor's hand lay flirtatiously on his arm, and he was intently listening to whatever she was saying. They presented quite a different picture from the one Laura had made with

Lord Farris, or so she imagined.

Looking about the room, Laura spotted a few other unattached gentlemen and said, "Let us try and focus on the other unmarried gentlemen present."

Disappointed, Allison said, "I guess you are right. At least with Miss Ashford's attention centered on Lord Collins, we have a much better chance with the other unmarried gentlemen. Otherwise, I am sure they would all be panting after her as normally happens. In fact," she added excitedly, "I noticed that Lord Harding is in attendance."

Laura groaned. That was the baron who had stopped courting her in favor of Eleanor. Allison knew the story but must still be holding out hope for them. Eleanor would probably not attempt to lure him away this time. Laura had never seen her cousin so focused on one gentleman, which left the rest of the gentlemen free. Maybe she would find someone at this very house party, although there were only two other gentlemen in attendance she did not know the identity of. Bidding her friend a good afternoon, Laura ascended the stairs to her bedroom for some rest before dinner.

Chapter 3

"Did you hear the news?" Mrs. Westfield exclaimed in an excited voice. "Lord Percival is here!" Eleanor and Mrs. Westfield had joined Laura in her room after Laura had taken a short nap. Eleanor, of course, was all aflutter about Lord Collins, and Mrs. Westfield, who had made it her mission in life to see the two girls wed, could not be more proud of her.

A plump woman, Mrs. Westfield had been a beauty in her younger days, and much of that beauty had not yet faded with time. "We are having the very best of luck. Not only are Lord Collins and Lord Farris present for Eleanor, but now we have Lord Percival here for Laura!" Lord Percival was a younger son to the Duke of Hartfurth and a well-known fortune hunter.

Laura could never understand why Mrs. Westfield set such a high bar for Eleanor and such a very low one for herself. She could only assume it was because Mrs. Westfield was related to Eleanor and not to Laura. No matter the reason, it was not like Eleanor could marry two gentlemen, yet clearly Mrs. Westfield allotted her just that. Laura may not possess the perfect English looks, but she was the daughter of an earl! Marrying a titled gentleman did not interest her, but she at least expected to marry someone she loved, and Lord Percival would never be that someone. "Oh, please promise me you will not push him at me. I do not want to spend time with him." She just could not tolerate a man as feminine as Lord Percival.

"Now, Laura, that is most inconsiderate. He may want to spend time with you, and a lady must always treat a gentleman with respect. Plus, he would make you an excellent match with his connections. He is exceptionally attractive, and you could do far worse."

"Mrs. Westfield," Laura said sternly. "I am afraid I just do not find the dandy sort attractive. Papa would never allow me to marry a man like that, no matter how much you applied yourself to matchmaking." Her father was a man's man, and strongly disapproved of the dandies. Her chaperone, however, had clearly set her mind to the task of setting the two of them up. Laura would just have to avoid him, and all would be fine.

"Well, I declare all this talk of Laura's prospects has made me utterly famished," Eleanor stated dramatically. "I believe dinner is about to be served. We may as well make our way downstairs."

The other ladies agreed and proceeded to join the rest of the party. Dinner was served, an elaborate seven-course meal that somehow was not satisfying to Laura. She could not focus on the food, and instead found herself wondering at the whereabouts of Lord Farris.

The conversation with Lord Percival, who was seated next to Laura, was lackluster. Lord Percival was blessed with very good looks, which somehow did not affect Laura at all. He had dark blond hair, which she assumed he spent a decent part of his day styling, brown eyes, and a pleasant nose thanks to impeccably good breeding.

Small talk was not something Laura excelled at, and she soon found herself exhausted. He was particularly interested in the musical portion of the night, not that Laura disliked music, but she was not one to obsess about who was going to play what at the pianoforte. By the time dinner concluded, Laura wanted nothing more than to go to bed. She smiled sweetly to Lord Percival and bade him goodnight before turning to her chaperone. Mrs. Westfield surprised Laura before she could depart from Lord Percival's side by saying, "Oh, Lord Percival, how fortunate we are to have you at this party."

"Why, thank you. I am always happy to be a member of a good party. I heard there was going to be music tonight, but Lady Laura has just informed me she is to miss the fun." Lord Percival certainly was a well-spoken, handsome, and kind man. These traits made her dismissal of him as a suitor much more difficult than it had to be.

"I hope you are feeling all right," offered Mrs. Westfield, with polite concern.

"I will be fine once I get some sleep. I am just very tired tonight."

"Oh dear. You go ahead then." Mrs. Westfield added conspiratorially as she turned back to Lord Percival, "She is probably tired from her ride this morning. She rides every morning, you know. I imagine she would love to have the company of a gallant gentleman such as yourself accompany her on her ride tomorrow."

Laura sent a prayer heavenwards. Please, do not say yes. He probably used a sidesaddle and needed her help to mount the horse. The image brought a giggle bubbling out, which, unfortunately, Lord Percival took as encouragement. "I would love to go riding with you tomorrow morning, Lady Laura."

Usually Laura was a quick thinker, but the best she could come up with was "Thank you, Lord Percival, but I am not sure yet if I will be up for a ride tomorrow morning." Laura coughed delicately and tried to appear frail.

"I understand. I will be at the stables tomorrow morning, and if you do not appear, I will just have to ride alone." Lord Percival was considerate and ideally suited for anybody other than Laura.

"Good night then." Laura curtsied and attempted to appear weak as she climbed the stairs. Now she actually needed to go to sleep so she could rise early and avoid Lord Percival. She sighed as she entered her room and changed into her dressing gown. She was tired and expected to fall asleep immediately. Her pillow was exceptionally soft, but instead of the welcoming arms of sleep, she was greeted by Lord Farris's wickedly handsome face. His image was not something she wished to dream of. If anything, she wished to cut him from her memory entirely.

She had spent a good deal of time with Lord Harding the previous season, and had felt a pleasant feeling of warmth for him when he was near. That feeling was precisely how she imagined love would be, and she certainly did not receive that feeling when she was around Lord Farris. No, Lord Farris was not the sort of gentleman to elicit anything mundane. If anything, he caused unusual tingles and spasms to occur within her. Maybe those were the feelings all rakes inspired, but those feelings were not what she wanted.

Chapter 4

Despite Laura's plan to avoid Lord Percival by rising at dawn, she unfortunately overslept and awoke at her normal time. Maybe she would get lucky, and Lord Percival would decide against a ride that morning. Laura hurriedly donned her riding habit, swept her hair into a serviceable bun that would survive a vigorous ride, and hastened down to the stables. She was delighted to find she was alone, aside from the groom who was saddling her horse. Laura gracefully mounted and breathed a sigh of relief as she guided her mare out to freedom.

"Hello there, Lady Laura!"

Laura cringed and halted her departure after recognizing Lord Percival's voice. She seriously had some of the worst luck. "Good morning, Lord Percival. I thought you had decided to forego our outing this morning." Hopefully her disappointment was not too obvious, as Lord Percival did not deserve outright cruelty.

"Of course not. My greatest aspiration for the day is to escort you on this ride, my lady. Please wait a moment while I garner a horse." He hurried over to the stables and began the task of selecting a mount.

Laura waited impatiently as the groom saddled Lord Percival's chosen gelding. He was dressed in a gaudy coral vest that only reinforced her opinion of him as a dandy. One of his calves appeared larger than the other, and Laura wondered if Lord Percival was wearing padding under his clothing to give the pretense of muscles.

The mare evidently sensed Laura's impatience and started prancing underneath her. "Why cannot my horse actually run off with me this time? I doubt Lord Percival would be able to overtake me on that." Lord Percival's horse was a stocky older gelding, which was almost on its last leg. That poor horse would have been set out to pasture long ago in her father's stable.

After a few moments, Lord Percival was ready to depart, and Laura noted with relief there was a groom trailing behind them. Laura could not help but compare Lord Percival to Lord Farris. Lord Farris exuded manliness, and his glance sent sparks down Laura's spine. When Lord Farris spoke, Laura's world ceased spinning as everything in her focused in breathless anticipation on what was about to be said. Lord Percival, on the other hand, was nice enough but felt almost brotherly to her, and a flying leap into a lake was preferable to conversing with him.

After approximately ten minutes of riding, unfortunately at a sedate trot, Lord Percival called out to halt. "We can take a small break here," he suggested as he dismounted next to a fallen log. "Let me help you down."

She hid her scowl with a cough. Why did men seem desirous of walking rather than riding? Laura again had a chance to compare Lord Percival to Lord Farris. When Lord Farris had helped her from her horse, she had felt tiny in his hands, as if he could break her in two. Lord Percival made her feel like she was a big, hulking weight, and he was attempting to cushion her fall instead of lightly helping her dismount. Feeling like an unmanageable weight was not a feeling she wanted to get used to.

"We only just started our ride. Why are we already taking a break?" This ride was not going to be very invigorating, that much was certain. Laura glanced at their chaperone and was dismayed to see he was leaving them. "And where is the groom going?"

"I wanted to take this opportunity to talk with you for a moment, so I convinced him to leave us. Come sit here, beside me." Lord Percival patted the spot next to him on the fallen log. Green moss added padding to her seat, and red, orange, and brown leaves surrounded her. It was very autumnal, but she sincerely wished she had just stayed in bed that morning.

"So what did you want to discuss?" she asked tentatively.

"Laura. May I call you Laura?" Before she could say no, Lord Percival continued speaking, "I know we have not known each other long, but after a smattering of balls and this house party, I feel I know you most intimately. Your sincere personality and serious nature speaks to my inner self in a way that I have never experienced before." He paused and tented his fingers as he considered his next statement. "What I am really trying to say is I have developed strong feelings for you. I know we will be happy together when we wed, if our previous discourses are any indication."

Shocked disbelief overtook Laura. Had he just offered marriage to her? And more shockingly, did he actually think they had held pleasant conversations? She had almost laughed when he had said she possessed a serious nature, but this was all too much. How does one respond to a declaration like his? Events of this nature did not happen to her, so why was it happening now? Her relationship with Lord Percival was superficial at best. For goodness sake, she did not even know the most basic of details about him!

Startled, Lord Percival stated, "Those matters are trivial, dearest. We will have plenty of time to discover things about each other after we are wed."

Laura's hand flew to her mouth at her lapse. He was so sure of his success in securing her hand. Despite her lack of experience, she knew this was not a normal offer of marriage. "Lord Percival—"

"Oh please, we needn't stand on such formalities."

"All right, Percival." Drawing a fortifying breath, Laura prayed for patience. "I am afraid you are mistaken about us. I do not have romantic feelings for you and am not going to even entertain the idea of marriage to you. There are plenty of women out there who would be flattered to hear of your intentions, but I am not one of them." Laura rose from the log and started to step to her mare across the lovely landscape. She did not want to hear his response, and really just wanted the whole matter to be behind her.

Laura was unprepared for Percival's sudden onslaught as he whipped her toward him and started to maul her with his mouth. She was reminded of a cold fish flopping over her lips, and her instincts of self-preservation took over. She hurriedly swung her knee upward into his groin area and heard a satisfying thud as Percival broke off the kiss while doubling over in pain.

"You bitch!" he roared. "I will make you pay for

that."

"Now, I assure you that will not happen, Percival," a deep voice rumbled. "I suggest you mount your horse and leave." Laura whipped around to see Lord Farris pulling his horse to a stop while expertly dismounting. "Actually, how about you leave the house party altogether."

Laura had never expected to be so happy to see Lord Farris, although she was positive she would have been able to handle the situation without his intervention.

"I cannot just leave the party," moaned Percival as he attempted to mount his horse, obviously still in pain.

"It seems you do not understand. That was not a suggestion. You do not want to know what will happen if I see you again." He could have been talking of the weather for all the emotion he displayed.

Lord Farris's words had their desired effect as Lord Percival whipped his horse into a gallop toward the house. Lord Farris turned to face Laura and he asked in a soft, reassuring voice, "Are you all right?"

Hot tears were welling in her violet eyes as she looked up at him. Even though Lord Farris annoyed her exceedingly and was not her favorite person, Laura was upset by Percival's behavior. Lord Farris was acting in a most chivalrous manner, and Laura decided in that moment to let her guard down. Shaking her head, she sank onto the log she had shared with Lord Percival. "I just do not understand how he changed like that."

Lord Farris sat down beside her and placed a comforting arm around her. "Please do not cry, Laura. The matter is finished, and he will not bother you again."

Sighing, Laura felt safe in his arms and began to calm down. He was just so warm, and he smelled so good. She smiled up at him wryly. "That was my first kiss. Are all kisses supposed to feel revolting?"

His eyes appeared to darken slightly as he held her. His hand caressed her arm and he said, "No, Laura. I would show you a true kiss..." He stopped speaking and suddenly grinned. "But I fear you would turn that move on me that you just employed with Lord Percival."

She giggled in response. "It was fairly effective, was it not?"

"Yes, but I have a suggestion so you may avoid the tactic altogether."

Laura's interest was piqued. "Oh?"

"You simply must dress even more outdated. Your garb is obviously not working."

Laura's smile froze as she realized he had just insulted her riding habit. Realizing she was still seated next to him, she quickly stood and said coldly, "Do you have a problem with my attire, my lord?"

He smirked as he surveyed her gown. "Aside from the gaping hole in your skirt? No, not at all."

Laura's gaze flew to her skirt, realizing with chagrin that he was speaking truthfully. She would have that darned immediately upon returning to the manor. "A gentleman would not admit to noticing such a minor flaw."

"And allow you to ride around the countryside in such a state of dishabille? That, my dear, would be the rude thing to do. Why do you wear such a garment anyway? Your father has money, and you should go buy a new one."

"Naturally, I wear this habit for safety reasons. Just imagine all the gentlemen I would attract if I did purchase a new one."

Lord Farris chuckled at her joke, and he stood and took a step closer to her, "Yes, but would you feel the same sort of attraction for any of them as you do for me?"

The sudden change in conversation prompted Laura's heart to beat erratically. She could recall his previous accusation that they shared a mutual attraction, and that was just not true. At least, she would deny it to the bitter end. "I hardly find you attractive, my lord. Dangerous, yes, but not attractive."

He smiled darkly. "Yes, but dangerous can be oh, so very amusing."

Laura began to tingle as she found herself mesmerized by his eyes. A compelling force caused her to lean toward him, but she had enough sense to stop herself. "Thank you, my lord, but I think it best to avoid danger." She straightened and took a step back. "I think I should return to the house now. Lord Percival bribed our chaperone for an unknown duration of time, and we do not need the groom to find us together. You know how servants talk."

"Then allow me to help you mount your horse." His hands circled her waist, and he swung her lightly on to the mare.

Laura arranged her skirts and looked down on Lord Farris. "Thank you, my lord. For everything."

"The pleasure was mine, my lady. I should think all matters between us are settled, then."

He handed her the reins, and Laura neatly took control of her horse. The look in his eye gave Laura the impression that matters were definitely not settled. She raised her eyebrow and nodded. "Just as you say, my lord."

Her mare broke into a canter toward the manor and away from Lord Farris. It had occurred to her that she might happen upon Lord Percival, but she also felt confident in her ability to outride him if she did. The courtyard was deserted as she rode in. What exactly did the other guests do in the morning? Eleanor's voice was audible from somewhere in the house, and Laura concluded that Lord Collins was likely escorting her.

"At least someone is having a cheery morning." She had to admit, at least to herself, that she had not actually hated the last portion of her outing. Lord Farris had shown a side of himself that had made an impact on Laura. She had never considered the notion that a rake could have a chivalrous side.

She wanted nothing more than to relax in her room for a spell and swiftly changed into her dressing gown once she arrived. Shakespeare beckoned to her, but she needed tea before she could fully relax. She ordered a tea tray sent up, and then waited on her bed until a knock resounded on her door.

"Come in," she called cheerfully, fully expecting the maid to bring in her refreshments.

Instead of the expected maid, Mrs. Westfield came swooping in. "So, dearie, how did your ride go this morning?"

Mrs. Westfield looked so hopeful that Laura hated to shatter her dreams. "He did not show up." Just as she had suspected, her lie had left Mrs. Westfield crestfallen.

"I was so sure he would go riding with you. This is

disappointing."

Another knock rang out, and this time a maid came in with the tea. Laura had planned on taking her tea alone, but it would not hurt her to share. "Would you like to join me?"

Mrs. Westfield nodded and said, "Sugar and cream, please."

Laura rose from her bed and prepared the drink for her chaperone as directed. There was only one chair in the room, so she repositioned it facing the bed and offered the use of it to Mrs. Westfield. Laura sat and faced her chaperone, prepared for whatever words Mrs. Westfield might impart.

Her chaperone began the conversation. "You know, when I was your age I married for love. I was my season's Incomparable and had my choice of gentlemen." She laughed softly and said, "You would not believe the number of offers my father fielded on my behalf. Instead of listening to common sense and marrying an earl or marquess, I succumbed to what I thought was love. It turned out Mr. Westfield, may he rest in peace, was not the man I thought him to be."

Laura inhaled the aroma of her tea and listened, transfixed.

"I had been blessed with a sizeable dowry, but Mr. Westfield convinced me he loved me and did not care about the money." Mrs. Westfield took a fortifying breath and sip of her tea before continuing. "The first year of our marriage was blissful, but after that, Mr. Westfield changed. He became more distant and began to stay away from the house for days on end. It was around that time that household items started disappearing. First the candlesticks, then the silver, and eventually I could not sit at home in denial anymore. I found out he had a gambling habit and had been selling our possessions to pay his bank notes. You see, my husband had burned through the entirety of my dowry in under a year. We lost everything, and just one more year into our marriage, my husband passed away. At that point, I could have remarried, but I was too jaded, and after a while lost my chance."

Laura's heart went out to her. Mrs. Westfield looked crestfallen as she had recounted her story. "I am so sorry, Mrs. Westfield. I had no idea." Laura was not always the best at consoling people, so she offered more tea.

"No, thanks, dear. I just wanted to share my story with you as a cautionary tale. I want you and Eleanor to marry well so you can avoid making my mistakes. That is why I have been pushing Lord Percival at you. He is just the sort that you can control, and not worry about squandering your dowry."

"Then why would you push Eleanor toward Lord Collins? He sounds like the sort of gentleman your Mr. Westfield had been."

Mrs. Westfield responded quietly, "Eleanor is the type of woman that can charm any man. Once she marries, she will control her gentleman, or at the very least, his finances. You and I are not of the same mold. We need a stable and grounded husband."

Well, that part made sense, although Laura was a trifle insulted. She could control a man if she ever found one to love. From now on, Laura would try to be a little more sympathetic when Mrs. Westfield tried to matchmake, and would make sure she only fell in love with a deserving man. "I truly do appreciate your help, but can we please rule out Lord Percival? He just is not someone I can see myself with."

"If you absolutely insist on the matter. Just remember to look past the outer layer. Friendship is a wonderful foundation for marriage." Mrs. Westfield finished her tea, rose from her chair, and added brightly, "I hear Lord Harding is also in attendance. We can focus our efforts on him. Now, if you will excuse me I should really track down Eleanor."

The door shut behind Mrs. Westfield with a click, which left Laura to reflect on her thoughts. She did not care to reacquaint herself with Lord Harding. She would never consider a man who did not place her above Eleanor. She had enough self-respect for that. At least Lord Percival had never tried to woo Eleanor. If Mrs. Westfield had told Laura her story before Laura had been mauled by Lord Percival, Laura might have been more willing to give him a chance to see if feelings would develop. Lord Percival was clearly out of the picture now, but when another man entered the scene, she would try to look past the outer shell.

Laura reclined back into her pillows and read for a while, until another knock sounded at her door. She did not have a chance to bid the visitor entry because the door swung immediately after the knock and Eleanor entered.

"What are you doing in bed? It is about time for the festivities to start." Eleanor was almost glowing with excitement and looked ready for whatever adventure Lady Songfeld had planned.

"What is on the agenda for today?" Laura asked.

Sometimes when Eleanor spoke, Laura wondered if she felt the necessity to breath, as typical humans did.

When Eleanor was excited about something, she tended to speak quickly without pause, as was the case in that moment. "We are having a scavenger hunt, so we can all become familiar with the house! Lord Collins has already asked me to pair with him. Things are going very well between Lord Collins and myself, and I think it is safe to rule out Lord Farris as an option. I know it is a little soon, but I think I hear wedding bells!" she gushed excitedly and clasped her hands together. Hopefully, Eleanor was not getting her hopes up, but knowing Eleanor, she had reason for her excitement. "But back to the topic at hand. The winners of the scavenger hunt earn a lovely set of pearl earbobs."

It was too early to say for sure, but Laura was starting to think Lord Collins was having a very positive effect on Eleanor. Eleanor's vanity was still present, but she seemed to be softening a little. Laura would have to observe and see if this was just a transient fad.

Laura stood and beckoned Anna over to help her change. Yet another example of why Eleanor seemed to be different, she had actually remembered Laura's need to use the maid and brought Anna along when she came to visit. "How wonderful, who does not love a good scavenger hunt? I will change quickly, and then we can go down." Laura chose a peach-colored dress and secretly hoped Lord Farris would approve.

Anna sent Laura a smirk as she helped Laura to dress. They both found Eleanor's antics amusing and would likely discuss her later.

"Shall we go, then?" Eleanor inquired.

Laura exited the room and wondered who she would partner with. She could not steal Lord Deering away from Allison, and she would prefer not to partner with Lord Harding. Lord Percival was out of the question, if he was still in attendance. That left Lord Farris, whom she would prefer to avoid. Her options overall were decidedly grim.

The ladies joined the other guests, and Eleanor immediately left Laura's side to partner with Lord Collins. Laura could tell that many members of the house party had already formed their groups and was cursing her decision to leave her room at all, when Lord Farris approached.

"I see you have recovered from your ride."

"Why yes, my lord, nothing a spot of tea could not fix."

"I am thrilled to hear that," Lord Farris said briskly as he surveyed the people in the vicinity.

"Everyone, please gather around." Lady Songfeld announced, "Our event is about to begin. Everyone is to pick a partner, and as luck would have it we now have equal numbers. Lord Percival was abruptly called away on business this morning, which is regrettable, but works well for our numbers. Now for the scavenger hunt. Each couple will receive a clue that leads to the ensuing clues. Whoever reaches the end first will win the prize! Everyone pick your partner, and we will begin in a few minutes."

This was the part Laura dreaded most. One never knew who would pair with whom, and Laura was always a little anxious until the matter was settled. Lord Harding began to approach her, looking roughly the same as the last time Laura had seen him. He had nondescript brown hair and eyes and was a fairly plain man. Just as he reached her side and appeared about to speak, his mouth abruptly closed as his eyes met Lord Farris's. He blanched and quickly turned to walk away.

"What just happened there?" Laura confusedly asked Lord Farris.

"That gentleman was about to ask you to partner with him before realizing you were already claimed," he calmly replied.

"I had not realized we were partners."

"Yes, well, we are."

Lady Songfeld signaled the beginning of the event by ringing a bell, and the couples started forward to receive their clues. Lord Farris garnered the first clue from a footman and read it aloud, "Where age only adds value."

Laura smiled. She loved riddles, and the excitement was vividly reflected on her face. "Hmm, what do you think? That rules out the kitchen but could be the portrait gallery. Maybe... oh I have it! The wine cellar!"

The two swiftly made their way to the cellar where another clue awaited them. Laura took the honor this time. "Where a twisted path leads to the heart." She considered the clue and asked in disbelief, "They cannot possibly mean the maze, can they? That could take all day."

"It does seem to fit the clue. Maybe the follow-up clue is located at the entrance of the maze," Lord Farris suggested helpfully.

Lord Farris escorted her through the house to the outdoors. The day had warmed up and was very pleasant without a single cloud marring the sky. A breeze greeted them and sent Lord Farris's scent wafting to her nose. He had a knack for smelling masculine, and Laura decided she approved.

She scowled when they reached the entrance of the maze, and there was nothing in sight. "We are not going in there, right? If the clue is in the maze, it is likely in the center, which would potentially require hours to find!" Those mazes were sometimes excessively intricate.

"Maybe we should skirt the outside and check to see if there is another entrance or place where the clue might be."

Laura agreed, and they began to stroll around the outside shrubbery. They had maintained an amiable silence until Laura brought up the topic foremost in her mind. "When we were supposed to pick partners, why did you not ask me to partner with you? Instead, you just assumed we were a set."

Lord Farris shrugged absentmindedly and said, "You were the closest female at hand. So why not?"

A dip in the lawn caused Laura to stumble slightly, but her gallant escort steadied her by placing a searing hand on her waist. His comment did not sit well with her. If he cared so little who he paired with, then why had he sought her out in the beginning? Well, two could play at that game. "I really wish you had not turned away that gentleman. I had been desirous of partnering with him, and I am sure he would have been the best choice for a scavenger hunt."

His eyebrow lifted and he sounded irritated as he said, "Are you saying you are displeased with my company?"

"Well, no. You are perfectly nice, but let us face facts. I must find a gentleman to marry. You are a waste of time, my lord." She uttered the statement in a nonchalant manner, curious to see how he would respond.

"Perfectly nice? That is how you view me? What happened to dangerous?"

"You have hardly been deserving of the title."

He sent her a piercing gaze and asked, "You do realize you are now in a perfectly acceptable social class, don't you?"

"I always was in an acceptable social class, but what does that have to do with anything?"

The pair rounded a corner of the maze and were now located outside of view of the house. "I could not behave the way I wished when I thought you belonged to a lesser class. Now I can."

"As a gentleman..." Her words were cut short as Lord Farris captured her in his arms. His lips descended on hers, engulfing her and chasing away all thoughts. This was not the same sort of kiss that Lord Percival had forced on her. Rather, Lord Farris's embrace was a heart-wrenching, soul-warming kiss that had her completely at his mercy. All she knew was she wanted this to continue indefinitely.

Instinct overtook her, and she brought her hands from their position on his chest, up to his hair. He growled encouragingly at her boldness, and she sighed against him, allowing him to expand the kiss. Her squeak of surprise as his tongue met hers only seemed to excite him, and she suddenly realized how wantonly she was behaving.

Grabbing a fistful of his hair, she pulled back sharply.

"Ouch!" Lord Farris exclaimed, breaking the kiss and rubbing his head. His other hand remained on her back, firmly keeping her within his embrace.

Laura tried to pull away from him, but his arm was immobile. "What is the matter with you?" She held her clenched fists firmly planted by her sides, because the dratted things apparently enjoyed the feel of his hair, and they could not be trusted.

"Nothing, other than I seem to suffer from an infernal attraction for you."

She glared up at him, and he laughed. "You know, you should not respond so encouragingly if you want to convince me you are not similarly attracted to me."

"I did not respond encouragingly!" Although she had definitely enjoyed the experience. "You just happen to kiss nicely."

He appeared to gloat. "Yes, I knew you would approve."

Laura bristled, unimpressed with his self-confidence. "Do not act so conceited. I am sure most any gentleman could kiss just as well, if not better."

"I can assure you, they do not."

He was too near to her, but his arm had not budged. Here was another situation that etiquette lessons had not covered—how to rid one's self of a rake. "I will have to take your word on that, my lord, but truthfully, I cannot see why my future husband would not be more accomplished. As I said previously, your kiss was nice, but it was hardly worth bragging about."

Laura was pleased to see the gloating look disappear from his face. Suddenly, his features were transformed by a wicked smile. "Are you sure of that?"

"Of course," she said boldly, while inside, she was trembling.

Lord Farris brought his other arm around her while

he slowly lowered his lips to hers. He stopped before they touched, and he said quietly, "You asked for this." Then his lips once again encompassed hers.

Not once had she verbally asked him for an embrace, but her denial was lost as he began to prove his point. His tongue forcefully engaged with hers, but she did not care. She was too lost in his presence, which was all around her. His entire body was pressed up against hers, and she wanted nothing more than to be completely engulfed by him.

****

Gavin growled as she wriggled against him. She was very obviously an innocent yet was more enticing than any courtesan he had ever known. His hands began to unbutton her dress, but he stopped. If he went down this road, she would be ruined, and he was not ready to get married.

Nothing was wrong with kissing her more, so he continued to explore. He never would have guessed that such a simple act would entice him so, but things were different with Laura. She was different.

He slowly disengaged himself from her but was left reeling by the enormous void her absence caused. He had suddenly lost a vital part of himself. How could such a slip of a girl have this much of an effect on him?

"Do not say anything, darling. You goad me too well," he growled and began to set her to rights. With her hair halfway undone and her bodice exposing some lovely cleavage, she looked quite wanton and utterly enchanting. She appeared dazed, but Gavin was skilled at repairing appearances.

That last kiss had been enjoyable, to say the least, but he did not need her to read into it. She was, after all, an innocent. "Your future husband will not be better, my dear. Make no mistake."

Her violet eyes sprang to life, and she said, "Maybe, but that is hoping I get the chance to find him."

That caught him off guard. "What do you mean?"

"If you insist on putting me in compromising positions, I might end up married to you."

He laughed. He could not help himself. "That would be disastrous. I have no plans to marry, you know."

Her eyes were expressive, and he could understand what she meant before she actually spoke. "I share the same sentiment. While I do wish to marry, I do not wish to marry you."

"We are in agreement then."

"Yes, but the question remains, why did you accost me then? Or partner with me for this forsaken scavenger hunt?"

He quirked an eyebrow and looked at her haughtily. She was bringing this on herself, after all. "I must find some form of diversion at this party."

Laura gasped loudly, turned, and began to walk away.

Gavin's stomach clenched as he was assuaged with guilt. He should be patting himself on the back for fulfilling his friend's request, but instead he only wished to bring the smile back to her face. He called after her, and tried to repair the damage he had just done. "Laura, stop. It is not like I planned on this happening. Let us just continue to look for the clue."

"Fine," she said sharply, and paused long enough to allow him to catch up. She accepted his arm, and they continued to search. Next to a different entrance, a footman stood holding a silver platter. "Thank goodness we had not entered the maze. Think what a waste of time that would have been."

Gavin made no response, and she continued to speak. "You know, I have quite the disastrous sense of direction, so I avoid mazes generally." Again he remained silent, and she continued. "Growing up, my father kept one of the best stables in all of England. I naturally had an adorable pony that I named Bessie, who I would ride around the estates with a groom trailing after me."

Gavin interjected, "You named your pony Bessie? Is that not a name reserved for a milk cow?"

Scowling, she responded, "Well yes, but I was young and had not quite understood what I was doing when I named her. But names aside, that poor groom always had to follow me on my adventures. One day I snuck away without my groom and found myself utterly lost."

He was strangely engrossed in her story. Normally, he would find a tale such as this repulsive, but watching her speak so animatedly was captivating. "Well, what did you do?"

"Remember now, I was very young and soon found myself hungry, so I simply lay down on a grassy knoll and waited for help to arrive while taking a nap. When they finally found me, Father was most displeased and would not let me ride Bessie for two weeks. Ever since that day, I am always forced to ride with a groom."

Quirking an eyebrow, Gavin put two and two together, "So basically every time you ride alone you get into trouble?"

"More or less. I told you I am a very good rider, but I have rather unfortunate luck."

He chuckled and picked up the next clue. Reading it out loud, he said, "Where the sun brings forth life."

Laura wrinkled her brow. "The gardens maybe?"

"I was going to suggest the orangery. I saw one located near the library."

"Yes, that does seem more likely. Shall we?" Gavin held out his arm. Laura accepted, and they walked along the pebbled path leading to the front door.

Not knowing why, Gavin decided to share with Laura his own memories best forgotten. "I also had a similar story from boyhood, except instead of getting lost, I was thrown from my pony very far away from the house. At least, it seemed very far to me back then."

Violet eyes wide, Laura listened with avid interest as he continued, "I imagine the grooms alerted my father when my pony finally made it back to the stables, and they sent out a search party. I remember being very cold and relieved when I finally saw help coming to get me. They brought me home to the welcoming arms of Mother, and I was so happy. Later, my father sent for me and gave me a thrashing to the point I could not sit a horse for a week." He had hated his father. Always ready to mete out punishment but never willing to give praise.

"That is horrid!" Laura exclaimed passionately. "How old were you?"

"I think I was four or five at the time. He said I needed to toughen up and be a man. Men do not get thrown from their horses. The thrashing did the trick though. I never was thrown from a horse again."

Laura's hand was at her mouth. "You were just a

little boy. How horrid." She exhaled softly as her hand pressed compassionately in to his arm. "Was he kind otherwise?"

"He usually was not so harsh. Normally, he just ignored me entirely. Mother was always the loving sort. I would say she tried to make up for his lack of interest by smothering me." Gavin had not intended to say so much, so he switched topics. "Why did Miss Ashford not accompany you on your rides? I thought you two grew up together."

Her eyes were filled with sadness. "Eleanor did not like to ride. We always rotated which house we were at. Mother passed away when I was very young, so Father thought it best I stay with Eleanor and her family. Summers were typically spent at my father's, and the rest of the year at her parents'."

"That must have been trying, to not have your father around."

"Yes, but I knew no different. He ensured I had my horses around, you know. Bessie came with me when I went to Eleanor's, but I rarely could convince Eleanor to join me on my ride. Right about the time we reached fifteen, Eleanor decided that riding horses was an important skill for a lady and then would come riding with me. I had naturally moved past Bessie at that point to a mare named Cleopatra. She was a wonderful mare."

"At least you chose a semi-appropriate name for that horse." He paused for a moment before continuing, "I had been under the impression that your cousin loved to ride." She had told Lord Collins she did, at least.

"Oh, do not misunderstand me, Lord Farris. She does not mind riding. It is just not her favorite pastime."

He would definitely have to mention the little tidbit about Miss Ashford to Lord Collins, in passing, of course. He could tell that Laura was holding back about her cousin, so maybe Gavin should suggest Lord Collins escort the lovely Miss Ashford on a trip to the stables.

Their conversation ceased as they entered the house. Their eyes took a moment to adjust to the dimly lit interior, and Gavin had begun to escort Lady Laura toward the orangery when she abruptly called out, "Hello! How is your scavenger hunt progressing?"

Miss Somers appeared inordinately pleased to see Laura. "We are doing fairly well. We just finished with the stables. What clue are you working on?"

"We are lagging behind a bit but are headed to the orangery."

A pitying look appeared on Miss Somers's face when she heard what clue they were on. "You truly must be terrible at these things. There is no chance we will win, so did you two want to join us?"

Laura looked at Gavin, who was more than happy to join the others, and then nodded to Miss Somers. "Who is in the lead? Do you have any idea?"

"We are not positive, but it seems like we are always two steps behind Lord Collins and Miss Ashford. There very well could be more couples farther advanced than them, but we have not seen any."

"Hmm," she muttered a touch bitterly. "Miss Somers, let me introduce you to Lord Farris."

Bowing low, he briefly kissed the back of her hand and said, "What a delight it is to meet you, Miss Somers."

Miss Somers blushed and curtsied, all while staring

at Lord Farris as though she wanted to eat him. After a long pause, Laura cleared her throat.

"Oh, I am sorry," Miss Somers said, having forgotten herself. "Lady Laura, this is Lord Deering."

Laura curtsied prettily. Lord Deering bowed over her hand and said, "I have been waiting to be introduced to you, Lady Laura. I am honored."

While she smiled and murmured a polite response, Gavin was annoyed. Lord Deering could not have been more obvious about his interest in Laura, and Gavin did not like it. "Where did you say we were headed, Miss Somers?"

"Well, our clue is 'where one thing fills while another empties.' Which we concluded must be the dining room. Shall we continue on our way then?" When no one disagreed with Miss Somers, she hurriedly latched on to Lord Deering and led the way for their little party.

Another clue awaited them in the dining room. Lord Deering picked it up and read in a pleasant voice, "Where unwed couples are encouraged to maintain close proximity."

Laura was quick to hazard a guess. "I am going to guess the ballroom."

Everyone was in agreement and had begun their journey to the ballroom when they heard a bell ringing from the foyer. "How unfortunate," exclaimed Miss Somers. "The game must be finished." The couples switched directions and entered the foyer to the sight of Lady Songfeld standing next to Lord Collins and Miss Ashford.

Lady Songfeld waited until several more couples filtered in and announced that the winners were unsurprisingly Lord Collins and Miss Ashford. She then proceeded to hand the pearl earbobs to Miss Ashford as Lord Collins jovially said, "Oh no, Lady Songfeld, I cannot possibly accept the earrings. Give them to Miss Ashford in my stead." This produced a chuckle from the guests, and Lady Songfeld invited everyone to return downstairs for dinner at a later time.

Gavin needed the break. He ought to check in with Lord Collins, away from Laura. He was not sure why he had decided to share one of his most intimate stories from childhood with her. It was those damn eyes that had induced him to trust her with information that he had never told anyone else. She somehow managed to get past his defenses, and it was not good.

****

Laura had almost started to ascend the stairs to her room when Allison asked, "Laura, I do not mean to impose, but would you be willing to meet with me in private?" Naturally she was, and the two ladies were soon ensconced in Laura's bedchamber with a pot of tea and some biscuits.

Allison demurely poured her tea as her cheeks heated. "Now that you have met Lord Deering, you must tell me your opinion of him."

"Well, I cannot say that I know anything about him, other than what you have told me previously." She literally had just met him for the first time an hour ago.

"Yes, but you have a first impression of him, so what is it? Do you think he would be a good catch?" Somehow her blush seemed to intensify as she added, "For me?"

The sweet girl was clearly in love, so Laura tried to be as uplifting as possible. "Allison, he seems like an extremely nice gentleman. Good looking, considerate, and he must be at least somewhat intelligent judging by how well you two did in the scavenger hunt. How is he circumstanced?" She might as well try to be the voice of reason, although love could make up for plenty of faults.

"He is not as rich as Lord Farris or Lord Collins, of course, but I have been told he is very comfortable. There is just something about him that makes my heart pound and causes me to fear leaving his side. Do you think he is interested in me?"

Laura could not say for sure, so went with the positive choice. "Well, he did choose you as a partner for a reason. He must at least find you more appealing than Miss Cannis. I can try talking to him for you if that would help?" As an optimist, Laura felt assured he would feel the same for Allison.

"That is true. He did choose me over Miss Cannis, but that does not mean he likes me. Maybe it would be for the best if you found out if there was anyone he was interested in. Do not be too obvious that I sent you, though."

"That should not be a problem," reassured Laura. "I will simply try to get to know him and very naturally bring you up in the conversation. That should do the trick."

The two shared the tea service and were chatting nicely when Allison decided to bring up the topic of Lord Farris again. "How was he as a partner? Is he as charming as everyone says?"

Laura had been doing a tremendous job of avoiding thinking of him until Allison asked her about the scavenger hunt. Lord Farris had a tendency to say things to her that made her irrationally angry, but at the same time, she enjoyed being in his presence. He was a rake, but he appeared to have a soft side. Overall, she felt she was softening toward him, but she knew she should not. "He is very charming when he wants to be, and he performed his duties as partner satisfactorily. I have no complaints, except he seems to act a bit brutish sometimes."

"Oh, how so?" Allison asked with wide eyes.

Laura tried to be vague. Examples were completely unnecessary. "He just imposes his will on people, whether they want it or not."

"How exciting. I like a man who knows what he wants. He is just such a handsome gentleman, probably one of the most handsome men of the *ton*."

Laura was not as impressed by Lord Farris's commandeering ways, but she had to admit there was something very appealing about him when he simply took what he wanted without caring what others thought. "So is Lord Deering a man who knows what he wants?" It was always safer to redirect the conversation away from her.

With a slight giggle, Allison blushed and said, "You must not tell anyone, but he kissed me during the scavenger hunt!"

"What! Why did you not say anything sooner? And why do I need to talk to him if he already kissed you?" Laura was truly happy for Allison. She looked so blissful.

"For all I know, he is the sort that goes around kissing every woman. Like Lord Farris. I hear he kisses a lot of women."

Allison had brought up yet another reason for

Laura to act warily around Lord Farris. She was just one of many to him, and as he said previously, she was something to keep him from boredom. Yes, she ought to avoid him, but that seemed increasingly unlikely, and how was she to say no when she knew he had such a chivalrous side? "Well, you can count on me to try to ferret out your gentleman's feelings. We will start immediately at dinner tonight."

****

Gavin was about to enter the library where he assumed Lord Collins would be when a footman materialized with a silver platter bearing a letter. "For you, my lord."

"Thank you." Gavin waved the footman away and glanced down curiously at the missive. His sister, Alexa, had apparently figured out he was in attendance. He entered the library and observed Lord Collins with Miss Ashford and her chaperone, Mrs. Westfield. Poor Lord Collins was constantly under scrutiny, and ironically, Laura was the one who had needed the chaperone. "Good afternoon," he stated to the room.

"Oh, good afternoon, Gavin. How has your day been going?" Lord Collins asked with genuine interest. Gavin had not been seeing as much of his friend lately, and he did not like it. If Lord Collins married, how often would he see him then?

"It has been invigorating touring the manor and surrounding areas. Congratulations on the win, Miss Ashford. I trust the earbobs were worth the effort?"

Miss Ashford visibly brightened under his attention and showcased her ears sporting the new earrings. "Can you not tell? They are glorious."

Mrs. Westfield agreed cheerfully. "They could not

look better on anyone else. I knew those two would win. Did I not say that very thing before the hunt began?"

Gavin could tell Lord Collins was exasperated by the chaperone as his friend said, "You most certainly did, Mrs. Westfield. Gavin, who wrote to you?"

Poor man. His friend was constantly monitored. It was much easier to woo a woman when unchaperoned. "My sister Alexa wrote. I have not had a chance to read it yet." He opened the letter and scanned the contents, after which, he paraphrased for the group. "It appears she has started to prepare for her upcoming season, procuring dresses and such. Mother is shocked I am at this house party, and Alexa sends her regards to you, Lord Collins. She expects you to dance with her at her come-out ball."

Gavin could have sworn he saw Miss Ashford's ears perk up as he read the letter. She asked indifferently as she paged through a book, "I had no idea you had a sister, my lord. Have you known her long, Lord Collins?"

Lord Collins waved his hand dismissively. "Of course, she is like a little sister to me. I did, after all, basically grow up with Gavin and Alexa."

"I will have to respond and alleviate my dear sister's concerns. She thinks someone has blackmailed me into being here. She must forget I attend this house party every year." He typically kept away from events such as these, and he understood his sister's confusion. Gavin pilfered a piece of paper, pen, and an inkwell from a writing desk and started to compose a letter. "I take it you send your regards?"

"But of course. Tell her I will even spare her two

dances if she should wish," responded Lord Collins kindly.

Gavin nodded and continued to compose the letter for several minutes. At the end, he signed with a flourish, folded the letter, and placed it in his pocket to send out later.

Miss Ashford and Lord Collins sat reading in companionable silence. When Gavin finished, Miss Ashford looked up from her book and began to converse. "I do look forward to meeting your sister, Lord Farris. You must tell me more about her."

"Well, my mother ensured she is quite accomplished. She speaks French and Italian fluently, plays the pianoforte, and does all manner of ladylike things without compare, or so I am told." Gavin poured a couple fingers of brandy, swirled it around, and took a sip while fixedly watching Miss Ashford. He had no idea if his sister did half the things he listed, although his pocketbook would suggest she did. Her tutors had not been cheap. He listed her possible accomplishments to see how Miss Ashford would react. Evidently, she reacted very interestingly.

"Does this paragon do anything poorly?" she asked coldly. Gavin could see she was jealous, but could Lord Collins? "I am sure I could be a great deal of help to your sister should she have need of it."

He doubted that very much. After all, Laura was still unmarried. If Miss Ashford was offering the same sort of help to his sister that she gave her cousin, he would prefer to refuse that help. "I am sure I will mention that to Alexa."

"Thank you, my lord. Now if you will excuse us, Mrs. Westfield and I have some personal business to discuss." Miss Ashford curtsied prettily and departed from the room with Mrs. Westfield on her heels.

Gavin waited until the ladies were well out of the room and then asked Lord Collins, "How are things progressing on the matrimonial front?"

Lord Collins appeared pleased with the mention of marriage and said, "Very well. I just wish Mrs. Westfield would leave us alone sometimes. I am not totally convinced yet that Miss Ashford is the one, but she possesses many traits that I find endearing. Who chaperones you when you are with Lady Laura?"

"Surprisingly, no one. I think that Mrs. Westfield does not care so much about Lady Laura's virtue. Granted, we are at a house party and surrounded by people, usually."

"Is there cause to worry?" Lord Collins asked with a penetrating stare.

"Of course not. I am not the one interested in getting leg-shackled, remember?" Gavin took another drink and thought of how much trouble could have been avoided if there had been a chaperone around him and Laura. Not that he was complaining, of course. Given the chance, he may very well kiss her again. "Have you spoken to Miss Ashford of your intentions yet?"

"Not yet. I want to give us more time. I do not see any reason to rush my courtship, especially when I am not positive I will offer for her."

Gavin was relieved by Lord Collins's admission. There was still time to prove to Lord Collins that marriage was a poor choice. "Lady Laura and I had a diverting conversation about her childhood. Did you know Lady Laura and Miss Ashford shared the same tutors and literally grew up together?"

"No, I had not known that. What is your point?" Lord Collins asked, unconcerned.

"Well, Lady Laura was talking about her love for horses, which Miss Ashford does not share with her. I distinctly remember your Miss Ashford mentioning she loved to ride, and it seemed odd to me."

Lord Collins gave him a look of annoyance. "People change. I doubt your interests are the same as when you were a child."

"Of course not, but I thought it was something you might want to watch out for. If Miss Ashford is lying about her affinity for equestrian activities, what else is she lying about? Just promise me you will take note of anything when she is around horses." Gavin needed his friend to at least watch out for clues. Otherwise, he may just follow her blindly in his smitten stupor.

"Hmm, I guess I can look for unusual behavior, but I do not think there will be anything to see." Switching topics he added, "Has Lady Laura given you any trouble?"

Gavin answered honestly, "No, she is actually an interesting little vixen, and I quite enjoy our discourses." Draining the rest of his brandy he added, "Her fatal flaw is she is an innocent, and thereby untouchable."

"We could have a double wedding," jested Lord Collins, although Gavin could detect a minute note of seriousness. "Care for another drink?"

"Why not?" Gavin held out his glass while Lord Collins filled it. "We both know I am not marriage material. Besides, she needs a man who can love her, and I would never be able to do that."

Gavin knew that much was true about himself. He

was incapable of love and did not want to be the one to crush the indomitable spirit that Laura possessed. He was much too jaded about *ton* marriages to want to enter into one anyway.

His parents had been blessed with a typical high society marriage, where they barely spoke to one another and were unfaithful. In fact, he doubted very much if his sister Alexa was his deceased father's child at all. He would never tell anyone his doubts, of course. Alexa was his beloved sister and deserved the best. If anyone cast doubts about her parentage, he would not hesitate to call him out.

For these reasons, Gavin avoided marriage like the plague. He did not have the stomach for it. Someday, he would take the plunge when he was older and better equipped not to care what his bride did. Bringing his mind around to safer topics, he started to speak to Lord Collins of parliamentary matters, where Laura was safely out of his thoughts.

Chapter 5

Dinner was served. The main dish was a very tasty roast beef and root vegetable dish that made Laura's mouth salivate by smell alone. The Songfelds' chef was a genius, as all the dishes served so far had been above reproach. The ladies left the gentlemen upon dinner's completion to partake of a bit of tea, although she opted for sherry, an indulgence she rarely allowed herself. She needed a little extra courage to talk to Lord Deering and determine where his heart lay.

The gentlemen eventually joined the ladies, and Laura got to work. Lord Deering took a position on the outskirts of the room, so Laura grabbed Allison to drag her over to him. "Why, Lord Deering, how do you do on this fine evening?" Laura asked invitingly.

Lord Deering glanced between Laura and Allison and bowed politely. "My night has been rather uneventful up until now, of course." Smiling, he showed a set of straight, white teeth. "Can I fetch you ladies a beverage?"

Laura and Allison both agreed to partake of another glass of sherry, and Lord Deering walked away to fulfill their request. "So what is the plan?" Allison asked.

"I do not have one," responded Laura dubiously. "It is not like I have done this sort of thing before. I am sure we can just see how the night plays out."

The sherry glittered invitingly in the glass as Lord Deering handed first Allison's over and then Laura's. "How wonderful. It appears Miss Ashford is to play on the pianoforte."

Laura glanced over to see her cousin take a seat and rifle through the selection of music. Shockingly enough, it appeared Lord Farris was to turn the pages. She would have guessed Lord Farris would be the last person to aid her, yet there he was. Suddenly, his dark gaze swung to her, and she blushed before quickly looking away.

The music started. Eleanor played a piece that showcased her extensive abilities on the pianoforte, and Laura relaxed. Her cousin knew how to play, and it was blissful to hear. Laura was startled from her trance when Lord Deering spoke. "Lady Laura, are you feeling quite right? Your face looked flushed, and now has changed color again. Would you care to get some fresh air?"

This was the perfect opportunity for Laura. Laura enquired sweetly of Allison with a wink, "Would you mind terribly? The cool air would be good for me."

Allison shooed them away and smiled secretively. Lord Deering extended his arm and escorted her from the room toward the gardens. Laura could not have planned this better if she had tried. She would hate to be in Allison's shoes right now, the anticipation would kill her.

Laura was too preoccupied to hear the music as Lord Deering led her from the room. Instead, she was too busy wondering why Lord Deering's touch elicited none of the same tingles that Lord Farris's did. The sherry had had a numbing effect on her brain, but she was certain Lord Farris would have been able to clear the fog, unlike Lord Deering.

The pair stepped out into the inky darkness, and Laura realized with dismay that they were very alone together. Maybe a clandestine walk with him was not the best idea, after all. She considered turning around but decided her mission was too important. "So, Lord Deering, did you enjoy the scavenger hunt?"

"The scavenger hunt was a delight, Lady Laura. I especially relished the company of my companion, Miss Somers. That is the main reason I had hoped to get you alone. I noticed you are good friends with Miss Somers, and I want to know if she was promised to anyone."

Laura could not be happier with the words he said and slightly relieved. He was interested in Allison.

They continued their walk, finally reaching a bench to sit upon. "Well, I do believe there is one certain gentleman."

Lord Deering looked decisively dejected at Laura's declaration.

Laura laughed and said, "Please do not look so sad. Allison is interested in you."

He looked up hopefully and asked, "Are you sure?"

"Of course. Who else could it be?" How sweet that the two could meet, and fall for each other. Just as Laura hoped she would do someday as well.

The baron's eyes widened and a wide grin spread across his face. "What luck! I have never met anyone quite like her and have to admit I am quite enamored of her. Naturally, I had worried she was already taken."

"She certainly is a gem, but do not tell me of your feelings. Go find her, and share your news. She will be overjoyed." Laura urged him to go immediately and was promptly left alone to her thoughts.

Sadness engulfed her as she thought of the two in love. She knew she should be overjoyed for the couple, but she was all alone. With no prospects or gentlemen even remotely interested, she was in the worst of positions and had never felt the pang of loneliness as strongly as she did now.

She sat down on the garden bench and tilted her head back with a sigh. The cold somehow seemed to suit her melancholy, and the stars only served as a reminder of her lonely existence. Yes, even the moon had its stars to keep it company.

"I am happy to see you are safe, but never do anything so foolish again," demanded Lord Farris.

Laura levelled a stare at him and whispered, "Oh hush. I am fine." She was not in the mood to spar with him. Her mood was too low for that. Funny how one could be surrounded by people, yet still feel completely bereft.

A thousand words were spoken in that one look from Laura, so Lord Farris sat, not saying a word.

Laura's gaze drifted to the moon as she asked, "Have you ever been in love, my lord?"

He paused for a moment before responding, "Once, when I was much younger than I am now." He sighed with melancholy. "She was a brand new debutante, and I was freshly out of school. I was too young to know what I was doing and was positive I was in love with her. It turns out she favored someone else, or that is what she gave as her reason to choose him over me. He was a much older gentleman who was a better match for her, and naturally, in possession of a higher title."

"What became of her?"

He sat beside her and took her hand in his. "She married him. The last I heard, she has numerous lovers, which do not include her husband. But you do not need to hear of such matters."

Laura knew there were some who did not honor the bonds of matrimony, so she was not shocked by his disclosure. "How tragic. Both for you, and for her."

"Yes, I suppose it is."

"You know, I plan to marry for love someday. If this woman is to be believed, she married for love but lost that feeling. What is to say that will not happen to me?"

His hand tightened on hers, and his voice held a faintly hoarse note as he said, "You are asking the wrong person."

"But you loved this lady. How did you get over her?"

"I am afraid I cannot tell you my methods. They are not entirely proper. Just understand that if you find true love, and if it exists, it is not so easily dismissed."

They sat silently, with her hand in his, as she contemplated the words he spoke. She could hardly believe that she sat alone with a renowned rake, speaking of matters of the heart, but here she was, doing just that.

"My lord?" she asked softly.

"Yes?"

"May I ask you a personal question?"

He chuckled. "Haven't you already asked several?"

She shifted uncomfortably and nodded. "I suppose I have, but here it is. Everyone knows you detest the idea of marriage. I would imagine someone who has found love would hope for a love match someday." She knew she did, even if it seemed somewhat unlikely at this point. Her optimistic nature was slowly crumbling down around her. It was hard to feel hopeful when she never received any form of encouragement, from any gentleman.

"Here is the thing. I thought I was in love, but looking back, I think it was just the idea of love that convinced me to fall for the lady. Since then, I realized that love is a false emotion created to convince people to marry."

He is so jaded. Love must exist though. Otherwise, she was completely wasting her time and should emulate Eleanor by choosing a man in a cold and calculating manner. Somehow that cynical world view only made her sadder.

She turned to regard the stars once more as a gust of wind blew a wisp of her hair over her face. She pushed it aside and looked at him with raw emotion shining in her eyes. "Would you do me a favor?"

"Yes," he said simply.

"Would you dance with me?" She knew it was absurd, dancing without music, but she needed a momentary connection to someone, even if that connection to someone would never be her someone.

"Of course, I would love to." Lord Farris stood and pulled her to him, beginning their dance. He led her in a slow, swaying motion with the rustling of leaves as their music and the stars as their candlelight. Laura could only describe this moment as a dream, and each step was on top of a billowy cloud. She knew in that exact moment that she was lost. Just as a leaf drifts from its tree, so she was also falling for Lord Farris. His magnetism had pulled her in, and she regrettably could not stop her momentum. She may have only known him a few days, but it seemed as if a lifetime had passed.

Lord Farris drew the dance to a slow, gradual end. He slowly lowered his head and placed a gentle kiss on her lips. Such a magical moment was now perfection.

Laura knew there was no hope for her as Lord Farris kissed her so sweetly. She also knew she had to leave before she did something to foolishly betray her revelation to him. The despair of a love that would never be returned was eating away at Laura as she stood in his arms. "Good night," she whispered, gazing into his eyes.

He slowly disengaged himself from her, and Laura stepped away. She left, not even turning to look back, only sending a whispered "Thank you" and hoping he heard it. A single tear escaped from her eye, and she vowed to never become as jaded as Lord Farris was. She would someday be successful in finding a lasting love, no matter how long it took.

Chapter 6

Laura was already on her way to the stables as the sun crested the horizon. The groom once again saddled the mare that Laura was starting to view as hers, at least for the duration of the party, and she was once more flying toward the copse of trees that seemed to be her riding destination of late.

Laura had done some thinking about the previous night and decided she had drunk too much sherry, hence her abnormal actions. She also decided that she needed to start avoiding Lord Farris. Spending time with him did not benefit her in any way, except to make her fall even harder for him. Finding love was her ultimate goal, but she yearned for love with someone who would return the emotion.

Lord Farris was incapable of loving her, and she knew he would never marry her. He was the sort to marry a woman when he was much older, after he decided to finally secure his lineage. He would marry a woman like Eleanor. Not a woman who preferred the country lifestyle, such as herself. Ultimately, she had concluded she was a strong woman, too strong to pine after a man, and she would move on before he realized how much she cared.

Focusing on other matters, Laura did not notice the doe that suddenly appeared, and she was definitely unprepared for the way her mare suddenly bucked her off. "Ouch," Laura moaned as her behind hit the dank ground with an audible thud. "Drat," she muttered as her mare ran off without her in the direction of the house. Luckily, she had landed on a relatively soft pile of leaves and was physically unharmed. Her pride stung a bit, as she was rarely ever bucked from a horse. Laura rose from the damp earth and reassured herself. "I am a strong woman. I will walk back to the house before anyone even notices I have gone missing." She felt very empowered and started on her walk back.

At least the view on her excursion was enjoyable. She was surrounded by the colors of fall, and even a little bit of green remained on display. There was still a touch of the morning frost on the grass that the sun had not kissed away, and Laura was glad to find something to appreciate, despite her circumstances.

She emerged from the trees and was dismayed to see the manor so far in the distance. She had not realized she had ridden so far. Only one obstacle lay in her way to dread, and that was the little brook. There was no way to avoid the brook. She would have to wade through it. She had barely noticed it when riding, but her boots were not meant for walking in water. She would just have to cross that bridge when she met it. She chuckled at her little joke.

As she walked for what felt like an eternity, her mind drifted to Lord Farris. He was incessantly present at the house party events, which made sense as he had nowhere else to go. Once the house party dispersed, she was certain she would never see him again. She had spent an entire season without running into him, and this next one would be the same. If she should happen upon him, it would be infrequently, and she could easily avoid him.

The brook was finally at hand, and Laura had no idea how she was going to get across. It was not deep, maybe a foot or two at its deepest point, but she did not want to ruin her boots. It was still fairly chilly, but Laura knew what she had to do. Sitting down on a rock, she started to remove her boots and subsequently her stockings. Upon removal, she lifted her skirts, and dipped a toe in the water. It was intensely cold, cold enough to immediately send a chill throughout her body.

"What are you doing?" Lord Farris asked pleasantly. She had been so focused she had not noticed him ride directly up to her. "If your intent is to bathe, might I suggest a hot bath at the manor?"

She blushed as she realized her ankles were blatantly exposed. She was supposed to be avoiding him, not showing even more of her body off. "Good morning, my lord. I am, very obviously, crossing the brook."

His eyes appeared as if glued to her ankles, until she coughed slightly. He focused on her and said, "Yes, I see that much, but why would you need to? Where is your horse?"

"I prefer not to say, Lord Farris."

"Oh please, darling, we know each other well enough for you to call me Gavin." He chuckled and asked teasingly, "Do not tell me your horse bucked you off?"

She avoided his eyes and said, "I will not call you by your given name, my lord." She felt it was best to avoid the latter query.

"Would you care for some assistance?"

"No, my lord, I have everything quite under control." She haughtily took a step into the water. "Bloody hell," she muttered as her entire foot was submerged. The water was cold.

Lord Farris raised an astonished brow and kicked his horse into action. He plucked her from the water and settled her in his lap. "What a naughty mouth you have."

"How dare you!" She had everything under control and would have been just fine walking across the brook. Also, her mouth was not naughty.

"Oh, do be quiet and settle down." His tone sounded as if he was impatient with her.

Laura stopped her struggle. They were on the other side of the brook, so it was pointless, and truthfully, she appreciated the fact that she would not have to place any more of her person in the cold water. "Well then, thank you for your assistance. Now, please set me down, so I can continue on my way to the house." She was very proud of herself for staying calm, despite being manhandled.

Gavin shifted her a little so he could start rubbing her feet. Laura gasped as he stroked first one foot and then the other. His touch sent shivers racing through her but was decidedly inappropriate. "My lord, stop your unwanted attentions this instant, and put me down."

The wind captured a strand of her hair and sent it to her lips. His eyes followed, and Laura gulped. Much to Laura's consternation, his lips descended on hers, and he kissed her lightly. His lips moved lower, and he nuzzled the sensitive spot right below her ear. Whispering, he said, "If I hear you call me my lord again, you will get more of the same."

Surprise flitted through her expressive eyes. He had kissed her because she had called him my lord? She hardly thought the crime justified the punishment. Not that she minded his lips on hers, quite the contrary, but she would not accept his attentions. She gritted her teeth and gave in. "Fine. As you wish. Now please, put me down." She would just avoid addressing him entirely.

"I am afraid I cannot do that until you say my name." He caressed her foot and snatched her stockings from her hand. He slowly placed one on and then another.

Laura glanced heavenward and braced herself with a fortifying breath of fall air. "Lord Farris."

"As you wish, Laura." Once again his lips settled on hers. He administered a thoroughly intense kiss that left Laura wanting so much more. He brought his lips to hover right above hers, and demanded harshly, "Say my name."

Laura was a bundle of nerves, with her mind having stopped working, coupled with an inability to move. The way his breath tickled her skin was almost more tantalizing than actually kissing him. She finally whispered against his sensuous, sinful mouth, "Gavin."

He smiled in exultation. "Thank you." He sealed his victory with a kiss.

Laura moaned. She was happy beyond words that she was already seated on him. Otherwise, she was certain she would have crawled on to him. Her body wriggled as she found herself yearning for more. With wanton abandon, Laura's hands were soon intertwined in his hair, and she pressed his lips to hers more tightly.

The realization of her actions dawned on her, and

she jolted away, breaking the kiss in an attempt to distance herself. She started to slide off the horse from her efforts and grimaced as she considered falling off two different horses in one day.

Gavin luckily stopped her descent and returned her to her former position as if nothing unusual had occurred. He began to calmly place her boots on her feet. He appeared unaffected by the exchange, which irritated Laura to no end.

Now that her boots were back on her feet, Laura saw no reason to stay atop the horse. She quickly propelled herself forward and slid to the ground before Lord Farris could react. Once her feet were safely planted, she determinedly started walking the remainder of the way to the house.

Laura only advanced a few steps before she was once again snatched from the ground and placed on his lap. "I would not try that again if I were you," he suggested mildly. "You are not walking back to the house."

Laura was imprisoned in his arms. She did not doubt what he said, but that did not mean she had to like it. She was seated sideways in front of him and chose to turn her head so she did not have to see him, even in her peripheral vision. Sitting with her back ramrod straight, she tried to make the ride as uncomfortable for him as it was for her.

He chuckled at her very obvious attempt to rebel. "You might as well relax, my dear. I have yet to hear a woman complain about riding with me."

She scowled. "Does this sort of thing happen often with you?"

"Laura..."

His voice held a warning, and Laura supposed she could comply. "Gavin."

He smiled. "What did happen to your mount? Aren't you the one that claimed to be an expert horsewoman?"

Laura tried to make her back even straighter, but it was apparently stretched to its limit. "It is not a claim, but the truth. Even an expert can have unfortunate moments."

He began to nuzzle the back of her neck, which tickled and made Laura squirm. Rather than allow his attentions to continue, she swung her face toward his. Which was, unfortunately, mere inches from her own. "Stop that." She growled angrily.

"Has anyone ever told you your eyes are like amethysts?"

Laura's heart stopped beating. His grin was lopsided, and his eyes appeared almost...unguarded. She did not know how much more of this she could handle.

She could dissuade him though. "Yes. Frequently."

Nothing she did seemed to break his unwavering façade. "Well then, my dear, has anyone ever told you that you smell like summer and taste like fall?"

She blinked. She could hardly say people told her she tasted of fall. "No." She finally answered grudgingly. "I like nutmeg in my muffins. That must be why."

His eyes drifted to her lips. "You know, I recently acquired a fondness for nutmeg, also. Would you care to share?"

"I am sure the cook will happily make extra muffins for you, my lord."

A shiver ran through her as she realized her error. His eyes darkened dangerously and he sent her a sensuous smile. "My lord? You know the rules."

Laura tried to whip her head around, but it was too late. His lips descended on hers in a conquering, all-encompassing manner. If she were honest with herself, she would admit she had purposefully turned her head too late. Instead, she kissed him back. Fully, and without reservation.

He drew away and whispered. "Why would I want muffins when you are so much more delectable?"

Irritated, she growled, "Oh, just leave me be already."

His smirk grew knowingly. "As much as I wish to continue our session, I am afraid I must ask you to behave yourself. The manor is at hand."

Laura swung her head around angrily. How could she help but be frustrated with him?

Once they reached the courtyard, Lord Farris whispered in her ear, "I do hope you call me my lord again. The consequences are most delightful."

She gasped as he helped her slide from the horse. Turning to glare up at him, she could tell he was amused, despite the stony mask he always sported. She curtsied and coyly said, "Thank you, my lord." Then she turned and started to make her way indoors. Unfortunately, she did not reach her goal as Mrs. Westfield came rushing out, clearly agitated.

"Oh Laura! Thank goodness, I had just been told your horse came back without you. What happened?"

Laura tried to answer soothingly. "Nothing. Just a minor fall. I am safe and sound."

"A fall! Oh dear. You know I am always worried

when you go out riding alone. However did you make it back?"

Hating to give him credit but seeing no way around it, she grudgingly stated, "Lord Farris found me and brought me home."

Mrs. Westfield turned to Lord Farris with tears of gratitude in her eyes. "Thank you, my lord, you have done us a tremendous service."

Lord Farris bowed gallantly and replied, "It was no problem. I am always happy to be of service to one so lovely as Lady Laura."

Laura wanted to smack him but instead turned to Mrs. Westfield. "I could really use some tea. Shall we go in, Mrs. Westfield?"

The door was almost in her reach when Lord Farris called out smugly, "Enjoy your tea, Lady Laura. I look forward to collecting on your debt."

Laura ignored him and marched through the door with Mrs. Westfield on her heels. "What did he mean by that?" her chaperone asked.

"He was just making a joke. Do not worry about it." She should be a bit nervous though, seeing as he was not going to forgive her jab of defiance when she had called him my lord again. She had an answer to her dilemma, which was to remain chaperoned at all times in the future.

****

Mrs. Westfield was kind enough to pour the tea this time. Per her chaperone's orders, Laura was in bed resting. Well, getting as much rest as she could with Mrs. Westfield in the room with her. They had already discussed Laura's fall, and even though she swore she was unharmed, Mrs. Westfield wanted her to be extra careful by staying in bed. If Laura was lucky, she might be able to go downstairs for dinner. She crossed her fingers and asked her chaperone hopefully, "Would you be willing to get me a book from the library?" Any genre would do for now, although Laura preferred an interesting romance novel to read.

"Of course, dear, I will go once my tea is finished," her chaperone cheerfully replied. "Can you believe we are almost halfway through the house party? Time is flying by. Of course, I have been especially busy monitoring Eleanor. You know Lord Collins's reputation. I cannot leave them alone for one second."

Laura wished her chaperone held the same zeal for herself. Much of her interactions with Lord Farris would have been different with a chaperone about. "Has Lord Collins done anything unseemly?"

"Oh no, but to tell the truth, he is not actually the one I am worried about. You see, I believe Eleanor would stop at nothing to secure a good marriage, and Lord Collins would be more than willing to oblige her."

Laura was in shock. She had never heard Mrs. Westfield say a disparaging thing about Eleanor. She was a bit vindicated that she was not the only one to see Eleanor's mercenary side. "Who is watching her now?"

"Well, it is now the lunch hour, so I know she is surrounded by people. Otherwise I would be down there with them." Sighing, she added, "The life of a chaperone is exhausting."

Although Laura appreciated the company, she was a little miffed to know it was only because Eleanor was in a crowd. In a short while, Laura would be left alone. "If you do not mind, I will ring for a bath."

"Oh, let me, dear. I will go fetch your book and be

right back." Mrs. Westfield stood, refilled Laura's teacup, and departed the room.

"Thank you," Laura sincerely said as her chaperone left. Maybe after her bath, she could escape out of her room for a walk. Unless she was provided excellent reading material, there was no way she would survive an entire afternoon in her room.

Mrs. Westfield eventually returned with a book and an apology. "I tried to hurry, but I ran into Miss Somers. She said she would stop by in a little bit to see how you are doing."

Laura thanked her and accepted the book Mrs. Westfield offered her. With an inward groan, she could see it was an entirely proper book that would likely bore her to tears.

"Well, I am off to see to Eleanor. I hope you rest up and are back to your old self again in no time!" Mrs. Westfield exclaimed as she departed the room again.

Shortly after she left, the maid arrived to draw Laura's bath. Laura particularly loved the smell of lemons and decided to add a bit extra lemon scent to her bath. Once the maid exited the room, Laura disrobed and stepped into the enveloping warmth of the water. "This is heaven," she sighed as she breathed in the lemony vapor. Not quite as heavenly as riding in Gavin's arms, but much safer.

She did not know what to do at this point. She had resolved to avoid him yet still found herself in his arms. Her quandary was off-putting, to say the least. Her feelings continued to grow with each kind gesture that Lord Farris made and each smile he bestowed on her. How, then, was she to fight him off, when internally she wished to welcome him with open arms?

Deciding that relaxing was the best answer at the moment, Laura sank further into the tub and let her mind clear, except it refused to behave as she wished it to. Lord Farris was not exactly helpful in her plight, either. She wanted to spend time with him, but he would never marry her. So why had her heart chosen him? She cringed slightly when she remembered his previous admonishment. He had already admitted she was simply a diversion to him. As a result, shouldn't her heart have guarded itself against him?

Laura could not dwell on Lord Farris any longer, or else she might end up in tears. She reached for her book and read the title. It was a book on etiquette, which seemed most appropriate, considering her actions lately. Why had Mrs. Westfield chosen that book out of all the options in the library? Laura stepped from the tub, toweled off, dressed, and decided to fetch herself a replacement book.

Once suitably attired, she left her room and walked into the library. So this was where Eleanor spent her time. Her cousin was seated pleasantly with Mrs. Westfield and Lord Collins. Laura performed a quick curtsy to Lord Collins and said, "My lord, Eleanor, Mrs. Westfield, how is everyone?"

Eleanor was the first to answer. "Oh, we are doing very well. I heard about your fall this morning. I trust you are better?"

"Oh yes, I feel marvelous. I just came down to exchange books before returning to my room again." Laura added that information for Mrs. Westfield's benefit. She did not want Mrs. Westfield to worry she had escaped from her room. Laura turned her back on the group and started to peruse the multitude of books lining the walls from floor to ceiling.

"I heard Lord Farris was there to rescue you. You certainly spend a good deal of time with him," Eleanor said, as she unabashedly fished for a reaction.

Lord Collins jumped into the conversation before Laura could respond. "He did what? He had not mentioned his gallantry earlier when we ate lunch." He paused, mumbled something Laura could not discern, and went back to the newspaper he had been reading.

Laura shrugged. "Yes, he did rescue me at a most opportune moment." Her hand grasped a promising book, a novel that was not considered entirely appropriate for unmarried ladies, and Laura excused herself.

She glided out the door, wishing word had not spread about her rescue. It was beyond annoying that everyone had to hear of her fall. Laura ran into Allison outside of the library. "Hello!" Laura exclaimed, genuinely happy to see her friend.

"Oh, hello! I was just on my way up to see you. We have much to talk about." She excitedly whispered, "Did you wish to go to your room, or would you prefer a change of venue?"

"If you promise not to tell on me to Mrs. Westfield, then I suggest we go for a walk." Laura would dearly appreciate a vigorous walk outside to work off some energy.

Allison giggled and agreed readily. They departed the house to tour the gardens, not even bothering to grab a parasol or hat. The day had warmed up considerably from when Laura had been out, although the sky was beginning to darken with the promise of rain. Linking arms, the two ladies walked slowly while chatting.

"You did a marvelous job last night." Allison was positively alight with love. "When Lord Deering returned, he asked me to take a turn around the parlor with him. He then told me he loves me and wants to be with me always. Our walk was in view of the assembled crowd; otherwise, I am sure we would have kissed!"

Laura could not help the bitter tide of envy that washed through her. That was how love was supposed to work. Not this one-sided misery she had. Why could she not be as lucky in love as Allison? "So are you two engaged to be married yet?" That was the ultimate goal that she felt was completely out of reach for her.

"Not yet. Brandon, that is, Lord Deering, wishes to speak to Father first. He is the very proper sort. I am sure we will have a very proper length of engagement, and then a hugely proper wedding." She giggled. "Like I said, he is proper, but I find it absolutely adorable. I just cannot wait. Mother will be so happy when she finally learns of the news."

"Well, I wish you both the best. You two are splendid together. I hope someday to be half so lucky." Laura could not look at Allison, fearing her friend would see the sadness in her eyes.

"Of course you will, Laura," Allison said reassuringly, and then once more became excited. "I heard Lord Farris rescued you today! How romantic. Are you sure you two will not be tying the knot soon?" She smiled archly. "I have seen the way you look at each other."

Allison was only teasing, but it still felt painful to Laura. Laura laughed forcibly and said, "One does not marry a man like that. Not if she wants a happy marriage. But yes, he did rescue me today, but it was completely unnecessary."

The ladies turned and entered the rose section of the flower garden. Some roses were still in bloom, which Laura was grateful for. Flowers always gave an uplifting boost to one's mood. "How has Miss Cannis been getting on?"

"Oh, she is doing very well. She told me that your cousin has been asking some odd questions."

"Interesting. What about?" Eleanor normally did not talk to ladies outside of family.

"Well, you know Miss Cannis grew up near to Lord Collins and Lord Farris." Laura had not known that. "It seems Miss Ashford is very curious about Lord Farris's sister, Miss Farris. Asking questions about her accomplishments, how she looks, and things of that nature."

She had not even realized Lord Farris had a sister. Was it possible to truly love someone without knowing more about him? She mentally shook herself and returned her focus to Allison. "How old is Miss Farris?"

"I hear she is to have her come-out ball this season." She paused and asked curiously, "Why would Eleanor care?"

"Who knows." It was very interesting news though. Eleanor typically did not care about the actions of other ladies, unless—"It is possible Eleanor sees Miss Farris as competition."

"In that case, poor Miss Farris."

"Yes, indeed. Hopefully, she knows how to fend for herself."

****

Gavin once again found himself in the library with Lord Collins, Miss Ashford, and Mrs. Westfield. He stood by the window with scotch in hand. From his vantage point, he could see Laura walking with Miss Somers. They appeared to be deep in conversation while touring the gardens. He turned and caught Lord Collins analyzing him and raised an eyebrow in answer.

"Miss Ashford," Lord Collins intoned. "Would you be kind enough to play some music for us?"

"Of course, my lord. Shall we adjourn to the drawing room?" Eleanor appeared more than eager to play for them and was soon seated at the pianoforte while Mrs. Westfield turned the pages.

"That was very smoothly done," Gavin said to Lord Collins. "We are basically alone without having to actually leave the ladies."

"Yes, sometimes I have quite the clever tricks up my sleeves," Lord Collins responded drily. "Now tell me of this heroic rescue you performed this morning. The one you forgot to mention earlier."

Bloody hell. It was bad enough that Gavin could not get the encounter out of his thoughts, but now even Lord Collins knew of it. He had often fantasized about an experience just like the one with Laura, albeit the day's version had been a very tame version of his dream.

"It was nothing. Everyone is enlarging the tale. Give it a week, and I will have slain a dragon to rescue the lady."

"Hmm. My main question is why you never mentioned it to me. No one will judge you if you have taken a liking to the chit," Lord Collins said as he focused on Eleanor playing before them.

"It is just the boredom of the house party. Once we leave, I see no reason ever to talk to her again." Gavin's heart skipped a beat as he said those words. He was not sure if he would stop talking to her as easily as he made it sound. "I just need to visit Lady Robbins again." He had an understanding with the woman, which unfortunately had not been understood for too long.

"Just so you know what you are doing," Lord Collins cautioned. "Lady Laura is Miss Ashford's cousin. I will not stand for you ruining her."

"I would never ruin an innocent," Gavin said, clearly offended, "and even if I did, we both know I would do the honorable thing and marry her."

"Very good," Lord Collins responded skeptically.

Gavin sighed and effectively ended the conversation by turning to listen to the music. Someday he would marry, but it would be an ideal marriage of convenience where he did not have to worry if he was being cuckolded. Laura may act like she would be the perfect choice for such a marriage, but he knew only too well that once wives grew bored, they quickly forgot their vows. Granted, husbands were no better, but Gavin wanted his offspring to be his.

****

Laura and Allison ended their walk, and Laura returned to her room to read. Her novel was extremely engrossing, with a love triangle, which even involved a peer of the realm masquerading as a pirate. Before she knew it, dinner time was at hand, and she found her way down for more sumptuous fare. She sat watching Eleanor with Lord Collins, and Allison with Lord Deering, and felt a surge of jealousy. Oh, how she wanted to have what those couples had!

She surreptitiously glanced over to Lord Farris and found him staring at her with a hungry look that made Laura's insides clench tightly. Exciting as Lord Farris's attentions were, those attentions promised nothing but disaster for Laura in the form of ruined spinsterhood. Frustration welled within her. She longed to spend time with him but needed it to stop if she was to move past him. She looked away but could still feel his eyes on her throughout the remainder of dinner. Her dessert finished, Laura gratefully departed with Allison and the rest of the ladies to the drawing room.

The women enjoyed a rousing discussion of the latest fashions until the gentlemen decided to join them. Once all members of the party were together in the drawing room, Lady Songfeld announced they were to play a game of charades, much to the crowd's delight. Everyone was to draw a number to be randomly placed onto teams. Laura's gratitude was almost palpable at the turn of events, as she was confident she would not have to be on a team with Lord Farris. Her head had started to pound, and if she had been paired with Lord Farris, she would have begged off using her headache as an excuse. Now, she would not have to.

A footman walked around the room, stopping at each member of the party so he could choose his number. Laura drew number two, which also happened to be the group Eleanor was in. Neither Lord Collins, nor Lord Farris were on their team, and Laura knew the night would be a pleasant one.

Eleanor and Laura were joined by a married older lady named Lady Foster and an older gentleman named Sir Archist. The game passed quickly, with Eleanor commandeering the attention of the crowd, which left

Laura to sit back and enjoy watching everyone else play. Allison kept sneaking suggestive smiles to her Lord Deering, while Lord Farris doted on an elderly woman named Lady Chadwick, who Laura learned was some sort of relation. It was endearing that he would show so much consideration to her. Before she realized it, the game was over, and it was time to go to bed.

Laura's mind drifted as she made her way to her chambers. The way Eleanor acted with Lord Collins and the way Allison acted with Lord Deering led Laura to wonder if her feelings were not a bit more advanced than she was acknowledging to herself. She truly hated the idea that she might have fallen for a rake, but the simple truth was she had. She thrilled every time he was around her, and every part of her detested the thought that he would leave her.

Laura entered her room and appreciated the warmth of the fireplace as she changed into her nightgown. She had been unusually cold all night, but the fireplace was soothing so she stepped toward it. She stared into the fire, watching its flames dance about merrily. No, she was truthfully in love with Lord Farris, tragically, regrettably, in love with him. She got into bed, snagged her book, and fell asleep to tales of high tides and pirate treasure. She remembered thinking it strange how the pirate looked similar to Lord Farris as she drifted off.

Chapter 7

The morning was a bit overcast, but this was England, and an overcast sky was entirely too normal. They had been experiencing unusually good weather lately, but Laura wished it had lasted one more day for this particular excursion. Today was her most highly anticipated event: a visit to an old castle ruin. Everyone was gathered in the courtyard when Laura emerged from the house.

She normally was not the last one to arrive at assemblies, but her head had been pounding that morning. She had tried several different methods to lessen the pain in her skull, but none had worked. Finally, she had given up and ventured downstairs to find her mare. There were several carriages assembled, and she could have ridden in one, but a carriage ride would only ruin her outing and aggravate her headache.

Lady Songfeld stood in one of the open carriages, and announced, "We are to go to the old castle ruins. Once there, we will have time to explore, and then luncheon will be served. Everyone prepare to leave. Those on horses please follow the carriages."

"Oh no," Laura muttered. She had not planned on being trapped in a slow ride behind the carriages. She observed the carriages and was dismayed to see Allison and Lord Deering seated in one. She had hoped to ride with Allison.

Not many guests had chosen to ride, only a couple of married gentlemen, Eleanor, Lord Collins, and of course Lord Farris. Laura grinned as Eleanor tried to hide her disdain for her mount, but Eleanor was a good actress and would easily hide her dislike from Lord Collins. She suppressed a giggle as Eleanor's mare tossed her head in an attempt to bite Eleanor. Apparently, the horse felt the same way for Eleanor as Eleanor felt for the mare.

Her attention was diverted as Lord Farris rode to her side. Maybe following the carriages was not such a bad idea after all, as they would be assured of a constant chaperone. House parties were wonderful events, but chaperones were sometimes more lax in their duties than at other events.

"I was worried about you last night. You disappeared quite suddenly after charades," he smoothly said to Laura, as if he had not been the reason she had departed.

"Why yes, there was something that quite disagreed with me last night." Now let us see if he was smart enough to figure out what that something was. She knew she should be nicer, but niceness did not convince people to leave them be.

Lord Farris narrowed his eyes. "Interesting how you enjoyed that particular, shall we say, dish, earlier that morning."

"I believe I was forced to endure the disagreeable 'dish' and avoided it as much as possible on both occasions." She blushed, despite her annoyance, and decided innuendos would not work best for her. Instead, she would try to bore him. "The weather looks quite dreadful." She actually was feeling a bit chilled, and that chill had added a stiffness to her joints that was typically absent.

He gazed at the sky melodramatically. He raised an eyebrow, and responded very seriously, "Yes, the weather does look inclement. Should you have any needs at all, please let me know. I do enjoy rescuing the damsel in distress."

The infuriating man made talk of the weather exciting even! She could not help herself. "You will be the last to know of any needs I might have, my lord."

He smiled slowly, a smile of a predatory nature. As if he was just waiting in anticipation for his next meal, namely her. "I do believe that is twice now," he informed her seductively.

The thought sprang to her mind, as she intentionally let *my lord* slip out, that she would have been much smarter to not goad him. Avoiding him would work better if he was not purposefully seeking her out.

She focused back on the party. After a few moments, the group began its slow ride to the ruins. Laura wished she could redo her morning and avoid Lord Farris altogether. She was sure she could have found a different riding partner. She sighed. Did she actually wish that? Her heart would prefer to be with him, but her rational side told her to stay far, far away.

The group travelled at a sedate pace until they reached the ruins. Laura looked about with awe as they approached. There was one tower still intact, with half of a wall extending from its base. The rest of the ruins were an extensive, crumbling mess and could potentially take hours to investigate. She could not help but wonder what remained of the corridors underground. She knew they would not actually venture below, but sometimes these castles had impressive underbellies. They rode into what must have been the outer courtyard, which would serve as their picnic area.

Lord Farris helped her dismount, despite her frown of disapproval, and she swiftly went to stand by Allison. Lady Songfeld had another announcement, so everyone quieted down to listen.

"I have a surprise for everyone! Please break up into couples, as we are to enjoy a treasure hunt! Every pair will receive a map with an X marking the spot. Find the landmarks to pinpoint the location of the X!"

Dread filled Laura as Lord Farris came to stand next to her. "I thought I would partner with that gentleman." Pointing at Lord Harding, she fervently hoped he would believe her. She had to at least try to avoid Lord Farris.

He leaned in to her and said, "Two times, darling. There is no way you can escape me now."

That was precisely what she had figured. A footman handed Lord Farris their map, and they began to look for landmarks. The ruins were much larger than Laura had anticipated, and she was not sure how much they should explore, as some areas looked about ready to cave in. The castle must have been huge in its prime, but the elements, and possibly a battle or two, had broken it down to a giant pile of rubble.

They strolled about for a bit, Lord Farris appearing lost in thought, and Laura distracted by his presence. Her headache was slowly growing worse, and she could not have focused if she had wished to. Both were relying on the other to play the game. After several minutes, Laura decided they should have reached their first landmark, and asked him about it.

"I have not been paying attention, darling," he replied honestly.

Well, that is frustrating, Laura thought, and turned to retrace their steps.

"Forgive me for frustrating you," Lord Farris replied with a speculative gleam in his eye.

Laura was annoyed. First off, she had spoken out loud again when she had not intended, and secondly, he had to turn innocent things into suggestive, inappropriate remarks. She let go of his arm, took a step away from him, and passionately told him exactly what she was thinking, this time on purpose. "You, Gavin, are no gentleman. You may rescue me and act nicely, but you are a bloody cad." She felt much better now.

"Now what did I do to deserve that?" he asked as he took an intimidating step toward her.

She took another step away from him and found herself backed up to a wall in the ruins. The palpable tension swirled around them, building up until it reached its breaking point. She responded acidly, "You should know. Every time I am around you, you find an excuse to kiss me, and I have had enough. I do not want any more of your kisses." He raised a skeptical eyebrow as she added, "No more. Just stop."

Gavin took the last step toward her, thoroughly trapping her against the wall. Escape was possible through him, of course, but that was the only way out. "Why the sudden change of heart? I thought you appreciated my attention?"

Now was the time for honesty, if she wanted any peace at the rest of the house party. "I told you before you are a waste of time for me, Lord Farris. I need to focus on finding a gentleman to marry." Despair swept over her. If only he was that gentleman.

"We have a problem then, my dear. I cannot seem to stay away from you, and we cannot marry. So what do you suggest we do?"

Laura was growing more and more agitated. How could he be this hard headed? "I suggest you leave me be, my lord. I cannot handle you kissing me every chance you get." Suddenly the skies opened up, and large, cold raindrops began to pelt them.

"You are just so hard to resist."

He leaned toward her, but she pushed him away and said, "You have your choice of any woman. In fact, I doubt I am the only one you have been kissing at this house party. So, please, just leave me be." The icy cold of the rain drenched her with its unforgiving chill, but she ignored it.

Gavin reached for a lock of her chestnut hair and began to wind it around his finger without actually looking at her. "You truly believe that?" he murmured quietly before bringing his dark, piercing eyes to meet hers.

"Why would I not?" she exclaimed loudly. "You are the one that admitted to using me to relieve your own boredom."

"What other excuse should I have used to spend time with you?" he asked calmly.

"If you had been interested in marriage, then you could have used matrimony as your excuse. Instead, you plague me with your incessant presence when you should not even bother with me. I do not act shrewish, as you put it, to entice you. I do it to ward you off, as I know you will never be a marriage candidate."

"The fact that I have appeared to court you should bolster your popularity for the next season. You will not have a problem finding a gentleman to marry at that point."

Dismay hit her, hard. "You should use your magic to help Miss Cannis then. In fact, use it on any one, other than myself."

He chuckled in disbelief and lowered his mouth to hers. His lips met hers briefly in the whisper of a kiss.

"Stop!" Laura commanded, striking his face with a ringing slap. "I am being serious. There is no reason for me to kiss a man I cannot marry, and we both know you will not marry me." A tear escaped her eye, luckily blending in with the rain quickly drenching her. She was getting colder, and her lips were starting to grow numb.

Lord Farris responded bluntly. "I would not make a good husband, and you deserve much better than I."

"Then leave me be, so I can find him," she begged in anguish. She felt like she was breaking into a million little pieces. If this was what love entailed, then she would be happier without it. She could not look at him right now. The pain was too great. Startled by the sound of thunder, she eyed the darkly foreboding sky. The rain was falling harder and was strangely calming to her furious thoughts. It felt cooling on her skin, and she closed her eyes. Her head was pounding, and she was so very tired. Every ounce of her energy had been used up in her confrontation with Lord Farris, so she leaned back against the wall. What else could he possibly want from her, now?

****

Gavin was feeling like the most insensitive cad in

all of England. He had not known she was so affected by him, aside from physically of course. This was precisely why he did not dally with innocents. Their hearts were too easily involved. He was sorry for hurting her, but he could not seem to resist her.

She had tried valiantly to hide her pain, but Gavin had seen the evidence in the tear drop commingling with the rain.

He decided to respect her wishes and whispered softly, "Just one more kiss for good-bye. After that, I promise to leave you alone." He bowed to her level and looked into her eyes. For once, he did not try to hide the emotion he was experiencing. All he knew was he wished to erase her sadness with his one final kiss. Placing his lips to hers, he sensed something was not right. Her skin was much too warm.

Gavin cursed as he realized she had a fever and was even now shivering uncontrollably against him. He scooped her slight form into his arms and raced back to the party. No one was around. They must have left at the first sign of rain. He did not trust Laura to stand, so he slung her over his shoulder, tied her horse to his, and mounted his horse. He held her tightly to him as he tried to shield her as much as he could from the rain. Gavin kicked his horse into a gallop and raced back to the manor.

His sense of urgency had overtaken all thought at this point. Laura mumbled something about practicing holding hands, and he knew she was delirious. Her fever had come on quite suddenly. Hopefully, she would be fine once she was in her warm bed.

After what seemed like an eternity, they finally reached the house. A groom came rushing out, despite the rain, to take the horses. Gavin dismounted and ran into the house, yelling to a footman to call immediately for a doctor. He defied convention and demanded a maid provide him the location of Laura's room. He deposited her on the bed and noticed how bedraggled she looked. Her hair was matted to her head, and her dress clung to her, weighing her down with its sodden weight. Not knowing what else to do, he stoked the fire to increase the temperature of the room and waited for help to arrive.

Mrs. Westfield came rushing into the room. She urged Gavin out, and he hurried to his room and changed clothes. He wanted to be at Laura's side, but knew if he did not change, he would end up sick as well. His worry was overpowering, and all he could do was wait with Mrs. Westfield for the doctor to arrive.

"Where is Gavin?" Laura asked shakily.

Mrs. Westfield frowned and motioned for Gavin to join them.

Gavin ignored Mrs. Westfield's evident displeasure and crossed to the bed. He took a seat and latched on to Laura's hand with his own in a death grip, while praying that she would be fine. He was entirely responsible for her sickness and would never forgive himself if she did not recover. This current situation was precisely why he was not worthy of her. She deserved a man who would not misuse her or leave her out in the rain when they should have returned long ago.

They waited for the doctor for what seemed an eternity. Finally, a gray-haired gentleman came rushing in with his bag of tools. Gavin had an aversion to blood-letting, except for more extreme sicknesses, of course, and would ensure nothing happened to Laura unless absolutely necessary.

The doctor addressed Gavin. "Please leave the room, my lord."

"No," Gavin responded. His tone suggested he would brook no argument.

"My lord, it is improper for a gentleman to stay in the room during an examination." He sent a pleading look to Mrs. Westfield, entreating her silently for aid.

Mrs. Westfield noted the doctor's dilemma, and joined in with his pleas. "Really, Lord Farris, please leave. We will send for you when the doctor is finished."

He sent them both a thunderous scowl that left the doctor and Mrs. Westfield shaking, and said, "I will not leave. Now get on with it, Doctor, and if I see any blood-letting, know that you will be hard-pressed to ever find respectable work again."

The doctor swallowed nervously but performed his check-up adeptly. After which he told Gavin and Mrs. Westfield, "It appears she has a cold. Her temperature is much too high. Normally I would let some blood out to help her, but you have insisted I do not. There is very little that I can do for her at this point. Keep a cool cloth on her brow, and try to feed her some bone broth. If she worsens, send for me."

The doctor left, which left Gavin and Mrs. Westfield to carry out his orders. Gavin turned to a maid and barked his order to her. "You heard the man. We need warm water, cloths, and broth. Get to it."

All the while he sat holding Laura's hand, wishing she would get better. "I will not leave you, darling." He whispered, hoping she would hear and be comforted.

He kissed the overly warm hand he was holding, and asked Mrs. Westfield, "What is taking the maids so long?"

"I am sure they will be here momentarily, my lord," Mrs. Westfield assured him. "Really though, I have everything under control. You may go, and I will keep you apprised of the situation."

"I think not. I will stay right here," he said very decisively. The maids then entered the room, and Gavin was occupied with trying to cool Laura's fever.

Mrs. Westfield whispered her urgent plea to a maid. "Please find Lord Collins, and bring him here immediately. If anyone can convince Lord Farris to behave, it is him."

After several minutes Lord Collins walked in, concerned. "Gavin, what are you doing in here?"

Gavin turned to him while still holding on to Laura's hand. "I have to make sure she gets better. She has to."

Lord Collins nodded calmly and turned to Mrs. Westfield. He apologetically shook his head. "He is hard-headed when he is in his right mind. Now, I can guarantee he will not be dissuaded." With that, Lord Collins turned on his heel and exited the room.

****

Laura's fever raged on for what seemed an eternity. In the middle of the night, she started to stir. "Water," she croaked. Gavin immediately brought some of the broth to her lips and helped her to drink. She managed a small sip and looked at him with a fevered gaze that plunged a knife of guilt through his heart. "You stayed with me." Grasping his hand in both her small, overly warm ones, she added, "My love."

Lightning struck Gavin's body. She could not really imagine herself in love with him, could she? He stood and placed a gentle kiss on her brow. "Of course I stayed. Now go back to sleep, and get better." Taking his seat again, he watched as her eyes drifted shut. She could not mean her words of love. It was just the fever talking. After all, he was not worthy of her love. Everything about this woman was perfect. So much so, he wondered if God had made her sick just to ensure one of His angels returned.

Gavin stayed with Laura the rest of the night, despite Mrs. Westfield's constant urges that he should leave. He would not hear of it and stayed right by her side. His was a tortured soul, filled with the gnawing guilt of having toyed with her until she innocently fell for him. He knew what he needed to do. He just was not certain he had the strength. When her fever broke, he would leave her and make sure he did not bother her again, precisely as she had asked him earlier that day.

Gavin's decision had been made, and he savored every remaining minute with her. He admired every minute detail of her face, right down to the curve of her lips and the tilt of her nose. Her face could not be more perfectly formed. Its delicacy was perfectly balanced by her temerity of spirit. His hand encompassed hers, tiny as it may be, and he would have it no other way.

He did not know what was wrong with him. Never before had he spent so much time caring about a woman. They were made to be played with and left. Not to savor and protect with all his being.

Laura's fever finally broke around noon the next day. Gavin could not have been more relieved, but he was exhausted and in need of a bath. He placed a soft kiss on her hand once more and bade her farewell. He stood and said to an exhausted Mrs. Westfield, "I will depart now. Please ensure she continues to recover. If she should relapse, you will send for me." He bowed and swiftly left the room in search of his own.

****

By the time Laura awoke, she was all alone with Mrs. Westfield in her bedchamber. Strangely, she swore she could recall Gavin sitting at her bedside. She must have dreamt his presence. No matter how lax Mrs. Westfield was in her duties, she would never allow a man to sit by her sickbed while she slept.

Laura was famished and asked Mrs. Westfield for some food. The only thing she was allowed was some hot broth, which was not going to be enough to fill her. She begged and said, "Mrs. Westfield, take pity on me. I have not eaten since yesterday morning. Please, anything other than broth."

"Oh, Laura, you have been sleeping much longer than that! Why, the trip to the ruins was three days ago!"

Eyes wide, Laura could not believe she had slept so long. No wonder she was hungry. "In that case, I really think I deserve a sandwich, or at least soup with some substance, please," she added, hoping her entreaty would result in any sort of solid food.

Mrs. Westfield chuckled and rang for a maid. Laura was still fairly sleepy, but she wanted to hear about any news that had occurred while she was sick. "So what did I miss when I was sleeping?"

"Not much. Everyone was pretty worried about you, so Lady Songfeld cancelled the events. After the fever broke, Lord Collins and Lord Farris had to leave for business or something of that nature. Now Eleanor thinks it is best we leave the party early, so she can be near Lord Collins. Once you are stronger and more rested, we will be making the trip. That is about all that has been happening. Unfortunately, it was nothing too exciting."

A maid entered bearing sandwiches and tea. Laura grabbed one and bit in, savoring the taste of cucumber. Hunger made everything taste so much better. She finished eating the sandwich and returned to her reclined position. She had filled up very quickly.

Leaving the house party was just fine with her. The sooner she got away from there, the sooner she could forget about Lord Farris. The manor contained too many reminders of him. She could not even go for a ride without thinking about his very masculine hands helping her to dismount or of his overbearing attitude when he forced her to ride with him. Yes, leaving the house would be fine with her.

She was a little hurt that he had left without saying goodbye, although it was easier for her this way. A sense of closure would have been nice, though. Leaving it this way made her feel a bit used, as if she had just been a random dalliance to pass the time. The worst part was that was exactly how their relationship had been. There had never been a promise of courtship, much less marriage. He may have rescued her a few times, but he had received more than his due reward.

Laura was happy she had come to terms with how their relationship stood; otherwise, his departure would have been a devastating blow. Instead it was just a blow. How was she supposed to move on from here? Find a new man? No one could compare to Gavin. He was too handsome, intelligent, and amusing. The best she could hope for would be a mere shadow of the man she loved.

Eleanor entered the room and interrupted her thoughts, just as Mrs. Westfield was departing. "I heard you were awake."

No inquiry into her health, and no how is your day going? So much for a nicer, more considerate Eleanor. Well, maybe it was too early to pass judgement. She would give Eleanor a bit more time to prove herself. "Why yes, I decided I had slept enough, and would rather sit in bed like an invalid."

Eleanor gave her an odd look as she plopped on to the bed. "Sometimes you say the strangest things. Now, I hear you spoke with Mrs. Westfield about our departure. When did you think you would be strong enough for a carriage ride to London?"

"I am only going to sit in a carriage. I do not see why I need to be in perfect health." Laura could never understand why people made such a big deal out of traveling when they had personal carriages.

"Excellent. Would you say day after tomorrow then?"

Laura nodded. She should be in perfectly fine health, physically at least. Emotionally, well, that was going to take time. "How long is the ride to London?" They had just come from her father's house, so the trip distance would be considerably different.

"I believe it will take all morning. I am so very excited to be in London again. Once we arrive, I shall send a missive to Lord Collins to apprise him of my location."

Laura could not help herself. She rolled her eyes at

the thought of Eleanor's successful love life.

Eleanor continued to speak, having failed to notice Laura's nonverbal response. "I am sure he will stop by for a visit in no time." Eleanor turned to preen in the mirror and wrapped a wayward strand of hair in her finger. She then attempted to place it back in her chignon. "It was such strange timing, Lord Collins and Lord Farris returning to London, and right after you were starting to get better. Lord Farris really should have known better than to schedule business during a house party."

"I am sure it was urgent for both to leave so abruptly." Laura was not sure why she was defending him. He certainly did not deserve it.

"Hmm, yes. I just wish Lord Collins had not accompanied him. I miss him terribly." Eleanor sniffed, which would usually elicit sympathy from anyone but Laura, who could see through her act.

"Oh yes, it would have been nice to finish out the house party. We still could, you know." Laura did not expect Eleanor to agree to stay, which was why she offered. If Eleanor had been inclined to stay, Laura would probably feign illness until the house party ended.

Surprised, Eleanor looked appraisingly at Laura. "You mean you will not mind Lord Farris being gone? I thought you enjoyed his company and would not care to stay at the house party without him."

"He is a pleasant enough gentleman, but not one I will miss greatly," Laura replied nonchalantly.

"I knew it! I knew you would not care to constantly be around him. I told Lord Collins it was not necessary to pair you up with Lord Farris at every event."

"What was that?" Laura asked, sitting upright. Had she just heard what she thought she had?

"Oh, you know, Lord Collins asked Lord Farris to partner with you so we would not have to worry about you. You did not think he chose you because he liked you, did you?" Eleanor laughed coldly. She was definitely unchanged.

Laura decided to act unperturbed. "Oh is that why? I had wondered why he was so annoyingly persistent." Not only had he used her, but it was as a favor to his friend. This hurt more than anything else he could have done to her. Yes, this was what love did. It set one's heart up to be torn from the chest and crushed. She did not want anything else to do with love, never again. In fact, she would find the type of man Mrs. Westfield would approve of. "Eleanor?"

"Yes, dear?"

"Who is the most eligible gentleman, after Lord Farris and Lord Collins, of course?"

"Why, Viscount Dunbar. He is not as wealthy as either Lord Collins or Lord Farris, and is in his midfifties, but he is still a great catch. He has never been married and is in the market for a bride. Why do you want to know?"

The man sounded perfect. Ironically, he sounded like the man Lord Farris would be in twenty or so years. "Well, Eleanor, I think that is the man I shall marry."

Shocked, Eleanor levelled a stare at Laura. Slowly, an approving smile spread across her face as she said, "What a delightful idea. I do not know what has come over you, but I heartily approve your discarding your ridiculous notion of love. I think we will need to change a few things about you in order to catch Lord Dunbar's interest though."

"What sort of things?" Laura asked curiously.

"Well, for starters, your clothes. You will have to dress a bit more enticingly than a nun in a convent to attract that sort of man. You will also have to learn to flirt a bit better." Squealing, she added, "This is so exciting! We will have to do a lot of shopping when we reach London."

Laura was not sure why, but Eleanor sounded overly enthusiastic about helping her. It must be that Eleanor thought she finally had found a kindred spirit, a mercenary and uncaring one. Sadly, that was exactly what Laura would strive to be, thanks to Lord Farris.

Chapter 8

Laura stayed as busy as possible for the next two months. She shopped frequently, until she had an entirely new wardrobe that met Eleanor's standards. When she did not shop, Laura went on rides in Hyde Park, accompanied by a groom, of course. Her interest in all else waned. Even her torrid romance novels held little appeal for her. She barely ate and withdrew from those around her.

She was in limbo. While she acknowledged her need to forget about Lord Farris, her heart kept her from doing so. She halfway expected to see him at Hyde Park every time she rode, but of course, he never materialized. The disappointment was almost too much for her, but the hope of a chance meeting kept her returning daily.

Eleanor, naturally, had no idea that Laura was internally a mess. Instead, Eleanor assumed Laura had focused all her attention on snaring Lord Dunbar. For two long, lonely months. And now, all the efforts Laura had put forth toward becoming Lady Dunbar would come to fruition. She would finally meet Lord Dunbar tonight at the theater.

"Oh, Laura! This will not do at all. You must stop losing weight if you are going to wear these gowns," Eleanor admonished angrily. She directed Anna to take in the waist on Laura's skirt and glowered prettily.

"Lord Dunbar will not want to bed skin and bones."

Laura blushed. Anna worked quickly, and Laura jumped when she pricked her with a needle.

"Anna!" Eleanor exclaimed sharply, "Do try and be careful. We do not need a bloodstain."

Laura's eyebrow shot up. Anna could read her easily, so Laura said sarcastically, "Yes, Anna. A stain would destroy our entire night."

Eleanor nodded absentmindedly and went to the wardrobe. She pulled one of the new slippers from a box and thrust them at Laura. "Wear these tonight."

The slippers were silver and matched the needlework on her gown. Aside from the thread, the gown was an ivory color, and possibly the most beautiful thing Laura had ever seen.

Anna stepped away, and Eleanor nodded. "You should do nicely." Laura turned to the mirror and looked at herself critically. Her hair was magnificently piled atop her head in an elaborate style and was intertwined with ivory silk ribbons that matched her gown. A touch of charcoal accentuated her pale lashes, and she had added some color to her cheeks.

"Do you really think I can attract Lord Dunbar?" Laura asked, skeptically. Aside from her plunging neckline and overly tight corset, she did not think she looked that much different.

"Absolutely. He will not be able to take his eyes off your chest."

Laura turned her eyes back to the mirror. Eleanor knew what she was talking about, but Laura would have preferred a slightly more modest gown. She did not appreciate feeling as though her chest would pop out of its confines at any moment.

"We really must hurry. Lord Collins is to meet us at the box," Eleanor said with concern marring her otherwise perfect face. "I have told him of your interest in the viscount, and he promised to make the introduction, should he be in attendance." Eleanor's eyes shone with approval as she observed Laura.

Laura shot Eleanor a look of gratitude. "Thank you. That was very considerate of you." Truly, it was very considerate, and Laura had to give her credit for a job well done.

"Are you girls ready yet?" a sophisticated voice called out from down the hall. Eleanor's mother was to act as their chaperone tonight. Lady Ashford adored the opera and would not miss it unless there was good reason. "If we do not get in the carriage now, we will miss the opening act."

Laura loved going to the theater, although she was a bit nervous at the thought of meeting Lord Dunbar. She drew on her gloves and hurried from the room. Eleanor followed down the stairs and into a carriage emblazoned with the Ashford family crest. Laura drew her shawl firmly around her shoulders to ward off the chilly night air. One of the problems with her new attire was she had a tendency to grow unusually chilled.

The carriage pulled up outside of the theater, and a footman helped the ladies down. They found Lord Rosing's box, which Laura's father had rented for the season, and entered quietly. Lord Collins stood and kissed Eleanor's hand. He greeted everyone warmly. "Ladies, I am so delighted to see you have arrived." They all took their seats, as they were eager for the show to start.

Laura was in a chair next to Eleanor, with Lord

Collins on Eleanor's other side and Eleanor's mother behind them. Laura whispered in Eleanor's ear, "Which one is Lord Dunbar?"

Eleanor took a moment to survey the sizeable crowd before responding. "The gentleman across the way and to the right. He is sitting with the notorious Lady Robbins, whom I believe is somewhat of a mistress to him."

Laura was shocked to hear Eleanor speak of this Lady Robbins. They were not supposed to know things such as mistresses even existed, although she knew she had better get used to the idea of mistresses if she was to have a traditional *ton* marriage.

She eyed the box Eleanor had directed her to. Laura could see a dark-haired gentleman whose hair was starting to gray. He looked like he would do just fine. He was not too stocky or old looking, although she doubted that would have swayed her decision to pursue him.

Laura was intrigued to see the woman besides him. She was stunning. The lady was a stylish creature who appeared to possess the typical English looks. Granted, Laura would have to see her up close to make a final decision.

Eleanor's eyes roamed the crowd as she whispered behind her fan. "Yes, I hear she had been Lord Farris's tart before he cut her loose recently. She is the widow of Lord Robbins, who passed away several years ago. Interestingly, she is only about five years our senior."

Once again, Laura was shocked by Eleanor's knowledge. If Lady Ashford could hear what her daughter had said, Eleanor would receive a verbal thrashing. She found it interesting that Lady Robbins used to be Lord Farris's mistress, though. Laura inspected Lady Robbins more intensely.

The woman was blonde. Even blonder than Eleanor, and was blessed with an extraordinary figure. Basically, she was everything that Laura was not, and the realization sank in that this was the sort of woman who enticed Lord Farris. Not women such as herself.

"How do you know Lord Dunbar will not consider marrying Lady Robbins then?" Laura asked curiously.

Eleanor regarded Laura pityingly and said, "Really, do you know nothing? Lady Robbins would never marry him. She is independently wealthy and can do whatever she wants. She had a son through her late husband and has no reason to marry again."

"Interesting," Laura said as the curtains opened. Maybe Laura would be situated like Lady Robbins one day. If all things went according to plan, she would at least be headed in that same direction.

Laura became engrossed in the opera and completely forgot all else. Before she realized it, the break was at hand, and Eleanor was whispering excitedly, "Now is the time to meet him! See, Lord Dunbar is rising."

Lord Collins escorted both her and her cousin down to procure some refreshments and promptly called out a greeting through the crowd, "Lord Dunbar, how nice to see you."

Lord Dunbar escorted Lady Robbins to them. Laura could now get a much more detailed view of her potential future husband. He did, in fact, have salt-and-pepper hair, but it gave him a refined air. His eyes were a dark cobalt blue, although currently rimmed with red from excess drink, or so she assumed. He had laugh lines around his eyes and a generous mouth that was quite appealing. Overall, he seemed like a pleasant gentleman and should do quite nicely.

"Lord Collins, how are you this evening?" Lord Dunbar asked in a pleasing baritone voice.

"I am excellent. I just wanted to stop you as there is someone here whom I thought you would like to meet. Lady Laura, this is Lord Dunbar." Lord Collins finished, as Lord Dunbar bowed over her hand.

"What a pleasure it is to meet you, my lady." He gazed into her eyes intensely.

"Thank you, my lord." He straightened as Laura curtsied. She could not help but notice his eyes leave her face and land on her bosom, for several moments. Yes, Eleanor knew what she was doing when she chose this gown for Laura.

"I do not believe I have met you before. Who is your father?"

"Lord Rosing," Laura answered.

His eyebrow rose, and he smiled. "Aah, good man. We were at Eton together, you know." An approving look crossed his face as he eyed her chest once more. "I take it you are enjoying the theater?"

"Very much, my lord, I am enraptured with it." Granted, the opera was quickly losing its appeal as his look was making her skin crawl.

Lady Robbins broke into the conversation with a polite ahem, which indicated it was time to go. Lord Dunbar smiled wistfully and once again bowed over her hand, saying, "You must save me a dance at the next ball you attend. Which one will that be?"

Laura blushed and was surprised she had caught his interest so easily. "I believe we are to attend the

Mansor ball next week." She smiled prettily and batted her eyelashes, just as Eleanor had taught her. "I look forward to our dance, my lord."

They returned to their seats. Laura should have been pleased with what had transpired but instead thought she might be sick. She was not supposed to be the sort to marry for status, and it revolted her.

She returned her attention to the unfolding scene before her and tried to become engrossed, but kept feeling a certain set of eyes on her from across the theater. She might as well get used to it. She met his gaze with a coy smile. If only he had not attended school with her father.

Once the final act closed, Lord Collins walked with the ladies to their carriage. There, he bowed low over Eleanor's hand and bade them all a safe trip.

The carriage door closed, and Lady Ashford asked, "Well, did you meet him, Laura? What happened?"

Laura was saved the trouble of responding, when Eleanor excitedly jumped in. "Oh, Mother, it was all so perfect! Laura behaved just as she ought, and Lord Dunbar has already reserved a dance at the Mansor ball." She clapped her hands together and smiled happily. If only Laura felt the same way.

"Congratulations, Laura." Lady Ashford beamed. "This is delightful news. Mrs. Westfield will be so excited to know that her services are needed."

"Why do you say that?" Laura asked curiously.

"Well, I must monitor Eleanor. You know how charming Lord Collins is. One cannot leave him alone with my innocent angel. Now that you have found a gentleman even more untrustworthy, we had better have two sets of eyes so neither of you is ruined."

Laura frowned slightly. She had already learned, courtesy of Lord Farris, not to defy convention by going off alone with a gentleman. Plus, there was no way she would allow herself to be ruined by Lord Dunbar. Her stomach turned at the thought.

****

Gavin threw back yet another pint of ale. He watched the waitress from across the room and wished for the hundredth time that he could get Laura off his mind. He had spent most of the last two months in a drunken stupor, unable to do anything but try to escape from her memory. Even the voluptuous blonde waitress in the bar looked unappealing to him. He scowled and signaled for another drink.

"Do you actually need another?" Lord Collins asked as he sat down.

Gavin growled slightly. His friend had pestered him incessantly about his drinking, and Gavin did not want to hear it. Just because Lord Collins had suddenly reformed did not mean Gavin had to. The waitress brought his drink, and he smiled charmingly at her. "Please fetch an ale for my friend. He is in desperate need of one."

She smiled invitingly and hurried away.

"I know you do not want me to talk about her," Lord Collins stated. "But I have some news I thought you might be interested in."

It was not that Gavin did not want to hear news of Laura. He was just sick to death of Lord Collins constantly thinking him in love with her. "Get on with it then," he said gruffly.

"Tonight we attended the opera, as you may recall me mentioning yesterday. During the interim, Lady

Laura was introduced to Lord Dunbar, who naturally has taken a liking to her and asked for a dance to be saved at the Mansor ball."

"She told him no, right?" Gavin could not imagine a more unlikely couple. Not to mention the fact that Lord Dunbar was a dissolute rake. He scowled. He was such a hypocrite, although Lord Dunbar was on another level than he.

"It appears she was delighted by the request and agreed to save a dance for him. During the rest of the act, I could see Lord Dunbar looking at her like he wanted to cross over to our box and ravish her right there."

The waitress returned and placed Lord Collins's drink in front of him.

Gavin was not happy with this information. How had Laura decided Lord Dunbar was acceptable? "How is that a concern of mine?" Gavin asked nonchalantly, trying to keep his consternation hidden from his friend.

"Well, it is rumored that Lord Dunbar is in the market for a bride, and Lady Laura would be an ideal match for him."

"But she's not," Gavin said calmly. He eyed Lord Collins's glass and asked, "Are you going to drink that?"

Lord Collins chuckled. "Why would you say they are not a good match?" He picked up his drink and took a sip.

"The bloke is too old for her."

"Is that the only reason?"

Gavin took another nip and nodded. "Of course."

"Well then." He gulped down his drink and stood. "You should probably inform her of her oversight. She is to attend the Mansor ball, in case you neglected to remember."

Gavin watched his friend go and cursed. He genuinely missed Laura but had to respect her wishes. Even if he did go to see her at this ball, what then? He still was unwilling to get married. The best thing that could happen to Gavin would be for her to marry, although he just could not grasp why she was interested in Lord Dunbar.

Laura seemed the type to marry for love, but she could not possibly be in love with Lord Dunbar. Maybe he should check on her. Just to make sure she was all right and not being coerced into a loveless marriage. He would definitely consider it at least. The waitress smiled at him from across the tavern, and he cursed again. His misery would have been much more bearable if he could at least enjoy the attentions of a lovely woman, but no. Laura had stolen that away from him, too.

Chapter 9

Laura entered the house after a brisk morning ride and hurried upstairs. The weather had been unsurprisingly horrid, having drizzled cold little pellets on her for the entirety of her ride. She rushed to her room, changed out of her riding habit and into her dressing gown, and sat before the fire. Her hair was a sodden mess, so she unraveled it and allowed it to dry.

The crackle of the fire was soothing, and Laura began to doze off. She forgot all sense of time until the door creaked open. "My lady." Anna entered, and whispered hurriedly, "You must get dressed quickly. A gentleman has called."

Laura's eyes flew open. She was used to receiving callers, but not specifically for her. With the aid of Anna, Laura got dressed in a charming, light green day dress and pulled her hair up neatly. She hurried downstairs and entered the drawing room.

Her eyes fell on Lord Dunbar, who stood immediately as she entered. "My lady," he greeted. "You are spring personified in that dress."

Laura's step faltered, and Eleanor smirked. Eleanor knew Laura did not approve of overly superfluous words. Laura ignored her cousin's facial expression and smiled engagingly at Lord Dunbar. "Thank you, my lord. You look exceptional, as well, this morning."

Lady Ashford rose and indicated the chair she had

just vacated, which was directly next to Lord Dunbar. "Sit down, Laura." She then crossed to Eleanor's side and joined her on the settee. "Did you see the flowers Lord Dunbar brought?"

A large bouquet of red roses rested on a small table, and Laura could make out a small, white card nestled amongst the thorns. "Thank you, my lord. That was very thoughtful."

"You are welcome, Lady Laura." He sat as Laura did the same, and said, "I had hoped your father would be in residence. He thinks very highly of me, you know."

Laura had not known that but nodded and agreed anyway. "He will be here when the Season begins, but at his townhouse."

"Understandable, although why he prefers the country, I will never know." The maid brought in the tea service. Laura raised her brow at his statement. She vastly preferred the countryside, but she doubted Lord Dunbar would care where she resided if they married and she provided him his heir.

He took a bite out of a biscuit and said, "Now that I think about it, I can distinctly recall your father mentioning you. I had not realized you would be so beautiful, though."

Eleanor chirped in with a smile. "I am sure he would not have mentioned her looks. She was quite the ugly duckling growing up."

Laura glared at her, but Lord Dunbar smiled pleasantly. "It is fortunate she turned out the way she did, then. In fact, I doubt I could imagine a lovelier swan."

Lady Ashford set her teacup down on the oak

parlor table. "Yes, we are quite pleased with her progress. You will have to dance with her, my lord, she is unwaveringly graceful."

"I am sure she is." He looked at Laura intently, then said softly, "It is a shame I was not in the marriage market last season. I am sure we would be happily married by now."

Laura was unable to tear her eyes from his. She doubted he would have spared her a second glance last season, but maybe she did not give herself enough credit. After all, Lord Farris had.

When Laura did not respond, he said calmly, "You do wish me to court you, don't you?"

She coughed. How had things progressed this smoothly? "Of course I do. I cannot imagine anything I would like more."

He appeared pleased, and his eyes swung to her chest. She really wished he would stop ogling her. "I am not a young man, and you are a worthwhile marriage candidate. If the rumors of your dowry are true, I am sure we will be wed shortly." He then stood and smiled at the room. "Thank you for gracing me with your time." Then he bowed and left.

The room was silent, until Eleanor laughed coldly. "Who would guess that our little Laura might marry before I do?"

"That has never been out of the realm of possibility," Laura said drily.

"That is true, but it seemed so very, very unlikely."

Laura's eyes narrowed. Eleanor stood and drifted over to the bouquet of roses. "He may be old, but at least he makes up for it." Eleanor snagged the card and removed it from the flowers. She then turned it over and read it aloud. "The most lovely lady in the room deserves the most lovely bouquet. Sincerely, Lord Dunbar."

Eleanor's eyes hardened, and she turned to Laura. She cooed, falsely sweet, "What a sweet gesture, no matter how untrue."

"What makes you think it is not true?" Laura asked. Why did Eleanor have to ruin everything? It was annoying in the extreme.

Eleanor's eyebrow raised haughtily. "Come now. Let's be realistic."

Lady Ashford rose from her chair and shook her head. Her features never changed, no matter how upset she was, all in an effort to avoid wrinkles. "You girls are too much." She glanced at the mantel clock and said, "I do believe we will not receive any more visitors, so I will adjourn to my room."

Laura also rose. She did not wish to keep company with Eleanor when she was in one of her moods. Before she could exit, Eleanor said scornfully, "I like how he even signed the card as Lord Dunbar. Does he not have a given name?"

The din of the rain increased, and Laura assumed it was raining harder. She could really stand for another ride to work off the frustration that was accumulating toward Eleanor, but knew that would not be possible. So instead, she clenched her fists, and said, "You have Lord Collins. Do not begrudge me my own suitor."

Eleanor inhaled sharply. "I never said anything of the sort."

She *never* intended to be mean, or at least that was the excuse Eleanor used whenever Laura held her accountable. "Of course you didn't." Laura departed the room, intent on getting as much distance between herself and Eleanor as possible.

Chapter 10

The next week passed quickly for Laura. There had been a whirlwind of engagements, including a visit to Allison's for tea. Laura had acted pleased to hear of Allison's official engagement to Lord Deering, but inwardly she could not escape her envy. Allison had met Lord Deering at roughly the same time Laura had met Lord Farris, so why had it worked for Allison and not Laura?

Finally, the Mansor ball was upon them. This was the first ball of the season and was sure to be a massive crush. Most of London's elite would be present, and Laura was confident this would be her start to forgetting Lord Farris.

Laura's feet mounted the marble steps to the ballroom. Her hand clutched her satin skirts tightly. She was not sure how, but she knew this ball would be pivotal in her life. She was announced, along with Eleanor, Lady Ashford, and Mrs. Westfield, and they entered the overcrowded ballroom.

The room was stiflingly hot and was sure to only grow warmer as the night progressed. Candles were mounted on every available sconce, and a myriad of flowers provided the room with a pleasing scent. Lord Collins and Lord Dunbar almost simultaneously stepped forward and offered their arms to the ladies. Laura smiled shyly and placed her hand on Lord

Dunbar's arm. She waited for the ensuing sparks to fly, but nothing happened. Despite her disappointment, she smiled up at him invitingly. She doubted very much that she would feel those sparks of attraction with Lord Dunbar as she had with Lord Farris.

"My lady, you look absolutely ravishing tonight." Lord Dunbar smiled down at her. "Your dress is stunning."

"Thank you, my lord. Did you notice the amethysts?" She gestured toward her train. Her gown was composed of white satin, with actual amethysts cascading down the back. She had included a few amethysts in her hair, as well, and had been pleased with the overall effect.

"Of course, my lady, those are what made the dress so noteworthy."

"I had worried they might be a bit too much."

"You are the daughter of an earl. If anyone deserves extravagance, it is you." He smiled charmingly and patted her hand.

She nodded in agreement and cringed at the ensuing awkward silence. She racked her brain but could not come up with anything to say but "The night is an absolute crush. Is it not?"

"Oh yes, the first ball of the season often is. I rushed forward before anyone else could steal the supper dance from me. May I?" he asked and indicated he wanted her dance card.

"Of course, my lord." Laura handed him her card, and he scribbled his name in the spot which claimed the supper dance.

"I look forward to later, Lady Laura." He bowed once again and pressed a sensuous kiss to the back of her hand, then quickly disappeared into the crowd.

Laura was then set upon by other gentlemen, and soon her dance card was full. She was amazed. She had never seen her card filled in its entirety. It was not like she had been desperate for partners before, but her previous experiences were nothing compared to this night.

Laura danced several sets and then excused herself to go to the retiring room. Her feet were going to be sore tomorrow, judging by the ache that had already begun to develop.

Mrs. Westfield had taken up residence with Lady Ashford on chairs skirting the ballroom where they could watch their charges and chat. Laura was determined to never do something her chaperone would disapprove of, which included any offers to walk in the garden or get some air. Walking to the retiring room was probably her most daring venture, which was actually extremely safe as the ball was so crowded.

Laura entered the room and checked herself in the mirror. Her cheeks were too lifeless. She pinched them and exited to return to the dance floor but stopped when she saw Allison. "Allison!" Laura called out, loud enough to get her friend's attention, while also attracting the attention of two older ladies, who immediately covered their mouths and started whispering to each other.

Allison walked over, and Laura gestured to the ladies. "What is that about?"

Allison glanced over and responded excitedly, "Oh it must be they heard the news about you."

"What news?" a bewildered Laura asked. She had no idea there was gossip about her going about.

Her friend looked particularly excited about what she was to share. "Why, Lord Dunbar's interest in you, of course! Everyone had heard that he is particularly taken with you, and then when he greeted you, immediately upon your arrival, the gossip was confirmed! I am so happy for you!" She surreptitiously whispered, "He is a very good catch, you know."

Shocked, Laura took a moment to let the information sink in. Her plan was working extraordinarily well. Who knew it would be so easy? Maybe that was the trick to marriage. Find someone for sure in the market, and ignore any details about him that were not ideal. Like his age. A pang of guilt seared her, but she thrust it aside. If Lord Dunbar did not choose her, he would choose the next young lady down the line. It might as well be her.

His age certainly had its benefits. He was stable, unlikely to suddenly squander his fortune, and worldly enough to know what to expect from a marriage of convenience. She really had chosen the ideal partner. Finally, she answered, "I had not realized he was so interested in me."

"Yes, well, it is rumored that he rarely dances with marriage-minded misses, as the gossips put it. Are you not happy about your situation?" Allison asked with a worried frown.

"Oh no, I am very pleased with the news." She changed topics by asking, "Tell me, how is your Lord Deering? Is he here tonight?" Laura tried to look very happy, and earnestly hoped she was convincing.

"Not tonight. I am sure he had important business to attend to." She added conspiratorially, "You know how these men are. They cannot dance too much attendance on us without risking looking overly enthralled. It is strange though, ever since Brandon began to socialize with Lord Farris, he has been less attentive to me and engages in games of chance more frequently."

Startled to hear his name, Laura questioned her friend, "Oh, I had not realized they were friends. Hopefully Lord Farris is not too bad an influence on your beau." Laura's heart was racing to hear Lord Farris's name, which was much more of a reaction than she would have preferred.

"Brandon told me Lord Farris has been drinking constantly for two months now. He is starting to get quite worried about him. And no, Brandon swears he only gambles small amounts, but I am worried."

Laura could tell her friend was concerned about Lord Deering, but Laura's thoughts were only for Lord Farris. Why had he been drinking ever since the house party? She knew she was not the reason. Maybe it was whatever business had taken him away so abruptly.

Either way, it was no concern of hers now. Smiling, Laura said, "I am sure you have nothing to fear. Shall we return to the ballroom then?" The two linked arms and gradually made their way back as Laura thought of yet another positive aspect to Lord Dunbar's age. He was not likely to acquire a new drinking problem.

The ladies entered the ballroom, and Laura's eyes alighted on a dark-haired figure that looked oddly familiar. The gentleman turned his head, and Laura recognized Lord Farris. She stopped immediately. Panic overtook her. What was he doing here, and how did he still manage to look so good?

Allison looked at her questioningly, which prompted Laura to mutter something about a rock in her slipper. Suddenly, Lord Farris's eyes met hers. Laura swore, turned the opposite direction from him, and quickly disappeared into the crowd. She could not think, only react to the sudden, searing pain in her heart. Normally, she did not run away from people, but her instincts had taken over in that instance. She should not have left Allison so abruptly, but hopefully her friend would understand.

Her mind started to calm down as her slippers led her farther away from Lord Farris. Eventually, her rational side kicked in. There was no way he was here to see her, so she should just stay focused on her dance partners and all would be fine. She peeked at her dance card and read the name of her next partner. She would find him and forget all about Lord Farris.

****

Gavin was annoyed. He had finally spotted Laura, and then she up and disappeared. From the glimpse he had received, she looked quite stunning, although she had lost some weight. He was not sure if it was from being sick at the house party or due to something after. Either way it was not a good sign.

He was growing more confident of his decision to attend the party and check up on Laura. Weight loss was always a negative sign, at least when the lady in question had already been in possession of a lovely figure. Now if only he could find her and have a two minute chat, so he could leave. He had already spotted his mother and sister in attendance, which meant they were sure to have dreaded questions for him about why he was there.

After several more minutes observing the crowd, Gavin's eyes finally alighted on Laura as she danced with some young buck. His eyes narrowed as he took in her attire. She was barely dressed, as her young dance partner was gleefully noting. He saw red as jealousy overtook him, and he abruptly took a step forward, waiting anxiously for the dance to end.

The final notes of the set sounded. Laura curtsied. He rushed to her side as yet another young man stepped forward to claim Laura for the next dance. Gavin growled fiercely, "She is already taken."

Laura's eyes turned to the source of the growl, and the color drained from her face. Her dance partner, who apparently was none too bright, said, "But, my lord, I already claimed this dance."

Gavin straightened to his full height and tried to calm his temper. He was acting a bit overbearing, but he would get what he wanted. "I think it would be wise for you to reconsider that statement."

The gears had finally started to turn in the young gentleman's head, because the lad slowly nodded in agreement and said, "Of course, my lord, I must be mistaken." He performed a small bow and left Gavin to his quarry.

"Shall we?" Gavin asked as if scaring away Laura's dance partner was something he did every day.

Laura nodded her assent.

Gavin offered her his arm and then escorted her from the ballroom to the terrace. He almost laughed out loud when he saw a rebellious light enter her eye. He had missed Laura.

"Why are we not dancing?" she asked, her voice holding a miffed note.

He quirked an eyebrow at her and stated in a matter-of-fact manner, "I want to get some air."

She swept her hand around her and indicated the nearly deserted, dark terrace where they stood. "I had been trying to avoid potentially dangerous areas, you know. Thank you for ignoring my desires."

He nodded. Her sarcasm never ceased to amuse him. "Any time, my dear. I aim to please you in any way that you will allow, aside from avoiding dangerous situations, naturally."

She blushed, and he smiled impishly. Her gown was quite low-cut, not that he minded, but he could not seem to drag his eyes away from her exposed cleavage. It was one thing for him to appreciate her assets, but the view was plainly on display for any gentleman that cared to look, which included every gentleman with a heartbeat. She must not realize how risqué her gown was, so he would inform her. "Are you not cold?" He looked pointedly at her bosom.

"No, my lord," she said, falsely sweet. "Although this trip outside, in the middle of winter, would normally cause a chill for anyone."

"Don't women typically wear more clothing in public venues?" Gavin asked and hoped she would understand his hint. He preferred not to have to bluntly tell her she was dressed inappropriately.

A blush rose to Laura's face. "I do believe I am dressed adequately, my lord, although I am grateful for your concern."

She was obviously not understanding his point, so Gavin pressed the issue by growling, "I cannot say that I agree with you. Your attire is rather provocative, and not something a young lady should wear in public."

Laura appeared shocked. Finally, she recovered and asked slowly, "What do you think the point of a season is for a young, unmarried lady, Lord Farris?"

Gavin blinked. This was rather off topic, but he would go with it. "To lure some poor man into marriage."

She began to explain, as if to a simpleton, "You are correct, although I am beginning to believe it is the woman who is led like a lamb to the slaughter, not the man lured into marriage. But I digress. A lady must dress in such a way as to attract eligible men, which is why I am dressed so provocatively, as you so flatteringly put it." She inhaled deeply and continued, "Please, look around us, and you will see I am quite properly attired."

Gavin heeded her words and glanced around him. He was surprised to see she was not so immodest, at least compared to the other ladies. Somehow, to him, she seemed almost naked, yet a different woman had strolled past, wearing much less fabric, and was just fine. Other ladies did not seem to have so many gentlemen salivating over their assets though. Not like Laura. Could it be that he had been that mistaken from jealousy? He shook his head slightly. She was just too beautiful.

He changed topics by stating, "You have lost weight."

"Thank you for noticing, my lord," she said flippantly. "I hear you engage in regular bouts of excessive drinking."

"Who told you that?" Gavin was surprised she knew about his habits, although he could imagine his dear friend, Lord Collins, had hoped she would "fix" him.

"Does it matter?" She eyed him none too kindly and accused, "I also hear you are causing one of the nicest of gentlemen to turn into a degenerate like yourself."

"What are you talking about and more precisely, whom?" Gavin had no clue what she was implying, but he did not appreciate accusations of that nature getting thrown at him, unless he deserved them. He would know if he had, though.

"I am talking about Lord Deering. You have influenced him in a most disastrous way, and now he has become a gambler. Lord only knows why you are friends with him anyway. He is a much better caliber of gentleman than you," Laura added scornfully.

Aah. Now he understood where she was coming from, although he had not heard Lord Deering gambled regularly. He could not idly allow her insult to sail past him, so he asked, "If he is a gambler, wouldn't that make him of the same caliber as myself?"

She scowled. "Maybe now, but he was a much better sort than you before you got your hands on him."

He laughed quietly, although internally her accusations were like small pin pricks to his skin. Normally, people held a poor opinion of him, but he wanted Laura to see him differently. "You make it seem as if my goal was to seduce Lord Deering into a degenerate lifestyle, when I never intended anything of the sort."

"Then why did you, my lord?" she asked hotly.

He glowered slightly and said, "He is my friend. What other reason could you need?"

"Any reason would be better. If he were your

friend, you would not wish him to engage in such activities. Your reason does not make sense when you could have chosen any other lowlife to associate with. Why him?"

She appeared undeterred, as if she were a dog that had caught the scent of wild game. Gavin did not wish to admit the reason, but he found himself answering her with the exact answer he had tried to hide. He took a step toward her and looked deeply in to her violet eyes. "So he could tell me how you fared, Laura."

She gulped audibly as confused understanding dawned on her. "Why would you care to know?"

He ran a hand through his cropped hair. He had immediately regretted his decision to tell her, but there was no going back now. "I was worried about you."

Her eyes locked with his, and tension swirled around them. He could tell she wanted to say something but changed her mind and backed away instead. She shifted her eyes from his and turned her gaze to a point past the terrace railing. Her voice was steely as she said, "Yes, well, Lord Deering does not deserve to suffer due to your curiosity."

He nodded. The tension was still there but had turned into something heavy and dark. This interlude was turning out much different from what he had planned. "I had not heard he had a gambling problem. I will be sure to check on him." He would not take this matter lightly. He may not be perfect, but he also prided himself on abiding by a strict moral compass, which did not include watching a friend turn into a profligate shadow of his former self.

Laura shivered slightly, and his eyes narrowed on her thin frame. They should return inside, but he had to ask, "Why have you been losing weight? Are you sick?"

Laura glared at him. "Have you been drinking tonight, my lord?"

He regarded her with nonchalance. "Of course not, my dear."

"And I suppose all the reports of your drinking have been exaggerated?" Her eyebrow lifted scornfully as she waited for his response.

He ignored her, which he knew would infuriate her. She looked adorable when she acted feisty. "Are you sick?"

Her eyes flashed. "I am in perfect health, my lord. I am sure any weight loss was from my sickness at the house party."

Gavin was not sure if he believed her. It seemed too easy an answer. Plus, would she not have gained that weight back by now? The sound of the music began to die down in the ballroom. He would escort Laura back in but could not deny his disappointment that he had not been able to establish a better answer.

The ballroom was overly warm but was a positive change from the chill outside. Couples were taking their places on the dance floor as Gavin and Laura vacated the terrace, and surprisingly, Lord Dunbar was waiting by the door to claim Laura. He appeared patently unhappy to see who Laura was with, and Gavin relished his disapproval.

Gavin could not resist whispering to the viscount as he walked past, "Treat her well, or you will rue the day you met her." He left Laura with a bow and a secretive smile that made her blush in response. The entryway loomed before him as he made his escape from the crowded dance floor. At least, it did until his sister Alexa accosted him.

"Gavin! Gavin!"

He stopped, turned, and then reluctantly walked to her side. His sister was quite pretty, with a petite frame and dark hair. She contrasted him drastically. Where he was dark in countenance, she had an approachable lightness. Her eyes were a deep blue, and he knew personally that when she was angry, they turned stormy gray. His sister was a younger version of his mother, who happened to be hovering right next to Alexa like a guardian angel keeping her from certain disaster.

"Mother, Alexa," he intoned as he bowed. He was prepared to depart for the evening, despite his misgivings about Laura's health.

Alexa responded first, "Oh Gavin! What a delight it is to see you here." She was positively glowing with excitement. "You have the most opportune timing, as the supper dance is to start. I have no partner for this set, so how about we sit, and then you can escort us for supper?"

There was almost nothing he would like less. "Sorry, I was just on my way out."

A devilish gleam came to Alexa's eyes as she patronizingly said, "Oh, dear, Brother, if you leave now you will raise all sorts of talk about tonight."

"What do you mean?" He did not appreciate it when his sister acted this way, all mischievous.

"Unless I missed something, you have only danced attendance on one lady tonight. If you leave now, everyone will wonder why you suddenly attended a ball, only to commandeer the attention of a woman for a set, and then mysteriously disappear. Who is she by the way?"

His mother took that opportunity to add, "Your sister is right, you know. There will be a slew of gossip about your actions tonight. I already heard one matron ask another matron the identity of the lady you were conversing with. You seemed extremely taken by the girl."

Gavin cursed his decision to come tonight. His mother and sister were right. He would have to stay for a while and dance with at least one other partner. Unfortunately, his sister did not count. "Fine. I will stay, but only to dissuade talk."

****

Laura should have been more pleased to see Lord Dunbar, but she could not help the tide of misgivings that passed over her. Not that she necessarily wanted to remain with Lord Farris, but she was not sure she wanted Lord Dunbar as his replacement. Lord Farris did need to leave, though. He had completely ruined her night, and why? So he could tell her he was concerned about her? How could she possibly get over her feelings for him when he said such things?

The fact was, she had been jarred from her deluded beliefs that she was over Lord Farris when her eyes had met his. That knowledge changed nothing and would only strengthen her determination to marry Lord Dunbar. Although she could not help but be curious over what Lord Farris had said to Lord Dunbar. Unfortunately, Lord Dunbar's expression gave no hint as to what Lord Farris had said.

Lord Dunbar smiled at her, and she firmly pushed Lord Farris from her mind.

"My lord, are you prepared for our dance?" She

smiled engagingly.

"Of course, Lady Laura. The light of the candles cannot compare to the shine of your eyes. How could I not wait with bated breath for our next dance?"

"Mmm." He must really like flowery compliments. She waited until he brought her to the dance floor, before replying coyly, "You make my eyes sound quite frightful, my lord."

He chuckled softly. "Of course not. If anything, they are the sort of jewels the king himself wishes he could have."

She quirked her eyebrow and made herself look pleased. In reality, she would prefer less sugary words, if he thought them necessary at all.

The set started, which was a quadrille, and the exchange of partners began. Each time that Lord Dunbar approached her, he stared at her intensely and smiled. While he never made inappropriate contact with her, she did not welcome his touch.

The next time he approached, she fortified herself and asked, "What are your interests, my lord?"

"I have quite a few. First and foremost is horse racing, followed closely by an appreciation for fine cigars." His smile turned condescending as he asked, "Do you ride, my lady?"

She was interrupted as her partner changed, but when he returned she raised an imperious eyebrow at his question. "I am sure you know my father has an impeccable stable. As a result, he felt it was essential I could ride."

He nodded and smiled. "Maybe we can take a ride in the park together."

"Of course, my lord, I would love that."

They danced through the remaining steps in silence. Eleanor had convinced Laura to acquire a new riding habit, one that was fashionably confining. She refused to wear it on her early morning rides, but she supposed she would have to don it if she rode with Lord Dunbar. She shuddered at the thought, but it would not do to allow Lord Dunbar to see her in her old, well-used one. No, he probably would not appreciate it the way Lord Farris did or, at least, appeared to.

Lord Dunbar escorted Laura to the table and considerately selected a variety of foods for her. They found a seat and began to eat. After some time, Laura broached the question foremost on her mind. "What did Lord Farris say to you before our dance began?" She had been dying to know.

"Nothing of any importance," he said, betraying nothing with his tone. "I thought it odd that Lord Farris is in attendance at all and even more noteworthy that he subsequently spoke with you. I had not realized you two knew each other."

"Yes, my lord, we met each other previously. He was just chatting with me to make sure I had recovered from a cold." Her response sounded unlikely, even if it was the truth. In all honesty, she was a little confused about why he had forced his attentions on her at all, especially if he had someone keeping tabs on her.

Lord Dunbar apparently did not believe her reasoning, as he raised his eyebrow questioningly. "He must be very worried, as he has been staring at you off and on from across the room throughout dinner."

He gestured to Lord Farris's location, and Laura looked over to shockingly find him in attendance, seated with two ladies she did not recognize. He was currently looking at her with his smoldering eyes, which immediately brought a blush to her face. She looked away.

She could only imagine what Lord Dunbar thought of her now. She modulated her voice in an attempt to appear indifferent and said, "I have no control over what he does, my lord. All I can say is he was concerned about me." There, that was better, although she could tell Lord Dunbar was still skeptical.

Laura did her utmost to enjoy the rest of the meal. She, very determinedly, ignored Lord Farris's presence and did not spare him a single glance.

At one point, her gaze drifted to Lady Robbins, who was seated a short distance away. Laura was startled to see the beauty was glaring at her. Laura raised her eyebrow questioningly, not intending to look haughty, but genuinely wondering why Lady Robbins had singled her out. Lady Robbins subsequently looked away, and Laura put the strange interaction out of her mind.

The supper ended, and Laura returned with Lord Dunbar to begin dancing. Her next partner approached, and soon she was happily twirling about once more. She could not shake the feeling that someone was watching her, but she would not allow herself to look around to find out. She could feel Lord Farris was still in attendance and could only assume it was his eyes on her.

Lord Dunbar had chosen to dance the set with Lady Robbins, not that Laura expected anything different. Even if Lord Dunbar was making his intentions clear toward Laura, at least in the minds of the gossips, it did not mean he would throw his lover aside.

She gave in to the tide of bitterness that overtook her. Her life was not supposed to turn out like this. She was supposed to be her knight in shining armor's one and only love. Instead, she was to act as her future husband's lavishly kept brood mare. She shut her eyes and let her dance partner lead her, not even remotely worried about a misstep. She could perform these dances in her sleep.

The set ended, and Laura was intent on giving her sore feet a break. She asked her next partner to fetch a refreshment. She was exhausted, and there was still much more night to while away. Laura sighed despondently. She watched the other dancers momentarily, until her eyes settled on one of the ladies who had been seated with Lord Farris at supper, currently standing next to her.

The lady beamed at her. "Hello," the mystery woman said, "how do you do? I am Miss Farris. I believe you know my brother?"

Ah, this was the sister Allison had mentioned. "Hello, Miss Farris. I am Lady Laura. It is an honor to meet you." So long as her brother was not near, at least.

"And I am likewise honored." Miss Farris admitted sweetly, "This is my first ball, you know. I was so surprised to see Gavin here tonight and even more surprised to see him dancing." She appeared astonished as she added, "Oh my. I do believe he is dancing even as we speak." Her eyes remained glued to Laura as Laura's eyes swung to Lord Farris. "It is not one-sided, then," she murmured quietly.

"Excuse me?" Laura asked, having missed the words Miss Farris had said.

"Oh nothing," Miss Farris chirped brightly.

Laura's partner returned with champagne. She thanked him and sent him back for more for Miss Farris. Laura was not finished talking with her. "Why do you imagine your brother is in attendance?"

"One can never be sure why men act as they do," she said, as if lost in thought. "Were you lucky enough to attend the Songfeld house party? We were all amazed that he was at that event, also."

"Oh yes, I was there, but we all just assumed he was in attendance because Lord Collins was there."

Miss Farris smiled, and Laura could not help but note the speculative gleam in her stormy blue eyes. The gentleman returned with Miss Farris's beverage. She thanked him and then asked Laura, "My come-out ball is next week. I would be honored if you would attend."

Laura had no idea what balls they were to grace that next week, and answered honestly, "I am not sure if we are already engaged for that evening. Did you invite Lady Ashford? She is my chaperone."

Alexa's eyes widened. "You are staying with Miss Ashford?" Her tone suggested disapproval, as she added, "Lord Collins insisted she be there, so I am sure we sent an invitation."

Laura nodded. "I look forward to your ball, then." She was not sure how exactly to respond to Miss Farris's evident disapproval of her cousin. The song ended, and Laura's next partner was at her elbow. Lord Collins also approached Miss Farris and greeted Laura, "Lady Laura, good evening. I see you have met Miss Farris." He then turned to Alexa without waiting for a response, bowed, and murmured, "I believe you promised me this dance."

Lord Collins promptly led Miss Farris away, and

Laura was once again dancing. Judging by the way Lord Collins and Miss Farris interacted, she could understand why Eleanor was worried. There was an almost palpable attraction brewing between the two. More of an attraction than she had felt between Lord Collins and Eleanor even. Miss Farris had seemed perfectly lovely, and under different circumstances, might have been the sort Laura would befriend. Hopefully, Miss Farris had nothing to fear from Eleanor.

The dance continued for several hours, and finally Mrs. Westfield came to collect Laura so they could depart. Laura had no idea how she would survive the season if every ball was like this one. She found her seat, and Eleanor stabbed her with a penetrating glare.

"Why were you talking to Miss Farris?"

That mostly answered Laura's previous question about Eleanor's intentions, and she responded, "We were just chatting. Why should you care?"

Eleanor ignored her query, and asked, "Chatting about what? Did she mention me or Lord Collins? I saw he was her next dance partner." Evident disapproval shone from her visage.

Laura had not wanted to believe it, but clearly Eleanor thought of Miss Farris as a rival. It was so unlike Eleanor to be worried about another woman. "Oh yes, we talked nonstop about you." Laura regretted her sarcasm, as Eleanor bolted up from her formerly reclined position.

"You did what!" Eleanor almost shrieked the question in an unladylike manner.

"Calm down, Cousin, I was only jesting. We only spoke of her upcoming come-out ball. She wants us in attendance."

Eleanor nodded slowly, relaxing an infinitesimal amount. "Good, you had me worried. You know she is trying to steal Lord Collins from me."

Lady Ashford interjected, dismayed, "What! How could she even imagine she is competition to you?" Lady Ashford was the sort of mother that held an over-inflated opinion of her child, which irritated Laura to no end.

"I do not know," Eleanor responded, perplexed. A typical person would wrinkle her brow, but Eleanor had a phobia of developing wrinkles and tried to always remain expressionless. "I can tell that she is interested. Normally, I would not care, but Lord Collins has a soft spot for her. He swears they have a purely platonic sort of relationship, though."

Laura settled in for the ride as talk of Eleanor's concerns dominated the conversation until they reached home. She was grateful to climb the stairs and see her bed looking soft and inviting in its pale pink coverings. Her room had been unchanged since she was much younger and reflected the girl she had been.

All she wanted was to sleep. She laid her head on her pillow and realized she was making progress with Lord Dunbar, but Lady Robbins's glare left her wondering what was going on between the lovers. Of course, the most perplexing event of the night came to mind—Lord Farris's attendance and attentions. She would prefer to be left in peace to overcome her broken heart. Otherwise, she would enter into a marriage with Lord Dunbar completely and unequivocally in love with someone else. And really, that was the most depressing thought of them all.

****

After Gavin's talk with his mother and sister, he decided he should listen to their advice, and dance with other ladies before departing for the night. He surveyed the crowd, and his gaze landed on Lady Robbins. She looked as beautiful as ever, and even more amazingly, he did not want to bed her.

She smiled at him from across the crowd and waved. Gavin sighed and walked to her side. He bowed and smiled, "My lady."

"My lord." She eyed him seductively. "It has been some time, has it not?"

"Indeed," he murmured.

"I cannot say that I am surprised to see you in attendance."

His eyebrows betrayed his surprise as they lifted. "Oh?" he asked calmly.

She began to fan herself and scanned the room. She had always been the astute sort. "It was only a matter of time before the rumors proved true."

"What rumors?" She really did not need to behave so cryptically.

She suddenly grinned at him and patted his hand patronizingly. "Why, the rumors about you and Lady Laura. She is quite pretty, so I cannot say I disapprove."

He scowled. He had not heard any rumors about him and Lady Laura. In fact, he had done his best to avoid them.

She laughed delightedly. "Of course there are no rumors, just my own suspicions. You appeared quite taken with her tonight, and there are bound to be rumors from that." Suddenly her smile dimmed and she fanned herself again. "I cannot say I understand her allure."

Gavin had always thought Lady Robbins did not get jealous, but suddenly, it was right there in front of him. "I thought you did not mind ending our dalliance?"

She smiled sweetly. "Of course I will miss you, Gavin, but we had reached our conclusion."

"So, what is the problem?"

Her eyes held traces of sadness, but she continued to smile. "There is no problem, but if you are interested in her, do not allow her to slip through your fingers."

Her fan dropped to her side, and she placed her other hand on his arm gently. "Do not think you are doing her any favors by leaving her to Lord Dunbar."

She left on a whisper. He frowned as she walked away. Laura would never be happy with him, but would she be with Lord Dunbar? Even if she did not end up with Gavin, Lord Dunbar was unacceptable. After all, Lord Dunbar was too flawed. He smiled bitterly at the notion. Lord Dunbar was no more flawed than he himself was.

He also was reasonably certain that his feelings for Laura would dissipate, but if tonight were any indication, they were going to take much longer than two months to pass. If he were being honest with himself, he would say that he probably would always have feelings for her, which was a terrifying thought. Ten years from now, when he did decide to marry, would he still be carrying a torch for Laura?

He certainly needed to decide what he was to do about his perpetual desire for Laura, but for now he needed to dance with some ladies and get out of this infernal ballroom.

His mother directed him to some harmless wallflowers, who almost swooned when he asked them to dance. He navigated his way through various sets, and once he reached his quota, prepared to leave by wishing his mother and sister good night. Before he could actually make his escape for the night, his mother made him promise to stop by to talk about his sister's ball. Naturally, he agreed to her request. He took a step into the cold night air and breathed a sigh of relief.

The evening was still fairly young, at least compared to how he had been spending them lately. He checked his watch fob, thought about heading home, and quickly nixed that idea in favor of his club. He had business to attend to. The sooner it was finished, the better.

Gavin entered his club and was greeted by an unrepentant cloud of smoke. The familiar embrace of his secondary home welcomed him after his absence. A waiter brought him a drink, and he sauntered over to the card room. Sure enough, Lord Deering was playing at a table. Gavin could see that Lord Deering had been drinking and appeared nervous with small beads of sweat on his forehead, combined with shaky hands.

He observed the table for several minutes with a scowl.

Finally, one of the gentlemen at the table looked at him angrily. "You need something?"

Gavin eyed the man coolly. "Yes, I do."

Lord Deering's head reared up at the sound of Gavin's voice. "Oh, Lord Farris. Wait for a few hands, and I will join you for a drink."

He could tell Lord Deering was deeply entrenched in his game, and it would be more than a few hands.

Waiting was not Gavin's forte, and instead he said, "No. You may call on me tomorrow when you have time."

The dealer dealt another hand, but Lord Deering paused before he picked up his cards. He paled slightly at Gavin's tone and said, "Of course. I will be there."

Gavin nodded and left to order another drink where he would not have to watch Lord Deering. A scotch was brought to him as he sat at an empty table. The liquid burned, but the punishing brew also soothed him. A chair scraped the floor, and Gavin glanced up to see Lord Collins joining him at the table.

"As usual, I know just where to find you, although if I had been trying to find you earlier I would have been dead wrong." Lord Collins smiled impishly.

Gavin glared at him, annoyed that Lord Collins knew he had been to the ball earlier. "Yes, well, I had an obligation to my mother and sister." He lied, although, once he had run into his family, they had created an obligation for him.

Lord Collins chuckled. "That explains why your sister was so surprised to see you." He sipped his whiskey and added, "Just admit you were there to see Lady Laura."

"Of course not," Gavin replied adamantly. "Well, maybe." He glared at his scotch, deciding finally to confide in his friend, whom he had sorely missed the past two months. "I cannot seem to get her out of my system. Try as I might."

Lord Collins whistled his feigned surprise. "So what are you going to do? You cannot allow her to marry Dunbar. Not if you love her."

"There is nothing that I can do. I am not in love,

just possessed of an infatuation that will not subside."

"That sounds exactly like love to me," dubiously responded Lord Collins.

Gavin did not acknowledge his friend's statement. If that was the case, then he truly was in a pickle. He did not believe in love, although the idea of love held an appeal like none other. If love existed, then he could have a relationship with a woman that went far beyond any physical satisfaction he had ever experienced. He could have someone to share all of himself with. Not just the positive aspects of himself, but also the flaws that were so numerous and seemingly insurmountable at times. Yes, love held its appeal, but how could one tell if he was truly in love?

"Do you love Miss Ashford?" Gavin asked, looking for an answer to his question.

"Yes. Yes, I do," Lord Collins responded, intensely serious.

"How did you decide it was love?"

"At first it was just a slight infatuation. I enjoyed her looks and personality." He paused to chuckle, as he became lost in thought. "Soon that infatuation evolved into a more serious feeling, where I wanted only to be with her. I enjoyed her spark of personality. The way she so easily overcomes every obstacle and in an exceedingly gracious manner. I think for me, I just feel when she is not with me, I am missing a piece of my very essence. The thought of going without that missing piece is a devastating loss I do not want to contemplate."

Gavin sat in silence for several minutes and watched the amber liquid slosh around in his glass as he tilted it back and forth. He shared many of the same sentiments toward Laura as Lord Collins held for Miss Ashford.

When he had fallen in love previously, the feelings had dissipated within a month. Yet here he was, over two months into this infatuation, and he swore he was more obsessed than ever. Could it be possible that this truly was love?

He abruptly sat up in his chair, almost spilling the liquid in his glass in the process. Everything that Lord Collins had told Gavin of his love for Miss Ashford was minimal compared to how Gavin felt for Laura. He was in love, and it had only taken him two months to understand.

Unfortunately, the fact that he loved Laura changed nothing. He was still unwilling to get married. He had never expected to find love, and he did not know how to respond to the emotion, as all he wanted was to find Laura and never leave her side. The problem was not his desire for Laura. The problem was his own inability to overcome his fear of marriage.

Realistically, he knew he could easily marry her and probably be happy with her for a time, at least until she grew bored of him. He also understood she had believed herself in love with him at the house party, but she was young, and he had been her first true kiss. His overall conclusion was, despite his love for her, nothing had changed. He may wish to be with her, but self-preservation dictated he was not.

Gavin rose from his seat, nodded to Lord Collins, and said, "I appreciate your insight. I am afraid I have much to do in the morning, so I bid you good night."

Chapter 11

Laura donned her worn riding habit and went downstairs for her favorite part of the day—her morning ride in Hyde Park. She vastly preferred riding in the country, but was grateful that she had the opportunity to ride at all.

Mayfair was almost deserted at this time of the day, although every one of the giant mansions she passed was filled with members of the aristocracy. Once she reached the park, she brought her mare to a canter, as a gallop would be too dangerous in such a busy place. The park looked beautiful, with a light dusting of snow covering the grounds and hoarfrost in the trees. She could not have asked for a more picturesque setting for her ride.

Sweet, sweet freedom enveloped her as she turned her horse to run along the sparkling waters of the Serpentine. It was not cold enough to have frozen over, which was just how Laura preferred it, as she liked to see where potential danger lay and avoid it. When the water froze over, she tried to choose a different path in the park for fear of roaming from her course and falling through the ice.

Laura turned her mare around to return to the house, after having covered a decent amount of terrain. The sight of another rider nearby made her jump. Normally, she was the only rider in the park so early.

Even more unusual was the fact that the other rider was Lady Robbins, who looked quite lovely in the crisp morning air.

Lady Robbins signaled to Laura and indicated Laura should stop. Laura pulled up on the reins and waited with trepidation to see what she wanted. "Good morning," Lady Robbins said brightly. "How is your ride? I thought I saw you and decided to track you down."

Funny how Laura had never seen the lady riding in the park before, and she would have noticed as few people were out at this time. "I do not believe we know each other," Laura said, not unkindly but still apprehensively.

"Oh I know, but we share a mutual friend, Lord Dunbar." She laughed and added, "And Lord Farris. We seem to have similar taste in men." She paused to calm her horse, which had been fidgeting. "Tell me, do you fancy yourself in love with Lord Dunbar?"

Laura was shocked by her bluntness. "I do not believe that is any of your concern."

"Hmm," Lady Robbins said knowingly, "I saw how you looked at Lord Farris when you danced with him. If I were to hazard a guess, I would say your heart lies more in that direction."

Laura blushed. Was she so easily read that everyone around her noticed, even complete strangers? Lady Robbins continued, "And if I were to make another guess, I would say Lord Farris feels the same for you."

Laura suddenly could not breathe. She sat completely immobile on her horse. Could it be possible that Lord Farris held feelings for her? She quickly nixed the notion. That road only led to more heartbreak. "What is your goal here, Lady Robbins? It could not possibly be to discuss my personal affairs."

Lady Robbins looked at Laura with a cold stare that sent shivers down Laura's spine. "You are in way over your head with a man like Lord Dunbar. You will never be able to hold him, and he will use you and throw you aside once he tires of you." Her gaze softened, and she added sympathetically, "I had the same problem when I was married." She laughed a bitter, lifeless laugh that prompted pity to well within Laura. "I just want you to know what you are getting into, because no one ever told me."

How sad, to have experienced a marriage like that and to probably never know any better one. She could appreciate the warning, although Laura was not fooled by Lady Robbins's declaration. Lady Robbins had ulterior motives, which also explained the glare she had received the previous night. "I was told you were uninterested in marrying again, but now I am thinking you very much want to marry. Are you interested in Lord Dunbar, then?"

Laura knew she had guessed correctly when Lady Robbins looked surprised and said, "You are smarter than you look, but what I said previously is true. Lord Dunbar will always have a mistress on the side. Is that what you want?"

Had Lady Robbins really just insulted her? Her ire was raised, and she said spitefully, "As far as I can tell that is the case with any suitable match in the *ton*, so why not marry Lord Dunbar? He is quite the catch, you know, and most gentlemen are looking for ladies such as myself. Not aged widows." Well, that was a little too mean. Laura softened and added, "Why would you want a second marriage if you know the man will keep a mistress?"

Lady Robbins showed no indication that she had even heard the insult and replied, "Sometimes, one must accept others' flaws. Even bad ones. If he comes home to me at night, I win in the end." She paused to assess Laura, and asked, "How can one as young as you be so jaded?"

Laura shrugged. "I am just realistic. Why do you not just continue your current relationship with Lord Dunbar, should we wed?"

Surprise flickered on Lady Robbins face. "I had not thought you would be aware of our relationship." She inspected her nails as she modestly said, "I am not the sort of woman who can be the other woman. I need to keep my self-respect, which would be lost if I were to engage in a tryst with a married man."

Well, that was completely understandable. Based on this information, it was also wise to disregard what Lady Robbins had said about Lord Farris. "Have you told Lord Dunbar your feelings for him?" Really, this conversation was most unusual, and just a little bit awkward.

Lady Robbins ignored her question and instead said, "You are young enough that you could find someone to love. Do not throw yourself away on a man old enough to be your father." She added softly, "As I did." She heaved a heart-wrenching sigh. "It is not too late for you to end the relationship."

Lady Robbins departed without another glance at Laura, which left only her words to echo. Evidently, Lady Robbins did not want Laura to marry Lord

Dunbar, but what gall to actually tell her. She spurred her horse onwards. She did not think she was capable of marrying a man that another woman loved, but who knew if Lord Dunbar returned the feelings?

Laura reached the house and hurried upstairs. She was so cold. Cold and weary, but instead of warming up in her room, she decided she needed to talk with Eleanor about the confrontation. Another woman's insight could be useful, although she was fairly certain Eleanor would not have any empathy toward the other lady's feelings. She knocked and heard a muffled voice bidding her enter, and when the door swung open, Eleanor looked quite pleased to see her. Eleanor's room was similar in décor to Laura's except where Laura disliked the color scheme, Eleanor thought it was superb.

"Good morning," Eleanor said tiredly, "how was your ride?"

"It was invigorating, to say the least." Laura perched on the edge of a chair next to the bed. How could Eleanor still look tired after sleeping so much? "I ran into Lady Robbins." Eleanor's eyes grew round as Laura recounted the details of the encounter. "I just do not understand her actions. You said she would never be interested in marriage again, yet she clearly loves Lord Dunbar."

"Some women are not as smart as you or I. They throw away their security for a made-up emotion." She paused to sip some tea and motioned for Laura to help herself to the refreshment tray. "Currently, Lady Robbins answers to no one. If she married again, she will be the property of her husband. Why risk your independence for a fleeting emotion?"

Eleanor shuddered. She did not believe in love, which hopefully would work for her better than love was working for Laura. "So you have no feelings for Lord Collins?" Laura secured a teacup and poured herself some tea. The steaming liquid worked quickly, as the cold receded from her body and was replaced by blissful warmth.

"Of course I have feelings for Lord Collins." Eleanor huffed with indignation. "He is a fine man, even if he does seem overly concerned with the entire Farris family. Did I mention Miss Farris is trying to steal him away from me?"

"But those feelings are not love?" Laura was not sure why she kept hoping others believed in the emotion. Somehow, it mattered a great deal to her. Strange that Lady Robbins was the only person to give her any assurance that love existed. Too bad she could not talk to her more. No, no, no. She no longer believed in love. She just had to convince herself of that. "How do you know Miss Farris wants to steal Lord Collins from you?"

"Sometimes one can just tell these things. Miss Farris must be watched, or I would be risking my future position as countess." Eleanor looked quite alarmed at the notion, but continued on by answering Laura's previous question. "No, I cannot imagine I will ever love Lord Collins. He has some rather annoying habits and enjoys his horses more than he ought."

"Don't we all?" Laura muttered. If Eleanor felt that way about Lord Collins, then she should really just let him loose. A nagging thought entered Laura's mind that gave her pause. If Laura disliked the notion of a loveless marriage, such as the one Eleanor was interested in, how likely would it be that Laura actually would marry Lord Dunbar? She at least had better reasons not to love the viscount, as opposed to Eleanor's reasoning. Maybe she should try to discern how Lord Dunbar felt about Lady Robbins before doing anything drastic.

Laura could tell that Eleanor was truly concerned about Miss Farris and tried to put her mind at ease, "I am sure you have nothing to fear from Miss Farris. Lord Collins will never deviate from you."

"Thank you, that is very sweet of you to say." Eleanor patted Laura's hand, and then added, "I have a plan to ensure Lord Collins will never prefer Miss Farris over myself." Eleanor's eyes held a wicked gleam that made Laura uncomfortable.

"What is this plan?" she asked cautiously.

"I am afraid I cannot say, although I am sure you will figure it out. The Farris household really ought to employ help that does not gossip." Eleanor laughed, a tinkling sound that normally was lovely, but this time had a cold note that did not resonate well with Laura.

****

Gavin entered the house in Mayfair where his sister and mother currently resided. He held separate bachelor quarters, which were far preferable for the activities he typically engaged in. "Where is my mother?" he asked to the aging butler who answered the door. Their butler, Munby, had been with them as far back as Gavin could remember.

"In the parlor, my lord," Munby answered with a small bow.

Gavin made his way to his mother's favorite room and found her seated demurely on her favorite chair with some needlework. "Hello, Mother."

"Oh, darling, it is about time you arrived."

Gavin glanced at the ornate clock on the mantel. It was only ten o'clock, and he had never specified when she could expect him. Just how long had she been waiting? "Terribly sorry to keep you," he said dryly.

"Yes, well you are here now. I have some urgent matters to discuss with you. Please, stop hovering by the door as if you yearn to flee, and sit down." She indicated a chair next to her, which Gavin obligingly took. He detested overly feminine décor, and this room was ripe with it. It was done in various shades of pink, and it made him rather uncomfortable.

Gavin watched apprehensively as his mother pulled out a jewelry box and handed it to him. "What is this?" he asked, although the box looked eerily like the one his grandmother's wedding band was kept in.

"Open it. It was your grandmother's, and now that you have found the woman you are to marry, you should have it." She looked giddy as she spoke of his supposed impending nuptials.

"Mother, it will be many, many years before I marry," Gavin said, aggravated that he was having this conversation with her… again.

She did not look as crestfallen as he had expected. "Of course you need it. I saw how you looked at that very eligible young lady last night. You cannot let a love like that pass you by."

Gavin swallowed. His throat felt suddenly very dry. "I will ring for some tea," he managed to croak out.

"Oh, I ordered tea earlier. It should arrive momentarily," she responded sweetly.

Gavin waited until the tea arrived, while trying to

figure out how to put his mother off. Once he had taken a gulp of his straight black tea, he said, "I have already told you my plans for marriage. Those plans do not include love, nor Lady Laura, so please take back the ring." He placed the box neatly on the table, finished off the remainder of his tea, and poured himself another cup.

This time his mother looked disheartened. "I do not understand your aversion to love. Why would you not want a marriage based on such a strong foundation? I have seen the way you two look at each other, and know you would be happy with her."

He did not wish to be cruel, but he knew no other way to stop his mother's hopes. Gavin bit out bluntly, "I saw the way yours and father's relationship turned out. I refuse to have a marriage that I am emotionally invested in subsequently turn out like that. Life is simpler if my expectations are much lower." Despair began to creep into his heart, because his view of matrimony was even depressing himself.

"Oh dear," Lady Farris said remorsefully. "I had no idea you felt this way. To think you formed your negative opinion of marriage from my example." She rose and began to pace. "I do not believe I have talked to you about my marriage with your father. Did you know our marriage was decided the day I was born? Your father was five at the time and had no more choice than I. When I reached adulthood, my family kindly gave me a season, although it was a complete waste of money seeing as I was to marry the next year."

His mother drew in a shaky breath. This was not an easy thing to talk about. "When I married your father, I was in love with someone else, and your father knew it.

I was so young and stupid. I should have forgotten about the one I loved and focused on your father, but I did not. After I had you, I am afraid I broke my vows. Granted, your father had not been faithful the entirety of our marriage, but there is always a different standard set for us women."

She sighed and continued pacing. "That is no excuse for my actions, of course, and I realized that after my one indiscretion." She took a shuddering breath, and Gavin saw a tear escape his cherished mother's eye. "That one night led to your sister's birth, who your father graciously acknowledged as his. I regretted my poor choice, but at that point it was too late for our marriage. He never forgave me."

She sat back down, and looked pleadingly at her son. "So you see, my marriage was a very poor example. If there is anything I can hope for you and Alexa, it is that you both marry for love and avoid the cold marriage I had."

Gavin lovingly cradled her hand in his. Who knew his mother had been in such a painful marriage? He had always assumed both his mother and father had led separate lives, instead of this lonely, one-sided thing his mother had endured. Is that the sort of marriage he was destined for? Protecting himself by waiting until he coldly selected a bride would only delay his misery.

He never had stopped to consider his future bride's desires, either. What if she was hoping for a loving marriage? He had never contemplated the possibility of fidelity on one person's side, much less both. He knew he could be faithful to Laura, but did he want to risk her dedication to do the same? Marrying Laura would be much riskier than marrying anybody else, because she could potentially break his heart. What happened if he let her go though? His heart would definitely be broken in that scenario.

Gavin rose abruptly and swept the ring off the table. He pocketed it as he left the room. He could hear the smile in his mother's voice as she called out, "We have not discussed the bills for the ball yet."

"Send them to me," he ordered gruffly as he left. He had more important things to focus on, such as winning his woman.

****

The previous night's activities had left Laura antisocial. Typically, she would have joined Eleanor and Lady Ashford in the drawing room to welcome any guests who might come to call, but she held different plans for the day. She had decided to take a trip to Bond Street under the pretense of acquiring a new shawl for a gown that had just arrived. Luckily, Eleanor already had plans to join Lord Collins on a ride, so Laura was free to take Anna as her sole companion.

Laura sighed at the dreariness of the day as the carriage rumbled down the cobbled streets. The rain had started that morning, but had now begun to turn into snow, rendering the streets a slushy mess. She turned to her maid and asked, "Has your mother's health improved?" Anna's mother had managed to catch a cold a week past, and Laura had not been updated.

Anna smiled brightly. "She is doing much better. The doctor you sent over really helped, thank you."

Laura was happy to hear of the improvement. She had spent a good deal of her pin money on that doctor and liked to see results. "That is good to hear. Have there been any new developments for you in the romance department?" She loved to hear Anna's stories and sat back to listen while Anna spoke of a young man she had recently met. She knew she should not be so familiar with the maid, but what was she supposed to do? Act as if the girl did not exist? Sometimes Anna helped her for hours on end, and Laura preferred to spend that time enjoying herself.

The carriage halted as it arrived at Bond Street, and Laura was pleased to see the usually boisterously busy shopping district was almost deserted. The inclement weather must have kept idle shoppers away. She entered an establishment to quickly choose a shawl. Once her transaction was completed, she immediately crossed the street to peruse a bookstore. She grimaced at the mud caked on her boots. Laura had tried to step daintily through the streets, but her hem was still a sodden fright.

A bell jingled as she walked in. The owner glanced up and gave her a look of disapproval when he saw the mud she tracked in. Laura pointedly ignored his rudeness and began to browse the books. Her eyes alighted on a particularly elegant volume of John Keats's poems. She happened to adore Keats and had never seen such a spectacular edition. She glanced at the price, and Laura was displeased to see the amount the store owner was asking. She had used most of her pin money for the month already, and Laura was a little short but decided she could ask the owner to negotiate.

She walked determinedly up to the man and laid the volume on the counter. "Good day. I was admiring this volume by Keats and wondered if you would negotiate on the price a little."

The shopkeeper pushed back the spectacles perched on the bridge of his nose, and said unyieldingly, "The price is firm."

Laura wanted that book. "Would you be willing to hold it until next month? I will have the full amount at that time."

"No," he said flatly, "I do not put books aside when someone cannot afford them. Especially women." He sneered derisively, pausing to smile as a patron entered the store. "Besides, you just tracked mud throughout my establishment."

An unusual mixture of shame and anger caused an unwanted blush to rise to her face. She glanced at the floor, noting she had not tracked that much mud around. He must truly despise women, to offend an obvious member of the aristocracy in such a manner.

"That is no way to talk to a lady." Laura whirled around to find Lord Farris standing there, looking perfectly tailored, and frustratingly, without a single speck of mud on him. "What is the problem here?" he demanded.

"Nothing," Laura spoke quickly. She added frigidly to the shopkeeper, "Do not worry about seeing me in here again." Not waiting for his response, Laura left, wishing she had not bumped into Lord Farris.

Laura could curse, she was so mad. Lord Farris had the worst timing, to happen upon her when she was in such an awkward situation. She was not actually upset with him, more just at the situation. She bit her lip and glanced down at her hemline. Even the weather was working against her today. If she had simply gone shopping yesterday, none of this would have happened.

She stepped daintily past a pothole in the road and

was irked when Lord Farris's hand shot out and grabbed her elbow. "You walk so slowly it is a miracle you do not get run over by a carriage." He hurriedly directed her to the safety of the sidewalk. His clothes were miraculously still unmarred by mud.

"I am certainly not that slow," Laura responded indignantly.

The snow was still falling, and Laura shivered. Lord Farris's hand tightened on her arm, and he led her into a nearby deserted café. A waiter approached, which allowed Lord Farris to order hot chocolates as he led Laura to an intimate table.

She sat down, annoyed that she was allowing herself to be guided so easily. "What are we doing here, my lord?"

He smiled wryly, which properly melted Laura's heart. "In several moments, we will partake of a beverage together." He shifted in his seat and asked, "Did you know you have a tendency to ask obvious questions?"

"When else have I asked obvious questions?" she asked, slightly vexed. "And for the record, my question was not as obvious as you think."

He laughed, and he caught her hand in his. Laura tugged gently, but he refused to let go. His eyes darkened slightly and he said, "I can still remember the sight of your naked ankles by the brook."

Laura gasped loudly and blushed. The rules of etiquette demanded he not speak of her exposed ankles. Ever. His eyes appeared hooded, and she asked sharply, "What is your point, my lord?"

"Nothing, except I believe I had been remiss in telling you how lovely your ankles are."

"They are just ankles, my lord." She added brusquely, "Now, when did I ask obvious questions?"

His hand stroked hers methodically, and his eyes landed on her lips. "You asked obvious questions on almost every other altercation we had."

She pulled much harder on her hand. Unfortunately, his grip was like steel.

"Now, now, Laura. Your chocolate will arrive shortly. Try and be patient."

She glared. He knew full well that she did not care about her chocolate. "And if I am not thirsty?"

He raised an eyebrow as he inspected her light frame. "The chocolate will help with your weight problem."

The waiter brought two cups of the thick, molten chocolate and placed them gingerly in front of the couple. If Laura had not been so chilled from the weather, she would have refused out of principle. She looked defiantly at Lord Farris, lifted her cup, and took a sip. It was delicious. "I had not realized I had a weight problem."

"Were you not listening last night?"

"Of course, but I was perfectly fine last night, and I am perfectly fine today."

He scoffed. "And I am sure you were perfectly fine in the book store."

She could not meet his eyes. "Of course I was. Why are you here, anyway?"

"I have an appointment with my tailor."

She looked meaningfully at the clock on the wall, then back at him. "I would hate to keep you from your appointment. Thank you for the chocolate. Have a good day." She hoped he would take the hint and leave.

Lord Farris sat back and smiled a gloating smile. "Do not concern yourself overly about me, darling. Where is your Lord Dunbar? Too cold outside for his old bones?"

He was not *that* old. Lord Farris excelled at picking out topics to annoy her with. She began to drink her chocolate in earnest and ignored him. The sooner she was away from him, the better.

"How old is he? If I was to hazard a guess, I would say about the same age as your father."

Suddenly, her chocolate went down the wrong pipe. She coughed and looked up. He was smiling wickedly, and Laura had a sneaking suspicion that he had consulted *Debrett's* in regards to Lord Dunbar.

"So is it true your father and Lord Dunbar attended school together?"

Her suspicions were confirmed. He had investigated Lord Dunbar. Laura quickly drained the last of her chocolate, almost slamming the poor cup down on the little table. She stood, which forced Lord Farris to also stand. "That is none of your business, now I must be going. Thank you for the chocolate," she gruffly admonished, swept a small curtsy, and left as Anna trailed behind.

Laura was relieved to be back in her coach travelling home. Lord Farris was the most infuriating man she had ever met. To think he had purposefully fed her rich food to put weight on her. She was not some cow getting fattened up for slaughter, and then he magically knew which topic to bring up about Lord Dunbar that aggravated her most. Dratted man.

Anna broke through her thoughts, asking inquisitively, "That was not Lord Dunbar. He was too young. Who is he?"

Again with the age. Laura spoke shortly, indicating she did not want to speak of the subject further, "He is no one." Anna closed her mouth and did not utter another sound the rest of the way home, which was just what Laura needed.

****

Gavin let her go and took a moment to appreciate the view of her backside, swaying as she walked. He signaled the waiter to bring his check and paid the man. Life was so much better with Laura in it. He stepped back outside and perused the streets. They were still empty, and it was still snowing slightly.

The bell jingled as he entered the little bookstore, and he was unsurprised when the shopkeeper rushed to help him.

"My lord," the shopkeeper groveled, "what an honor that you would choose to grace my shop with your presence."

Gavin stared at him coldly. "What was the lady interested in when I stopped by earlier?"

The little man wrung his hands nervously. "Just some of that romantic drivel young ladies find so interesting, my lord."

"Byron?" Gavin had not pegged Laura as the type.

"No, my lord. Keats."

Gavin's eyebrow rose in surprise, which was the only emotion he betrayed. "I would like to purchase it."

"Of course, my lord. Allow me to wrap it for you."

The book was small, but the binding was unusually well made, seeing as Keats was not very popular. The shopkeeper handed the package to Gavin, and Gavin said quietly, "Now, you will also write a letter of apology to the lady."

He sputtered in surprise. "For her? But my lord…"

Gavin glared harshly. "You have insulted a future viscountess. It is the least you can do."

The man gulped and scurried away to do as told. Gavin checked his timepiece while he waited. He was considerably late for his appointment with his tailor, but his tailor would never send him away. Even if he did, Laura was more important.

****

Gavin had not sat at home alone for quite some time. Carousing every night was exhausting, and he was happy to enjoy the stillness for a change. He had asked his chef to prepare a simple meal and serve it to him in his study, as he did not want to waste time adjourning to the dining room. He needed time to dwell on the best course of action for winning his Laura.

She would be in attendance at his sister's ball. Lord Collins had mentioned more than once that Miss Ashford required an invitation. Aside from that one event, he was unsure where she would be. His most likely recourse would be to tag along with Lord Collins to any events he attended, as logic dictated where his friend went so would Laura.

Gavin pulled his grandmother's ring from his pocket and contemplated it. A large, circular opal was surrounded by amethysts, which somehow seemed to suit Laura perfectly. Maybe it was how the fire in the opal reminded him of her fiery personality, or the purple of the amethysts were reminiscent of her eyes. Placing the ring back in his pocket, he realized he had a lot of work to do. He knew Laura had only just begun a relationship with Lord Dunbar, but he could imagine the older gentleman was in a hurry to get things finalized. Maybe he needed more time with Laura, but finding out her schedule was imperative and would cost him. Gavin called for a footman and waited impatiently for his hurried arrival.

"I need you to go to the Ashford residence and gather some information for me," he demanded, as he pulled an envelope filled with money from his pocket. The amount would ensure he received the information he desired. "Use whatever means necessary to find out the schedule of Lady Laura Rosing. Primarily any daily habits she may have." He knew Laura enjoyed riding and was hoping she was still maintained that daily practice in London.

The footman agreed readily and departed to complete his mission. Who knew how long it would take for his man to accomplish his mission, but Gavin was confident it would be successful. Now he had another dilemma. To win Laura, it was imperative he convince her he'd had a change of heart about marriage. If he were to simply approach her and propose marriage, she would laugh in his face. He could easily compromise her, but he would keep that as a last resort for when all else failed.

He knew himself, and he realized he would have to convince her through sheer force of will. Forcefully, just as he did everything else in his life. Scaring away suitors would not be a problem, except Lord Dunbar, whom he must somehow convince to leave the picture. Above all, Laura needed to feel the choice was hers to come to him, even if he manipulated events to suit his desire.

Gavin was interrupted by a knock on the door.

"Come in," he said gruffly.

Lord Deering entered the room and smiled curiously. "I have arrived as directed."

"I trust the rest of your night went smoothly?" If Gavin had to hazard a guess, he would say Deering's night was not terribly pleasant, as evidenced by the dark circles under his eyes.

Lord Deering hesitated. "I suppose it could have been worse."

"Care for a drink?" Gavin stood and poured two glasses. After handing one to the gentleman, he went to stand in front of the window. The city was spread out before him in all its glorious splendor. As much as he enjoyed the perks of city living, he would always prefer the countryside, and unless he had missed something, so would Laura.

"Not that I don't appreciate the scotch, but why am I here?" Lord Deering asked pleasantly.

"There is some concern over your gambling lately."

"Why, I never!" Lord Deering sputtered and stood.

Gavin looked behind him at Lord Deering. The man appeared agitated, but there could be any number of reasons. "Sit down." He waited until Lord Deering obeyed him, and said gruffly, "I will be blunt. I am the one who introduced you to the world of chance. After all, you barely knew how to throw dice when I met you. In two months' time, you have progressed from a complete novice to a wastrel, and I will not stand for it."

"I am not some child in leading strings, to be ordered about, and I am hardly the first gentleman to engage in games of skill," Lord Deering declared sharply.

"Skill?" Gavin scoffed and returned his gaze to the lights shining before him. "Just how much money have you won, then?"

Charged silence followed his query.

"Well?" Gavin asked.

"I think you know the answer to that."

Gavin appreciated Lord Deering's honesty, despite his grudging tone. "I cannot allow myself to be your downfall. I am the last person to tell you to quit enjoying your vice entirely, but I would suggest you ease up."

"Or what? You cannot do anything to me, so your threat is useless." Lord Deering's eyes gleamed from his boldness.

"Do you truly believe that?" He levelled a stare at Lord Deering until the chap was forced to look away. "I will not do anything, but you have a choice to make. Miss Somers does not seem the sort to marry a degenerate. You might hide your predilection from her, but you know how rumors abound. Something tells me she will find out."

The chime of a clock echoed in the house, signaling the start of a new hour. Both gentlemen ignored the noise, focusing instead on the other in a silent battle of wills. Finally, Lord Deering stood, tore his gaze from Gavin's, and said wryly, "I can only imagine how she would find out." He swept a mocking bow and said, "Good day to you, sir."

His feet whispered softly on the carpet as he departed the study. Gavin sighed audibly. His message had been delivered, but only time would tell if it worked, and if he had lost a friend. The room was starting to darken as night fell, but light was unimportant. He had only to wait for his footman's return, and then he could ascend to bed.

Finding out Laura's habits was essential to his plan to woo her, but he was starting to doubt his luck on gaining insight. Some servants were paid well enough to know better than to betray their mistresses, although everyone had his price. He returned to his desk and started to pay the accumulating charges for his sister's ball. He was always shocked to see how much one of these events costed, and this one was astronomical. After finishing the last one for the night, Gavin rose and started to make his way to bed when his footman finally found him.

"My lord, I have the particulars on your lady," he said proudly as he puffed out his chest.

"Very good, please tell me," Gavin demanded impatiently.

"Well, my lord, I tried talking to another footman, but he would not say anything." Gavin raised his eyebrow, indicating the man should get to the point, at which, the servant hurriedly continued speaking, "The lady's maid says she rides in the morning at Hyde Park." He swallowed as his chest deflated a bit.

Just as he had suspected. "Did she say where in Hyde Park, or at what time?"

"Well, no, my lord."

Oh boy, that meant he would have to go early and hope to bump in to her. He could ride near the entrance, but morning was not exactly a short period of time. "Very good, thank you for your services." Tomorrow morning could be most promising.

****

Laura rose as she did every morning, dressed in her worn riding habit, and ventured downstairs to begin her ride. Her groom was waiting for her as usual, and she was shortly entering the park. The air was colder than Laura preferred. She could see her breath clearly, which meant she would have to ride that much harder to keep warm. She found herself once again taking the Serpentine route she had used yesterday. The view had been so lovely the previous morning that she wanted to appreciate it again.

As she rode, she thought she heard a voice call her name. "Not again," she muttered. She did not welcome interruptions to her riding ritual. She turned in her saddle and could have sworn she saw Lord Farris riding behind her. As he drew closer, she had to rule out the notion that her eyes were playing tricks on her, because it was indeed Lord Farris. He smiled as he approached, which meant she could not continue riding as if she had not heard him. How frustrating.

"Good morning, Laura," he stated as he reached her side. "What a pleasure it is to happen upon you this lovely morning."

Laura scowled at him. "Yes, my lord, my day is now complete." He was only being polite by greeting her, so she attempted a smile. "I hope you have a good ride." With a polite nod, she continued on her route but was surprised to see him keep pace with her. She raised an eyebrow in inquiry, and disdainfully asked, "Are you just returning home for the evening?"

"My, aren't we prickly this morning?" His eyes swept over her attire, and rather than the frown of disapproval at her old riding habit that she expected, he looked almost appreciative. "I hate to disappoint you, but I recently had a change of heart about staying out all night." He paused as he steered his mount away from a hole in the ground, and then continued, "I have decided I should start a new exercise regimen, which includes riding in the morning. Tell me, do you ride every morning also?"

He could not possibly intend to ride at the same time and place she did, did he? That would be disastrous, although she supposed she could be prevailed upon to share, but not happily. "I hear there are many trails in the park that you could consider using for your *solo* enjoyment." Hopefully he would catch the obvious hint.

Lord Farris smiled wryly. "My dear, why would I ride alone, when riding with you is infinitely more pleasurable?"

"I am sure there are plenty others you could find to share your ride. In fact, I believe Lady Robbins also rides at this time. Maybe she would enjoy a riding partner."

"I think not. You are, by far, my first choice."

"But that was not always the case, was it?" she asked softly, enjoying the flash of surprise in his eyes.

He recovered quickly. "That appears to bother you. Why is that?"

Laura glared at him. "It does not bother me. You are hardly the sort to only ride with one lady, without exception. The fool is the one who would think you capable of commitment."

"Something tells me we are not speaking of riding horses anymore."

"Of course we are." She turned to ignore him. She would just keeping riding and hope he would not follow.

"Are you not curious to know why I am riding with a package?"

Odious man. She lifted an eyebrow and stopped her mare as Lord Farris also stopped his stallion. She could care less about his package. "Tell me, my lord, who asked you to accompany me this time? Perchance Lord Collins asked again, as he did at the house party?"

His eyes narrowed. "Who told you that? Never mind, I am sure I know." He paused for a moment and said softly, "That request made no difference to me. I would have still chosen to escort you over any other member of the house party."

"Because you had so many options?" Laura retorted acrimoniously.

Lord Farris appeared to consider his words carefully and then said, "Maybe at first I partnered with you due to necessity, but as I got to know you, I would have chosen you over any other lady in my acquaintance." He held up his parcel and smiled engagingly. "What if I told you this is a present for you?"

"Then I would tell you to keep it, as I am not interested in presents from you," Laura retorted haughtily.

"In that case, I will simply send it to your home. I am sure the gossips and Lord Dunbar in particular will be interested to see you are receiving gifts from other gentlemen."

Odious, infernal man. She could not allow him to send her a gift, and he knew it. She looked at his wickedly charming smile and yielded. "Fine." She submitted as she walked her mount closer to accept the gift. Lord Farris handed her the present and allowed his hand to linger excessively during the exchange. She shifted uncomfortably from the touch, then snatched the gift, and her hand, away. "Thank you."

"You are welcome, now open it," he ordered.

Slowly peeling away the wrapping, Laura was thrilled to see the volume of poems she had admired so much at the bookstore. She looked worriedly at him. "This is too much. I cannot possibly accept this gift."

"Of course you can, you nonsensical woman. You have no other choice."

Laura paused for a moment, lost in thought, then finally a bright and engaging smile overtook her face. "Thank you then. I will cherish this always."

Her smile vanished as she swiftly turned her mare and began to ride. She had lost herself in the kindness of his act. Clearly, he had purchased the book after she had left the bookstore. That was just the sort of action that would make her love him all the more. She turned to see that he was keeping pace with her on his beautiful, black stallion.

The couple rode silently for some time, until they changed direction to return from whence they came. Lord Farris called out as they slowed to turn, "I say we call a truce and agree to be friends."

She gave no indication she had heard Lord Farris's suggestion but continued riding, which gave her time to mull over his proposition. If she did not accept his offer, she would seem very unladylike; however, accepting his offer would probably result in more time spent with him.

She knew it was likely she would have to see him on occasion. Eleanor would soon marry his best friend, and Laura would see him whenever she saw Eleanor. Having made her decision, Laura continued to ride until they reached the entrance.

"I accept your offer, my lord. We may be friends," Laura stated graciously.

"Same time tomorrow, then?"

"I suppose, my lord. Please do not feel obligated if you change your mind," she offered hopefully.

****

The couple parted ways, with Laura heading home, and Gavin riding to Lord Collins's house. He was cold, hungry, and he had a strong inclination to utilize his friend in his wooing endeavors. The morning had gone unusually well, but he had spent a good hour riding back and forth in Hyde Park until Laura had appeared.

His chill had been momentarily warded off when he had spotted Laura. Not only was she wearing her old riding habit, but she appeared to be completely without artifice in the brisk morning air. No matter how lovely she looked in a fancy ball gown, the Laura he saw this morning would always be his Laura.

Gavin knocked on Lord Collins's front door and did not bother waiting for a response before opening the door. He immediately went to the dining room and entered as Lord Collins looked up from his newspaper in surprise. Gavin had always used to breakfast with him, but had not in the past two months.

Lord Collins acted as if nothing was amiss and Gavin's arrival was expected. "Good morning. Are you hungry?"

The food looked divine, and Gavin loaded up a plate with some tasty morsels. He sat and dropped a bombshell. "I am going to marry Lady Laura."

Lord Collins was suddenly overtaken by a coughing fit. He eventually cleared his airway and laughed. "I knew this would happen. I was just waiting for you to come to the same conclusion." He eyed Gavin, and asked curiously, "Does the lady in question know of your intent?"

"She does not." He grimaced. "In fact, just this morning she agreed to be friends." What a distasteful word.

Lord Collins proclaimed with a smile, "How wonderful! The man who never has problems with women cannot seem to ensnare the one he wants most."

Gavin could not see the humor in the situation. "Yes, well, I would not have so much difficulty if you had not told Miss Ashford of your request at the Songfeld house party."

This revelation wiped all traces of humor from Lord Collins's face. "You mean she told Lady Laura? Why would she do that? I specifically asked her not to mention it to anyone."

Maybe because she is not such a nice woman. His friend would hopefully figure that out soon enough. "I do not understand it either. There would be no benefit for Lady Laura to know." Gavin took a bite of food and silently allowed Lord Collins to form his own opinion on that bit of information. "Either way, you will have to make up for it by helping me."

Lord Collins raised his eyebrow, which indicated Gavin should continue.

"You obviously go everywhere that Miss Ashford goes, and now I will also." Determining Laura's whereabouts would be easy.

"That is a tremendous sacrifice for me," Lord

Collins said sarcastically. "I could not be happier to have you accompany me, so I am not plagued by females constantly."

The matter settled, Gavin and Lord Collins continued to eat their breakfast. They had some catching up to do, but they easily fell back to their old rhythms as was typically the case for most great friendships. At breakfast's conclusion, Gavin asked, "So what is on the agenda tonight?" He could not miss a single chance to win Laura.

"Well, Miss Ashford told me they are to attend the theater tonight as Lord Dunbar's guests. I had no plans to attend, but if you wish I am more than willing."

Gavin did not like the idea of Laura with Lord Dunbar, seated next to him for an entire evening. "Do you have a box?" he asked practically.

"No. However, your sister has informed me that you do," Lord Collins replied drily.

What? That secured Gavin's attention. "I had not realized that. How thoughtful of Mother to have such foresight." He would have liked to have been notified of the decision. He suspected the bill had been snuck in with the charges in relation to the ball.

"Indeed." Lord Collins chuckled. "I wonder if we will be escorting your mother and sister tonight?"

Of course they would. Gavin knew if he attended without them he would never hear the end of it. "Send a note over," he grudgingly said.

Lord Collins nodded. "Right away."

Chapter 12

Laura enjoyed any genre of play, but comedies were by far her favorite, which was what they were to see tonight. Lord Dunbar had greeted the ladies as they arrived at his box with delight, although he had saved the warmest welcome for Laura. She was accompanied by Eleanor and Lady Ashford, although Eleanor had been practically dragged screaming to the theater. Eleanor had thought it a complete waste of time, as Lord Collins would not be in attendance, but her mother had given her no choice.

Lord Dunbar had kindly seated Laura in the most visibly advantageous spot and subsequently sat next to her. He smelled nice, and Laura assumed it was some sort of tobacco product. "What is the scent you are wearing?" she inquired softly.

"I am not wearing any scent. I imagine you are smelling the cigar I recently smoked." His eyes drifted to her décolletage. "Do you like it?"

"Yes, I was just thinking how appealing you smell. It is a soothing scent." She had done a marvelous job at continuing to converse, despite the fact that his eyes had remained firmly planted on her chest.

"In that case, I shall ensure I smoke that cigar should I smoke around you."

Laura had no idea how she was to determine if he was interested in Lady Robbins. Every time she thought of marriage to Lord Dunbar, she pictured the lady's face, and then guilt ate at her stomach. That was not exactly the feeling she wanted on her wedding day.

Suddenly, Eleanor's voice rang out behind her. "Lord Collins is here." She sounded excited until Eleanor noticed who he was with, then her tone turned scornful. "He is seated next to Miss Farris. That scheming jade has got to be stopped."

Laura's gaze searched the crowd, as she unwittingly held her breath. In a box not far from her father's sat Lord Farris. He was attentively listening to someone she could only assume was his mother. Why was he here? As she enjoyed her unobserved moment to scrutinize him, his gaze locked with hers, and Laura swore quietly. "Bloody hell." Her cheeks colored, and she quickly looked away, but not before Lord Farris's face was transformed by a lazy smile, which suggested he knew exactly the effect he had on her.

Lord Dunbar's question was a welcoming distraction. "Is everything all right?" He looked charmingly concerned. "Ladies are not supposed to know such language, but I am sure you had a worthy reason to use it."

Laura smiled up at him and lied. "I certainly thought so, my lord. I seem to have bit the inside of my cheek." She realized her falsehood was a poor one. People generally did not bite their cheeks while sitting quietly and especially when not chewing anything.

"That is most unfortunate. Is there anything I can do for you?"

Laura placed a hand on her cheek, as if in pain, and said weakly, "No, my lord, I think it best we just sit in silence and observe the play," which would fortunately begin momentarily.

Lord Dunbar patted her hand and agreed, although his hand lingered for several moments longer than Laura thought necessary. After several more minutes of waiting, the first act began, and Laura tried to focus. Unfortunately, she found her gaze wandering to Lord Farris more often than it ought. Frustratingly, he was unceasingly prepared for her glances with a smile. Why was he at the theater if he was not going to actually watch the play? She was so focused on her thoughts she did not realize they had reached the interim. She snuck one more peek at Lord Farris and realized he had disappeared.

Laura excused herself to use the retiring room but had not managed to depart before Eleanor volunteered to accompany her. As they exited the box, Eleanor remarked, "Did you see how Miss Farris was hanging on to Lord Collins? It was shameful, and I will not just stand by and watch her steal him away."

Laura had been occupied and failed to observe anyone hanging shamefully off anyone else. She suggested, "Maybe we will run across him, and you can apprise Lord Collins of his shameful actions."

Eleanor looked as if she wanted to attack the next person who eyed her crossly. "Did you not hear me? *She* is hanging on *him*. Lord Collins is not at fault, but I did, in fact, accompany you to hopefully warn him of the scheming harpy."

Laura had not realized the extent of Eleanor's dislike for Miss Farris. Just how serious was the information Eleanor had on Miss Farris? Laura was unsure if she should intervene or simply let nature take its course, but if she did nothing she would hate herself when Miss Farris suffered. The whole matter was terribly disconcerting. Maybe she should warn Lord Farris.

The two ladies parted ways until Laura concluded her business and set out to find Eleanor. "Figures," she exclaimed after she searched and could not find her cousin. She began to navigate her way back to her seat. Suddenly, a hand was on her elbow, forcing her to stop.

Awareness from his touch coursed through her, and she knew without looking that Lord Farris had accosted her. "My lord," she asked as she glanced into his eyes. "May I help you?"

"Not really," he said, still holding her elbow as he guided her toward a quieter location between two ivory columns. "Lord Collins and Miss Ashford are discussing some matter of the utmost importance, and I decided I should act as your escort."

"Of course you did." She glanced at the strong hand holding her and attempted to nonverbally remind him of propriety, which he frustratingly ignored. She was not too concerned, though. They were in full view of several passing theater patrons.

She paused as she remembered Eleanor. Should she warn Lord Farris of Eleanor's intentions toward his sister, or brush it aside as an unlikely occurrence? Laura knew herself. If she did not tell him, she would feel responsible, but she also did not want to betray Eleanor.

Finally her conscience won out, and she spoke very seriously to Lord Farris. "I have something important to tell you, but you must promise you will never betray that I am the one who told you."

He nodded.

"I am not positive anything will actually happen,

but I worry that Miss Ashford views your sister as a threat to her relationship with Lord Collins. She claims to have bribed one of your servants into betraying a secret that will ruin your sister's reputation." Laura cringed, it sounded much worse when said aloud.

He stilled. "Thank you, Laura," he said distractedly. "Your cousin is not too bright. Revealing this secret will not cause Lord Collins to abandon Alexa. Rather he will cling to her more in order to help."

Laura nodded. "I will try to talk some sense into her, but I felt you should be warned."

"You have my sincerest gratitude."

"Why do you not thank me and return me to Lord Dunbar, then?" She smiled impishly.

"All in due time, Laura," he murmured seductively as his hand moved from her elbow to her gloved hand. He lifted her hand to his lips and kissed it sweetly, all while his eyes remained glued to hers. She could not tear her gaze from his, until he smirked at her. He was fully aware of the effect he had on her.

Laura tingled all over from his touch and abruptly jerked her hand away. They were supposed to be friends, per his suggestion, so why was he holding hands with her? "What are you doing here tonight?"

Lord Farris leaned against a column and smiled wryly. "Rest easy, my prickly pear. It is not as if I ascertained your location this evening from Lord Collins, only to procure a box so I could see you."

Laura blushed furiously and rushed to say, "Of course I do not think that. That would take way too much foresight on your part." There, now she felt better.

Lord Farris placed a hand over his heart in feigned hurt. "Ouch. I will have you know I am capable of great foresight."

She scoffed in disbelief, and he asked, "How is your new book? You know, the one that required great foresight on my part to obtain."

All the myriad of feelings Laura had been fighting in regards to Lord Farris disappeared as she smiled. "It is wonderful. I almost do not want to read the volume for fear of hurting it." Her smile dimmed as she said, "I found the most unusual letter in the book. It would appear the store owner has apologized for his behavior. You would not know anything about that, would you?"

He shrugged absentmindedly. "I was a little surprised you were interested in Keats. He is not a very popular poet. Byron would have been the more typical choice."

Laura looked at him skeptically. "I have begun to notice a trend with you. Whenever you do not want to answer a question, you change the topic. Why is that?"

"I cannot say that I have noticed this peculiar trend." Switching topics once more, he asked, "How are things with your beau?"

She scowled. "Splendid, my lord, although I see we are once again changing topics." She would allow it, as the crowd was beginning to thin. "Is it not time for the next act? Maybe you should bring me back, or at least help me find Eleanor."

"Are you that excited to return to Lord Dunbar?" He took a step toward her and brought his hand to her cheek. He swept an eyelash from her face and returned his hand to his side, but not before she had to fight off an overwhelming urge to step into his arms. His eyes positively sizzled as he looked down on her. "You know I could make you forget all about him."

And then her stomach clenched tightly. She lost herself in his overpowering nearness, as vertigo overtook her. How could she ever imagine marrying such a man when she could not function properly in his presence?

She shook herself. "I am in a hurry, my lord. Lord Dunbar will begin to worry if I take much longer."

"I doubt he will worry overly much. He will soon put two and two together when neither of us returns."

He was probably right, which should have worried Laura more. Lord Dunbar held no emotional attachment to her, but at least he was honest about his intentions, unlike Lord Farris.

She still could not determine Lord Farris's motives. After all, it was not typical behavior to act as though he wished to pursue her and then offer friendship. His actions hurt. He might present her with the most thoughtful gift she had ever received and say endearing things, but his unwillingness to wed only made his actions cut like a knife to her very soul. Her heart constricted. She should contribute his actions to the fact that he was a rake, but she wished to believe better of him. She sighed. She was simply too naïve.

She averted her eyes from his overly handsome face. Her breath was coming too quickly, but she had an iron will and would not exhibit her emotions. Instead, she squared her shoulders and smiled at him. She teased, even though the words hurt her. "If Lord Dunbar can deduce we are together, who else will? I thought you did not wish to wed."

He nodded, his fixed gaze intense on her face.

"Shall we return, then?"

He stopped at the entrance to Lord Dunbar's box. The corridor was empty and dimly lit, and he turned toward her with a sensuous smile. He raised her right hand, which was once more in his, and slipped the glove off. Laura's body began to shake from her desire to rush into his arms. He kissed the inside of her wrist, and Laura sighed.

"My lord," she whispered faintly. "What have you done to me?" She blushed as she spoke the words.

"Believe me, my dear, the feelings are mutual."

Her lips parted, until a slight rustle emitted from the doorway, and Laura looked up to see Lord Dunbar emerge from the box. Lord Farris held on to Laura's hand for an extra moment, and he took a step closer to Laura in a proprietary manner. The scowl on Lord Dunbar's face forced Laura to remember herself. She jumped back with a blush and pulled her glove back to its rightful place.

"There you are," Lord Dunbar said flatly to Laura. "Come, my dear." He extended his hand to her.

Laura hung her head and walked to his side. His arm came protectively around her shoulders, and he pulled her toward him. "I was worried about you." He stated loudly.

"She was perfectly fine," Lord Farris said gruffly, but his eyes held a look Laura had never beheld before. He appeared angry. Angry enough to leave Laura speechless, but for what? Laura knew better than to assume he could be jealous.

"Was she?" Lord Dunbar asked reproachfully. "You may wish to steal her from me, but it shall not happen in *that* way."

Laura's eyebrows skyrocketed. Was Lord Dunbar truly under the impression Lord Farris had designs on her? "My lord…"

She broke into the conversation, but Lord Dunbar sharply raised his hand to indicate she should be silent and said, "Not now."

"Dunbar. Watch yourself." Lord Farris stepped threateningly toward him but stopped himself.

Lord Dunbar smiled and grasped Laura's elbow. "Shall we?"

Laura did not want to go, but her future was with Lord Dunbar and not Lord Farris.

She turned to go, and Lord Farris said pleadingly, "Do not go, Laura." Her eyes went to his, but truthfully, what did he expect? She could not leave with him. She shook her head slightly.

Lord Dunbar turned also, and whispered snidely over his shoulder, "Well, Lord Farris, it appears your women prefer me, without exception."

She tensed but entered the box in front of Lord Dunbar anyway. Her heart was numb, and her shoulders were slumped in defeat. She had wanted so badly to go with Lord Farris, but his direction held disaster for her. He should know better than to toy with her this way, but asking her to leave with him was absurd.

"Where have you been?" Eleanor's mother whispered worriedly, as Laura sat.

"Looking for Eleanor," Laura replied simply.

Laura breathed a sigh of relief when Lord Dunbar smiled at her and took her hand in his. "I was quite worried about you, you know." His eyes darkened and he said, "Lord Farris can be quite the lady's man. I want you to know I do not fault you for his actions."

"Thank you, my lord. He is hard to dissuade."

"That is what I had assumed." He turned his attention to the stage, and asked as the curtains opened. "Would it be acceptable for me to call on you tomorrow… alone?"

Laura stilled. The meaning of his words had hit her, hard. "Of course, my lord."

He smiled, and his attention was absorbed by the performers on the stage.

Laura relaxed. At least he was not upset with her. Quite the opposite, in fact. His suggestion that he call on her alone implicated a much more serious turn to their relationship was at hand.

The second half started, which drew their attention away from each other. Laura was relieved Lord Dunbar was not causing a scene about the awkward moment, but at the same time she was a bit disappointed. She would like her future husband to care about what she did, although realistically, she knew they would lead separate lives after marrying.

Shortly into the second half, Laura noticed Lord Farris's party depart. Why were they leaving so abruptly? Unless it was due to the secret Eleanor had obtained. It must be a big secret, if it caused the family to leave so early.

The play continued for a good amount of time, and Laura was thankful it had ended. She had not been able to focus for the entirety of the second half. Lord Dunbar readied himself to leave but first kissed her hand and whispered seductively, "Tomorrow cannot come too soon." Laura agreed and was soon warm and comfy in the confines of her carriage.

"So, Eleanor, did you enjoy this evening's

interim?" They were hardly hiding the fact that Eleanor had seen Lord Collins from their chaperone.

Eleanor looked quite dejected as she said, "No. Lord Collins thought I was being overly dramatic, as his attentions toward Miss Farris are platonic." She slumped into the carriage cushion. "I just do not understand why he cannot see how Miss Farris throws herself at him, most inappropriately."

"Yes. That is most perturbing." Laura still did not see what Eleanor saw. "What is this secret you previously mentioned about Miss Farris?"

Glancing furtively at her mother, who appeared asleep, Eleanor whispered quietly, "I started my plan tonight. I mentioned to one of the biggest gossips of the *ton*, Lady Chadwick, that Miss Farris was not sired by the late viscount." She laughed coldly, causing a chill to run down Laura's spine. "The old hag was more than willing to believe me, especially when I mentioned my source was one of Miss Farris's own maids."

Laura could not determine why that name sounded so familiar. Either way, this was much worse than Laura had feared. People were always willing to believe gossip, no matter how unlikely. "How do you know Lord Collins will not figure out you were the one to start this rumor?"

Eleanor scoffed and said, "Do not be ridiculous. This particular lady is extremely tight-lipped about her sources. My tracks are well covered. Besides, why should he care once he understands her dubious parentage?"

Laura was unable to understand her cousin. Starting gossip of this nature was cruel, and to think Eleanor believed Lord Collins would disengage himself from Miss Farris when she needed him most was laughable. Laura was now vindicated for telling Gavin about Eleanor's intentions. If only she had told him sooner.

Chapter 13

The cold had almost managed to numb Gavin's hands completely, but he ignored them and waited patiently. He had been awaiting Laura's arrival for some time now. She must have overslept, or at least, that was what Gavin hoped. The other option, that she had decided not to come, was unpalatable.

He could not fault her if she chose to remain home rather than to ride with him. The previous night had been disastrous. No scenario he had considered had played out that way, especially her choice to leave with Lord Dunbar over himself. Granted, he never should have presented her with the choice, but he had. His heart had almost torn in two when she had looked at him with those sorrowful, violet eyes and shook her head.

The wind howled through the trees, and Gavin thought he could make out a rider in the distance. His heart lifted, and he smiled. Her decision to come today made up for all the barbs Lord Dunbar had thrown at him, because she may not realize it, but her arrival signified her ultimate desire for Gavin and not Lord Dunbar.

She reached his side, and he said, "Good morning, Laura. You look lovely, as usual." He bowed and was a little perturbed by the worried look on her face.

"Good morning, my lord. I have grave news to

relate to you."

Not liking the sound of that, Gavin indicated she should continue.

"It appears my dear cousin has already started to talk of your sister." Evident shame was written all over her face.

As Gavin remained stoic on the outside, inside he was fuming. Obviously, he would deny all accusations of Alexa's dubious parentage, but there would still be some who believed the rumors. And rumors of that nature would not help Alexa's success in finding a husband. "Tell me what happened," he urged as they started on a much slower ride than the previous day's outing. Once again they rode along the Serpentine, but neither one took the time to appreciate the scenery.

"Well, Eleanor told me she was upset by Lord Collins's attentiveness toward your sister last night. When she had the chance, she told Lady Chadwick of your sister's questionable parentage. That is all I have heard so far. I can only imagine how quickly the news is spreading." Laura hung her head in shame. "I am so sorry."

Gavin had spent the remainder of his evening worrying about Alexa. How would she react to gossip of that nature, and how badly would it hurt her chances of making an advantageous marriage? He had decided he would raise her dowry to a ludicrous sum if need be, but when he heard Lady Chadwick's name, he smiled a large and relieved smile.

Laura raised her head from its position of shame, saw the smile, and asked, perplexed, "Are you feeling all right? You have not hit your head lately, have you?"

Ignoring her question, Gavin said, "Do you know

anything about Lady Chadwick?"

"Only that she is a renowned gossip."

Gavin's laughed loudly, which only made Laura appear even more confused. "I imagine that is all Miss Ashford knows about her, also. Many people forget that she is my mother's second cousin. I would not remember except the lady thinks it imperative to remind me every chance she gets. She would never spread malicious gossip about my family, despite her love for gossip. In fact, I will be visiting her once our ride reaches its conclusion."

Laura giggled and appeared to relax. "You must let me know how that goes."

The sound of her giggle enchanted Gavin. He would enjoy making her laugh for the rest of their lives. But first things first. "I actually was planning on stopping by after my visit with her. Will you and your cousin be available?"

All color quickly faded from Laura's face. "We will," she answered slowly, "but Lord Dunbar may also be there."

That was one roadblock Gavin needed gone. "Oh, interesting. Is there any special reason for his visit?"

Suddenly shy, Laura responded, "I am not positive, but I believe he may propose. Of course he has not asked my father, but he made it sound as if he wanted to speak to me in private." Usually, a gentleman did not talk to a lady in private unless it was for one special reason: marriage.

Dammit, the bloody man was moving much too quickly. Gavin's mind raced. How could he convince her not to marry him? He needed to get past this friend zone quickly. "That does sound suspiciously like he wants to propose." Gavin paused. "What would you say if I told you not to marry him?"

Laura tensed. "I would say that is none of your business, my lord."

Gavin wanted to curse, loudly and extensively. Talk about eliciting the opposite reaction to the one he had wanted. He hoped she would have at least concluded he was interested in more than friendship. Maybe he needed to be more direct but in a believable way. Pulling his horse to a stop, Gavin dismounted. Laura noticed his movement and followed suit.

Helping her from her horse, Gavin watched as the groom approached. He beckoned the man over, handed him the reins for both horses, and told him to ride out of sight. The groom started to voice his disapproval, but Gavin's arched eyebrow and scowl convinced the man to do as told. "Walk with me," Gavin ordered Laura as he extended his arm.

"I will not. I wish to ride, not stroll about with a high-handed gentleman such as yourself."

"Laura, Laura." He tsked. "What am I to do with you?" He knew what he wanted to do with her, but unfortunately now was not the time nor place. "When your Lord Dunbar directs you to comply, do you defiantly disobey him also?"

Fire flashed in her eyes. "I am not a child that disobeys out of ill-temper. I sometimes disagree and choose to ignore directives, but Lord Dunbar does not order me about without good reason, unlike you."

"So the answer is no." He considered her demeanor and stroked the side of her face with his hand. Her face was cold, and he wished desperately to warm her. "One as passionate as you should not be wasted on a man like him. Tell me, will you remain faithful to him?"

"Of course," she declared vehemently, "I will never break my wedding vows."

"Even when he breaks his?" Gavin was well aware just how lonely many of the young matrons of the *ton* were. "I think you will change your mind when you rarely see him, much less have him there to warm your bed at night."

Laura gasped, and pushed him away from her. "I cannot say how I will feel should he treat me that way, but I know with certainty that I will not make a cuckold of my husband." Her comment was aimed squarely at Gavin, and he felt the blow smartly. Laura covered her mouth with her gloved hand. "I am sorry, my lord, I did not mean to insinuate…"

Gavin interrupted her, "Forget about it. I just want you to understand the life you will lead, should you marry Lord Dunbar. Eventually, you will grow lonely enough that you will convince yourself you have fallen in love with someone else and will forget your vows for that fleeting momentary connection. If you are lucky, you will have a child to dote on, but that is all your life will be."

"What do you suggest I do then?" Laura questioned passionately, her eyes shining with sorrow. "I must marry, and if I wait for some magical love match, I might never wed at all."

"I would suggest you have faith and wait for something truly magical to come along," Gavin whispered, as he stepped closer to her. "It very well could be closer than you think." Quickly scanning the surrounding area, he noted they were alone before covering her mouth with his. The realization that he loved her somehow made the kiss that much better. He growled and deepened the kiss, forgetting all about the frigid air swirling around them or the possibility that someone could happen upon them.

The sparks flew as she leaned into him. The chill of the day was chased away, replaced with the warmth of their commingled breath. Gavin ignored all common sense as he lost himself in the embrace. Her curves were slight, but his hands could attest to the fact that they were perfect. Her response to his kiss was not shy either, which shook him in a way no other kiss had.

"Oh dear," a refined female voice said, "this is a most unusual sight."

Laura jumped away from Gavin, surprised shame written all over her face, as if she was a naughty schoolgirl caught stealing a cookie. Gavin adjusted his clothing and scowled at the interloper. Lady Robbins sat on her horse, casually observing the two as if it was a common sight for her. Lady Robbins cooed, "Why, Gavin, you used to have more finesse than to be caught with your pants around your ankles..." She paused for dramatic flair. "Figuratively speaking, of course."

"Lady Robbins," Gavin said stiffly.

Laura interceded, not wanting to make matters worse. "We were just discussing something very important and..."

Lady Robbins interrupted, "With your mouths? Normally verbal communication is required for a discussion, but I see you discovered a different method." She laughed, although she was the only one amused. "You see this works very well for me. You, Lady Laura, have something I want, and now I have something you want me to forget."

Laura stilled and eyed her in a calculated manner. "You intend to blackmail me? I cannot be blamed for this oaf's actions."

The tension was palpable between them, which left Gavin scrambling to catch up. What was happening between the two? Before he could ask, Lady Robbins said, "No one will care whether you wanted his attentions or not. All I have to do is casually mention how I saw Lord Farris ravishing you in the park, and you would be ruined." She swept a dubious glance at Gavin. "Unless he marries you, of course."

Laura looked extremely unhappy but agreed. "Fine. I will break off the relationship between myself and Lord Dunbar." She glared daggers at Lady Robbins, then turned on her heel and walked away.

Gavin finally understood what had transpired and asked Lady Robbins, "You want Lord Dunbar?" Their previous conversation suddenly made a lot more sense.

Lady Robbins nodded and winked at him. "You are welcome." She raised her voice to Laura's receding back and said, "Consider my memory erased then." And promptly departed.

Even though he could tell by the set of her shoulders that Laura was angry, Gavin was overjoyed by what had just happened. He could not have planned it better himself. He hurried to Laura's side and walked with her in silence. Why speak when his goal for the day was accomplished? Although upon reflection of the scene, he would not mind if Laura was ruined and he was forced to marry her. That would certainly lessen the difficulty of his situation.

"Hmph," Laura muttered loudly and broke the silence.

"Do you have something caught in your throat?" Gavin asked politely.

"Of course not." She paused and then blurted out hurriedly, "I know you do not want to marry, but you could have at least offered to marry me to save my reputation."

Maybe she would be open to an offer of marriage already. Gavin smiled at her enticingly, he loved to goad her. "Would you like to marry me?"

Laura blushed and quickly said, "Of course not, I have no desire to marry you, but it would have been nice at least to know you would offer."

The blasted woman was such a contradiction. She wanted an offer of marriage but did not want to marry him. If he had not heard her declaration of love at the house party, he might have been a bit put out by that. "If you do not want to marry me, why do you care that I did not offer for you?"

Laura glowered at him. "It is a matter of principle, my lord. You should offer marriage to ladies you compromise."

Unable to resist, Gavin stepped nearer to Laura and took her hand. He placed a kiss on the back of it and whispered, "Good to know. Once I compromise you, I will offer."

Laura snatched her hand away. "You would make a joke out of this." She turned her back on him and began to walk once more.

"Who said I was joking?" He smirked and caught up to her. He could not help himself.

Her gaze took in his smirk, and Gavin could tell she was on the brink of all-out anger. "This is not funny." She stomped her foot, which was quite impressive, seeing as she was still walking. "If you insist on bothering me incessantly, then I think I deserve some reassurance that you will either behave yourself, or promise to make amends should you ruin me."

Her walk had turned from graceful to a jerky movement that no lady should engage in. He also noted, with a good dose of amusement, that she had another gaping hole in her skirt. "I thought you had that repaired."

"What?" She whirled on him suddenly. If Gavin had reacted any slower, he would have run into her.

"Your skirt." He gestured toward the hole in her riding habit and said, "You evidently have a new hole in it."

With a cry of indignation, she threw her hands in the air. "I have had enough of you, my lord. I do not know what your agenda is, but if it is to see me sent to an insane asylum, you are performing admirably well."

He smiled lazily, and she promptly swatted him on his arm. His mind barely registered the feeble blow. "Contrary to your belief, my goal is not to drive you to Bedlam." He drew her toward him, although she kept her back rebelliously straight, and he lifted his hand to the side of her face. She was so soft and inviting. "I cannot keep myself away from you, and I think you prefer me around."

Her eyes flashed. "I know you are just toying with me again, my lord. I am not an idiot. You toyed with me at the house party, and here you are doing it again." The wind blew strongly, but neither felt it as the tension between them warded it off.

"I am not toying with you."

Suddenly, her anger disappeared and was replaced by sorrow. "Then what is this? You offer friendship, and then kiss me. Now, I have to start over in finding a husband, but how is it possible with you around all the time?"

The look in her eyes reminded him of the day at the ruins. They haunted him, and he could not allow her to feel despair anymore. "Lord Dunbar is not the right man for you. I am not toying with you, and if I did compromise you, I would certainly marry you."

Her mouth opened in shock, and she gazed with her violet eyes into his. She had never looked more kissable. Suddenly, the sound of horse hooves broke the stillness, and Gavin stepped back. The groom had infuriatingly chosen that moment to return.

Gavin helped Laura into her saddle and mounted his own horse. They rode quietly until they arrived at the park entrance. Gavin looked at her and promised, "Until later then." Laura nodded in acknowledgement, and he began his ride to his relative's house. It was a bit early to make calls, but Lady Chadwick was family.

He mounted the steps to the doorway and lifted the brass knocker. Lady Chadwick was a bit of an eccentric, so one never knew what she had going on. He waited, and within a few moments, the door swung open. He could not recall the last time he had visited, so was unsurprised the butler did not recognize him.

The butler performed a smart bow and said condescendingly, "Lady Chadwick is not receiving guests at this time." He then began to shut the door.

Gavin shoved a foot in the doorway. "She will receive me." He moved past the butler into the hallway. "Tell her Lord Farris has arrived and is awaiting her in the library." Pausing on his way to the library, he ordered, "Send a breakfast tray to me while I wait." He did not wait to see the butler's expression but imagined he was unhappy. He knew his aunt, as she demanded he call her, would not mind his sudden visit, and that was what mattered. Several long minutes passed before a maid brought in a tea tray and a newspaper. She promised to bring more substantial fare shortly and left, leaving Gavin to wonder how long his wait was going to be.

Halfway through the newspaper, he heard footsteps and the butler appeared. "My lord, your aunt awaits you in the dining room." He bowed and led the way, not waiting to see if Gavin followed.

Evidently, the butler had been apprised of Gavin's relation to Lady Chadwick and was now slightly more accommodating as a result. Lady Chadwick had insisted he call her aunt and she had called him nephew since before he could remember. He had asked her why when he was still at Eton and was told the term made her sound younger than other titles he might call her. So aunt it was and always would be.

"Good morning." Gavin cheerfully greeted his aunt as he crossed the room to kiss Lady Chadwick's cheek. She had just awoken and was wearing a dressing gown with her long gray hair braided down her back. He knew she was at least seventy-five and in perfectly good health, although a bit too frail for his liking.

Lady Chadwick shooed him away, gesturing to a chair that he was supposed to use next to her. Once seated, she asked, "I always wished you would visit me, although I would have preferred if it was not under these circumstances." She glared at him. "Would that be too difficult?"

Gavin swallowed. "I will be sure to visit again in the near future." He smiled his most dazzling smile. "Or maybe you will grant me the honor of escorting you somewhere? I have a box at the theater, you know."

She flashed a sardonic look at him, saying, "I will hold you to that." A maid carried in a small glass of chocolate and placed it in front of his aunt. She sipped daintily, and asked, "Should I assume you are here because of a certain piece of gossip I heard recently?"

Gavin appreciated how she did not beat around the bush. "Yes, dear aunt, and to share breakfast with you, of course."

"I do not know how you found out so quickly, but I am going to guess it has something to do with your Lady Laura. Does she know of your feelings for her?"

Now Gavin remembered why he did not visit more frequently. Lady Chadwick was much too astute for his liking. "It may have something to do with her. However, she would like to remain anonymous in this ordeal, if in fact, she did play a part."

"Hmph. Normally I do not approve of people who betray their own family, but I can make an exception this time." She eyed him as though she had just snuck a peek at his soul. "Now, tell me what is happening with your family."

Gavin and Lady Chadwick conversed for two full hours. He kept trying to steer the topic of conversation back to the gossip about his sister, but his aunt seemed to want to prolong his visit as much as possible. Finally, she stood and withdrew an envelope from the sideboard. "Give this to Miss Ashford. It should solve your problems where she is concerned quite effectively."

He accepted the envelope and prepared to leave. He would be able to venture immediately to the Ashford residence to finish his business, once he collected Lord Collins. As he said his goodbye, Lady Chadwick said, "Good luck with Lady Laura. I look forward to meeting her soon…" She giggled. "As your wife."

Gavin could only shake his head and thank her. He was about to have a very difficult conversation with Lord Collins. He was worried how Lord Collins would take the news of Miss Ashford's scheme to hurt Alexa, but knew his friend would appreciate knowing the real person he had desired to marry.

****

Laura scurried up to her room and ordered a bath. She supposed she could at least smell nice for the upcoming ordeal she was to face. The tub was filled quickly, and Laura sank in to the steaming hot water. The idea that she would soon be turning away Lord Dunbar as a suitor was shocking.

Having declared two months prior that she would marry the viscount, the thought had never crossed her mind that she would be the one to say no. Her own sense of inadequacy had prepared her for the chance that Lord Dunbar would be uninterested in her, but never the opposite. She was left scrambling to come up with the words to say to him.

One thought had crossed her mind. She could ignore Lady Robbins's blackmail attempt, but she had quickly nixed that idea. A part of her was relieved to be free from Lord Dunbar, but part of her preferred him over the struggle of finding a new suitor. If she did ignore Lady Robbins, and the lady went through with her threat, Laura would end up with a scandal on her hands and a husband that did not truly want her. There really was nothing left for her to do but agree.

Laura emerged from the tub and toweled off. Anna helped garb Laura in a smoky blue day dress. Her maid was nervous about something, so Laura asked, "Is everything all right?"

Anna swept her a frightened look. "I am so sorry, my lady." She was shaking, and was clearly overwrought about something. "He was just so handsome."

Laura stopped combing her hair and confusedly asked, "What are you talking about?"

Anna wrung her hands and then blurted out, "He was just so handsome. I knew I should not care, but it seemed innocent enough, so I may have mentioned you liked to ride in Hyde Park."

Laura's hands stilled. "Calm down," she said sternly and set her brush aside. "Now, what man?"

Anna was pacing agitatedly at this point. "I know you will dismiss me, but I could not live with myself if I did not confess. A footman belonging to some lord—I believe he was a viscount—wanted information about you. I swear I only told him about your daily ride!"

Tears pooled in the maid's eyes, and Laura took pity on her. "Calm down, Anna. I am not going to discharge you." There were only two viscounts in her acquaintance, and only one had happened upon her in the park, but why? Why would he go to such lengths to see her?

Anna's countenance brightened, and she looked gratefully at Laura. "He really was irresistible."

Laura knew all too well the powers handsome men could use on unwitting females. "Just make sure you never speak of me to anyone else, ever, or you will get dismissed."

Anna nodded and helped Laura into a pair of slippers that matched her gown. Laura had not been sure what outfit would be appropriate for breaking off her relationship to Lord Dunbar and had decided on her current gown, which should be somber enough, but not too somber. After all, Lord Farris was stopping by later.

Anna began to style her hair, and Laura stared unseeingly into the mirror. To think, Lord Farris would stoop to such levels to find out her whereabouts, when she had purposefully been avoiding him. She could vividly recall the frustrations she had dealt with at the Songfeld house party, and now, this season was turning out eerily similar. Everywhere she went, Lord Farris appeared.

She had thought she loved Lord Farris before, but what she felt for him now went far beyond any feelings she had known previously. It aggravated her to no end that he would not simply leave her alone. He evidently wished to happen upon her, and then say confusing things to her, but to what end? Despite his actions, Lord Farris had plainly expressed his disinterest in marriage, and she could do nothing but assume his sentiments were still the same. No matter how many times he told her not to marry someone or informed her he could not leave her alone. She had no other choice.

Laura left her room to join her cousin in the parlor for tea. This was the typical routine for them, unless they were going out to call on friends. Both Eleanor and Lady Ashford were waiting for her with a tea tray.

Laura tried to act as if everything was normal by taking a seat in her typical spot by the fireplace. After eating several biscuits and drinking a cup of tea, Laura began to relax until a knock sounded on the door. Shortly after, the butler led Lord Dunbar into the room.

Lord Dunbar bowed crisply. "Good morning, ladies. I trust all of you are in good health."

Lady Ashford spoke for the room. "We are all in excellent health, my lord. Care for some tea?"

"No, thank you. My visit is to be a short one. I was hoping to speak to Lady Laura." He paused and smiled, fully aware how important his next word was. "Alone."

Lady Ashford's eyes shone with joy as she beckoned to Eleanor. They gracefully exited the room and closed the door firmly behind them.

Laura was incapable of moving, even if she had wanted to.

His masculine voice was the first to break the silence. "Lady Laura, I know we have only known each other a short while, but I want to make my intentions clear." He searched Laura's face for a moment, until suddenly his open expression shifted to a hard mask. "Aah. I will not waste any more of your time, then."

The feeling returned to her limbs which allowed Laura to hasten from her chair. She could not allow him to leave like this. "My lord, please understand, it is not you."

His smile was grim. "Lord Farris has beaten me. I had worried that might happen."

"No," she quickly interjected. "He is but a friend. I could not marry you knowing how Lady Robbins feels about you." That was mostly true.

An expression passed quickly over his face that

Laura could not identify. "Not to be vulgar, but why does it matter how my paramour feels for me?"

"I do not mean to overstep, but I think if you were inclined to ask for her hand, she might give it." He stopped and considered her words. He was apparently much better at hiding his emotions than she, because Laura could not determine the direction of his thoughts.

"Thank you for the information." He bowed stiffly. "Have a good day." As he exited the house, Eleanor and Lady Ashford quickly joined her once more.

Eleanor spoke first. "Well, are you to be the next Lady Dunbar?"

"No," Laura said simply. They did not need to know the details.

"Well, why not?" Eleanor asked, surprised.

"It was just not meant to be."

Evidently annoyed, Eleanor huffed and sat back, only to bolt upright as the butler announced Lord Collins and Lord Farris.

"My lords, how good of you to join us," Lady Ashford cooed.

Lord Farris snuck a smile at Laura, as Lord Collins spoke coldly. "This will be brief." He crossed to Eleanor's location and extended Lady Chadwick's letter. "This is for you. Understand if you should try something like this again, your prospects will be narrowed to the truly desperate." Both gentlemen bowed and left.

"Well, that was most odd. What is the letter he gave you, Eleanor dear?" Lady Ashford asked.

Her hands shook, but that was all the emotion Eleanor betrayed as she opened the missive. She quickly read its contents and then answered, "Lady

Chadwick is a relative of Lord Farris. If I ever speak of Miss Farris again, she will make sure I regret it."

"I have never heard they are related!" Lady Ashford said indignantly, as if that was the most important point contained in the letter.

"That hardly signifies, Mother," Eleanor said woodenly. "I seem to have a megrim. Excuse me."

She departed, and Lady Ashford muttered, "What a horrid day this has been." She grimaced and rose. "I too shall retire for a while."

Laura was left all alone. She had abhorred the thought of this day's events and was surprised they were over so quickly. Eleanor seemed subdued, so would likely behave henceforth regarding Miss Farris. Now Laura would just have to decide who she would attempt to marry this time.

*****

The following morning, Laura rode to Hyde Park and met Lord Farris in the same location as the previous day. "Good morning," she greeted.

"Good morning." Lord Farris's welcoming smile acted as a balm to Laura's heart. Somehow it always worked to calm her. At least, when he was not aggravating her. "Did you miss me?"

She laughed. "I just saw you yesterday, and even that was not long enough." She joked, but in all honesty she was always missing him.

"Well, I missed you," he replied seriously.

Laura's heart skipped a beat. "Do not be ridiculous." She began to ride. "Yesterday went fairly smoothly." Eleanor had stayed locked in her room the rest of the day, and Lady Ashford decided to stay in for the night, although Laura had not minded their absence one iota.

"Yes," he responded grimly. "Unfortunately, Lord Collins did not take it so well. After we visited, he departed for the country."

"I feel sorry for him, but he is better off. Miss Ashford is incapable of love. It is just unfortunate it took so long for him to see it," Laura stated in a matter-of-fact manner. After all, it was just Eleanor's nature.

"Agreed." Lord Farris paused. "You know my sister still wants you to attend her come-out ball. She will be quite upset if you are not there."

"I am sure we will still come, if you are sure your sister shall not mind Miss Ashford's presence. My cousin must continue to circulate amongst the *ton* in order to save face. Once people know Lord Collins has departed, they will come up with all manner of gossip about her, unless she acts strong."

Gavin nodded. "She is a necessary evil, I understand."

"Yes, well, Lady Ashford thinks it wise if we allow Eleanor a day or two to recover, so we will be staying in until your sister's ball."

"Of course. A couple of days will be good for her, I am sure. I hope to see you still on our morning rides."

"Speaking of which, I recently became aware of a very strange interaction my maid had with a footman." She paused. Here was yet another person with more schooled features than herself. She could not even tell with any certainty that Lord Farris had heard the words she imparted. "It would seem a viscount bribed my maid for information on my riding habits."

His tone was banal as he said, "It must have been some other viscount."

Laura looked at him skeptically. "Right." She tapped her chin softly and appeared lost in thought. "Although Lord Dunbar would not bother bribing my maid, and you magically appeared the morning after the event transpired."

He smiled evasively. "I guess we will just never know. How did your talk with Lord Dunbar go?"

Bloody aggravating man. "It went well enough." She brightened as she said, "I even managed to inform him of Lady Robbins's love for him."

"I wonder what will come of that bit of information." His tone suggested he did not actually care.

Laura beamed at him. "I wonder also. I hope they will be very happy and end up married." Her smile turned to a self-satisfied look. "Naturally, it will all be due to my timely intervention."

"You mean the intervention you were forced into?"

She glared at him. "We will simply forget that part of the story."

Lord Farris chuckled and stated patronizingly, "Of course we will." They continued to ride for a while in amiable silence until he brought up another important topic. "I hear your father has come to London."

Laura had not realized he was in town. "I would not know. He rarely tells me anything." Her countenance darkened. "I knew he would come to London eventually. I am sure if there was anything important he would tell me."

"Does he not check in on you?"

"Not usually, but he really is a good father. He ensured I received the best education, best clothing, and everything else I could ever desire. I have no reason to complain."

Lord Farris glanced at her skeptically. "Obviously, things like that are important, but a father's love is more important than any material good he can provide. Believe me, I know the pain of a father who did not care."

Glancing over at him, Laura could see he truly commiserated with how she felt. She always hated to say anything disparaging about her father, especially when he had done so much for her. He had provided, but she always wished she had the sort of father who doted on her or even wanted her around instead of sending her to her aunt's. Lord Farris looked at her, and they shared a mutual understanding.

She scrambled to think of some other topic of conversation. "Would you do me a favor?"

Lord Farris raised his eyebrow questioningly.

"You should think of potential suitors to replace Lord Dunbar. I need all the help I can get, you know." She smiled charmingly at him, hoping to entice him into aiding her. She was exceptionally proud of herself for her outward show of indifference to Lord Farris.

He appeared to freeze briefly, until his visage was transformed by a dark smile. "I know of the perfect gentleman for you."

She pulled up on her reins and stopped her horse beneath the branches of an oak tree. She lifted an eyebrow and asked with bated breath, "Oh?"

He nodded. "Yes. He is charming, titled, wealthy, and you are particularly fond of him."

Laura was puzzled. Who could he possibly mean? Her heart stilled, and her pulse began to race. He could not be speaking of himself, could he? She shuttered her eyes and looked into his. It was too good to be true, and she should not get her hopes up. "Who could you possibly know that fits such a description, my lord?"

His dark brown eyes bore into her, and he said, "Oh, I think you know."

"Then tell me." Please, get her out of this misery.

"Me." He exhaled the word, and Laura almost did not believe she had heard him.

"What?" she asked sharply.

The corners of his lips twitched, but he said somberly, "I had thought the answer obvious. You should marry me, Laura."

"What happened to your hatred for marriage?" She could not believe her ears. He must be toying with her, again, but this time the game was painful.

He scowled. "I wish we were not riding horses right now. In fact, this was terribly poor timing on my part."

"And what exactly did you have planned, my lord?" Laura's tone grew frigid. Her mind began to connect the dots. He was a rakish scoundrel who had kissed her at every opportunity. Now, he suddenly expressed a desire for marriage that defied his previous sentiments, but he should have planned it better? She had not thought he was the sort to deflower innocents, yet the evidence was pointing in that very direction.

"I planned on holding your small hand in mine and kissing your soft lips. Then, I would get down on one knee and ask you to be mine."

He had whispered his romantic words softly and promptly melted Laura's heart. She steeled her resolve and ignored the way her heart shriveled within her. He could speak all the words he wanted, but they would not change the fact that she knew he was opposed to marriage. However, all her resolve could not hold back the burning hot tear that escaped from her eye. "I do not believe you, my lord."

He stilled, and all the emotion was erased from his face. "What do you mean, you do not believe me?"

Laura said numbly, "One does not simply do an about-face when he despises marriage the way you do." She placed her hand on her hip and asked defiantly, "What did you truly have planned? Did you wish to seduce me and leave? Is that why you continued to plague me after the house party? To finish what you started?" It all was so very clear now.

His hand ran through his hair. His eyes showed their frustration, and he asked hoarsely, "What must I do to prove myself to you? I want nothing but the best for you, Laura."

And therein was the crux of the matter. She did not know how he could prove it. She shook her head. "I do not know if you can. I think I must go."

She turned her horse and brought the mare to a gallop. She knew he could catch her if he tried, but he was evidently allowing her to run away. The tears began to flow as she rode. She was just too confused right now. Could he truly want marriage? Despite all the things he said?

The tears had dried by the time she arrived home. She would sequester herself in her room for the remainder of the day, but her desire was soon shattered. Eleanor was on the warpath.

"I know if Miss Farris had not been such a horrible harridan I would be getting engaged to Lord Collins," she stated as she threw herself on Laura's bed, just as

Laura was changing out of her riding habit.

Laura regarded her numbly. Why was this even an issue at this point? She spoke flatly to Eleanor. "I feel the matter is settled. You cannot retaliate against her without earning repercussions from one of the biggest gossips of the *ton*. Why not focus on finding a new gentleman? Who is a worthy catch at this point?"

"There are some promising leads, but now that we are competitors, I think I will have to keep their names a secret," Eleanor said unhelpfully. "Although truth be told, you are not much competition."

Laura archly asked, "Then why not tell me who you think are the best catches?"

"Very well. There have been rumors that the Duke of Waking has recently returned from the continent. People do not know much about him, but he may be an even better catch than Lord Collins. I personally do not believe we will see him this season, so I ruled him out. After that, there is a very old earl whom I will be setting my cap for, so do not even attempt to try to capture his interest. Lord Farris is still available, but you will not have much luck there." She paused as she thought of other gentlemen. "You could always steal Lord Deering from Miss Somers or instead go after an almost equal catch in Lord Harding."

The options were seemingly endless, yet Laura could not recount any of the names Eleanor had just spoken. Her mind was too full, and a strange humming had developed in her brain.

Eleanor continued to speak loudly, unaware of Laura's turmoil. "Now then, we must decide where to go two nights from now. We were to attend the harridan's come-out ball but now must decide on a different location."

Laura's heart sank. She had promised Miss Farris she would attend. She spoke off-handedly and effectively hid her feelings. "I thought we should still go to Miss Farris's come-out. You would not want people to think it odd you are not in attendance. Also, most of the eligible gentlemen will be at that ball." Laura did not look at Eleanor, instead looking at the design on her bedding.

Eleanor tilted her head, lost in thought. "Yes," she said slowly, "I do believe you are correct. Are you sure we will be welcome?"

Laura nodded. "Yes. Miss Farris expressed her desire for our attendance, despite the slight altercation."

"All right, I will inform Mother of our plans." She paused on her way out of the door to look in the mirror, saying as if in a trance, "I will be a countess, just you wait."

****

The following day was dreary and wet. Allison had kindly sent over an invitation to accompany her to Bond Street, which was why Laura was waiting to go out in the rain. She would have vastly preferred to remain in her room, but some fresh air would do her good, seeing as she refused to ride. She was not ready to see Lord Farris yet, and she would not be ready until she had come to a decision on his intentions.

All she knew was he was purportedly a rake, and there must be reason that title was thrown around. All his kind gestures did not change the fact that he was a degenerate and had led Lord Deering into a similar lifestyle as well. For now, she had determined he could not be trusted, and many tears later, she still felt the same way.

Allison's carriage stopped in front of the townhouse, and Laura rushed out. The ride to Bond Street was short, and when they arrived, the ladies were amazed at the number of people out shopping. The decision was made to shop and then grab a bite to eat when the restaurants were less busy.

Laura and Allison entered a store and began to peruse a plethora of ribbons. Laura selected a few and asked the shop keeper to wrap them for her. As she waited, Allison asked her, "How is Lord Dunbar?"

Having neglected to tell Allison of the previous day's events, Laura concisely updated her, leaving out the precise gossip about Miss Farris. After all, it was not her secret to tell. She also neglected to mention Lord Farris's unusual behavior.

Allison appeared to be in a state of shock. "How does so much drama happen around you?"

Laura sighed in exasperation. "I wish I knew. Either way, both Eleanor and myself are once again in the market for a husband." She sighed wistfully. "You are so lucky you know. You have the man of your dreams."

"Lord knows how I found a man while both you and Eleanor have not." Allison smiled brightly. "You remember how I mentioned Brandon had been gambling lately?"

Laura nodded. "Yes, I thought you were worried about the situation."

"Yes, well, Brandon told me the most extraordinary story. It would appear Lord Farris has convinced him to avoid gambling."

"And how exactly did he convince him?" she asked

dubiously.

"Just by speaking with him." She spoke drily. "Brandon swears he does not have a gambling problem, but for some unknown reason, Lord Farris thought it necessary to address it."

"That is extraordinary." Allison's news could only mean that Lord Farris had listened to Laura's concerns about his effect on Lord Deering. Oh, why did he have to perpetually do things to further engrave himself in her heart? Her heart began to hammer in her chest. If he had listened to her, did that mean he was more of a gentleman than she was giving him credit for? If so, did that mean she had misjudged him and made a horrible mistake the previous day?

The clerk handed over the wrapped parcel, and the ladies continued on to the next store. Allison needed new undergarments, which this particular shop abounded in. "I think it is interesting how things have progressed between Lord Farris and yourself," Allison casually remarked.

Laura was caught off guard and asked cautiously, "What do you mean?"

"Well, there was the house party. You were sick. He left abruptly and developed a drinking habit. Next he sees you at a ball, monopolizes your attention for a dance, and magically overcomes his drinking problem." She paused to examine the stitching on a chemise. "Next thing I hear is you were seen riding with him in Hyde Park. It almost seems to me that there is more going on than either of you lets on."

How had Allison learned of her rides with Lord Farris? She supposed one of the other riders in the morning had seen them, but did gossip really spread that quickly? What else did the gossips know of her and Lord Farris?

"What else do the gossips know?" she asked suspiciously.

"Oh, not too much more. There is just plenty of speculation." She leaned in and confided, "Once word gets out that Lord Dunbar is out of the picture, everyone will think Lord Farris is next on your agenda. People think you really like viscounts." She laughed at the absurdity. "It also appears you are becoming popular with the men, as they all want to know why both Lord Dunbar and Lord Farris are so interested in you."

"First off, Lord Farris and I are just friends." Laura did not appreciate Allison's dubious look. "Secondly, how do you know all of this?"

She smiled secretly. "Oh I have my ways." Gesturing with her eyes, Allison asked, "Is that not Miss Farris?"

Laura looked in the direction Allison had indicated, and sure enough, it was Miss Farris. Laura extended a greeting, and Miss Farris made her way to their location.

"Good afternoon, Lady Laura, I trust you are in good health?"

"Oh yes." Laura swiftly performed the introductions and asked, "How do you have time to shop with your ball tomorrow?"

Alexa sighed. "I needed a break from all the commotion. Thus, I thought up an excuse and left."

This was very fortunate for Laura, bumping in to Miss Farris like this. "I can understand the need for a break. My breaks are typically in the morning when I ride."

"Like when you rode with Lord Farris?" Allison asked deviously.

Laura sighed. "Yes. He has a habit of accompanying me, not that I encourage him."

Alexa asked casually, "So, you ride often with him?"

Laura looked confusedly at Allison. "I thought it was common knowledge?"

"It is common knowledge that you went riding together, not that it is a frequent event." Allison giggled.

Drat. She would have preferred to keep that secret. It was too late now, and she would have to accept her unwanted admission. At least they did not know of the previous meeting on Bond Street. "We ride every once in a while." That was all they needed to know.

Alexa responded with a twinkle in her eye, "You know my brother has recently changed his views on matrimony." She regarded Laura intently and said, "Mother even gave him my grandmother's ring, and he accepted it. Every time prior to this visit, he had refused the ring."

"I am sure he had a perfectly good reason for that, aside from wanting to marry." She tried valiantly to appear nonchalant, but inwardly, she wanted to scream. What had she done? If Miss Farris were to be believed, she had accused Lord Farris of terrible things when he had truly been proposing matrimony.

Alexa did not respond and turned to accept a package from the clerk. She said her goodbyes and vacated the shop.

Allison was all aflutter about what had developed.

"See! Lord Farris is interested in you! This is exceptional news. Imagine how upset Eleanor would be if you snagged one of the top marriage prospects and she did not." She tittered. Laura had not thought how Eleanor would react, but she doubted it would be happily.

Laura and Allison spent another hour shopping, after which they adjourned for lunch. The restaurants were not as crowded at this point, so they did not wait long for a table. After enjoying a light meal, the ladies departed Bond Street, stopping to drop Laura off at home. They agreed to see each other that evening at the Farris ball.

****

The rest of Laura's evening was uneventful, and in the morning she went to see her modiste. Another dress was finished, one which boasted an extremely daring neckline. The color was a faintly purple color, which showcased her eyes and complemented her complexion exceedingly well.

She returned home to the sight of a single red rose. Her breath caught, and she rushed to pull out the card. Unfortunately, Eleanor had beaten her to it and was standing in the doorway to the parlor with the message firmly in hand.

"Well, well." She smirked at Laura and said, "Haven't we been busy?"

"Hand over the card, Eleanor."

Eleanor threw it to the floor in front of her as her eyes hardened. "So that is why you denied Lord Dunbar. You had Lord Farris lined up to take his place." She scowled darkly. "How you managed to pull that off is anyone's guess."

"So the flower is from Lord Farris?"

"Yes." She regarded Laura briefly, and then smiled. "You will never hold him, you know. He might show an interest now, but he will throw you aside before you ever make it down the aisle. If he proposes, that is."

Laura usually had an exorbitant amount of patience for Eleanor's mood, but she had had enough. "You should keep your comments to yourself. After all, you could not keep Lord Collins entertained."

Eleanor narrowed her eyes, and Laura internally shuddered from the hatred Eleanor sent her. "At least I had his attention based on my own merit. The only attention you receive is from my discarded suitors and gentlemen who must be asked to entertain you." She smirked. "Which is worse I wonder? Knowing you are so unwanted that men only escort you out of obligation, or being second choice?"

Shocked, Laura procured her rose, turned, and walked away as Eleanor's cold laugh accompanied her. She entered her room as the words haunted her. She could have stayed and fought with Eleanor, but what good would it do? Granted, it might have behooved her for future altercations if she had stood up for herself more. She knew Lord Farris had originally escorted her out of obligation, but he was doing so lately of his own choosing, and this rose was proof.

She sighed and sightlessly stared at her rose. Love was supposed to be easy, yet she could not determine what her love's intentions truly were. One did not simply desert a lady and then resurface months later. And if he did, how should Laura interpret that?

She closed her eyes as the memory of his touch

returned. She could almost feel his lips skim across hers, but of course, that was nonsensical. Placing her fingertips to her mouth, she reopened her eyes and sighed. Even in his absence, she could not drag her mind from his addictive touch.

She crossed over to her nightstand, which contained her favorite book, the only tangible link to Lord Farris she possessed. He should not have purchased such a dear gift for her, but did he purchase it as a way to compromise her, or to marry her?

Her fingers slid over the leather-clad volume, and she cringed as the realization hit her that she would not be able to marry any other gentleman than Lord Farris. Even if he did not want her, she would not want any other man. A wave of tiredness overtook her. This love business was exhausting.

The ball was a few hours away, and Laura decided to take advantage of the quiet by taking a nap. She thought of Lord Farris as she drifted into her slumber. Would he be as excited to see her tonight as she was to see him?

Chapter 14

When Laura finally awoke, she noticed it was much later than she had planned on waking. She would have to hurriedly get ready with little help from Anna. She crossed to the vanity, splashed water on her face, and looked in the mirror. Her hair was a mess. She must have had a troubled nap. She applied her touches of makeup and began to undo her serviceable bun.

After tying her hair into a quick chignon with a few tendrils escaping, she pinched her cheeks and stood. All that was left was to dress, and as if on cue, Anna came bustling in. "She is in a mood today."

"Oh yes, I had noticed." Anna helped Laura draw on her new gown. She thanked Anna once everything was in its proper place and exited her room. Lady Ashford and Mrs. Westfield were waiting on her, with Eleanor nowhere to be seen. A loud sound of glass breaking, coupled with Eleanor's shriek, indicated she was not yet ready.

Laura and Mrs. Westfield exchanged glances. They were going to be waiting a while. Eleanor descended the stairs, after a seemingly endless amount of time, and looked perfectly pieced together.

Mrs. Westfield greeted Eleanor as if nothing was amiss, and they promptly left the townhouse. The carriage ride did not take long, and the ladies entered the receiving line. Laura could see Lord Farris, which caused breathless anticipation to overtake her. He had never looked more handsome, outdoing even the Lord Farris in her dreams.

As they reached the Farris family, everyone was greeted warmly with the exception of Eleanor, who was largely ignored. Lord Farris claimed two dances from Laura, and then their arrival was announced. She was shocked to see how many gentlemen swarmed to her. She imagined Allison had been correct. Once one gentleman showed interest, the rest were soon to follow.

She danced under the light of the candlelit room, until Lord Farris approached to claim her for the next. She did not know if she could talk to him, especially when she had not come to a decision on his character.

He bowed. They asked about each other's health, and spoke of other polite nonsense. All attempts at conversation by her were met with noncommittal responses. Their conversation slowly wilted, almost to the point of silence.

His behavior was completely unlike anything she was used to, so she attempted to engage him in chatter. "Your sister is enjoying herself."

No response, except an almost inaudible "Hmm."

"She looks very comfortable here. My first ball was a fright." She had tried her best to hide in a corner the entire night.

Again, he responded with "Hmm."

Growing very annoyed, Laura said, "Oh dear. It appears her dance partner is ravishing your sister on the dance floor." When he did not respond at all, Laura purposefully stepped on his foot. This finally caught his attention.

"Did you just step on my toe?" he asked in surprise.

"Hmm, I had not noticed, my lord," Laura responded, happy to finally have caught his attention.

"I had not thought you capable of such a misstep."

"It is possible that I make the occasional mistake here and there."

His arm tightened on her back as he asked, "Is your corset too tight? I hear that can cause a lady to stumble."

She gasped in outrage and hissed, "How dare you speak of my corset?"

His eyes twinkled, and he smiled at her. "I am just looking after your well-being. The contraption does appear a trifle tight, although it does augment your assets delectably."

That may have been a compliment, but it was not a compliment she would accept, outwardly, at least. She scowled at him and asked, "What do you know of corsets, my lord?"

"More than you would think." He laughed softly.

"I suppose your mistress shows you hers enough." In all honesty, she did not know what a man liked to look at, but corsets were off-limits in polite conversation, so there must be a reason.

He laughed, loudly. "Why, Laura, are you jealous?"

"Of course not!" Laura responded a little too quickly. "Why would I be jealous?"

"Why, indeed?" Lord Farris murmured as the dance came to an end.

Laura was swept away by another gentleman. Lord Farris was lost in the crowd. It had bothered her that he might have a mistress. Why could he not have simply answered her question, so she could know if he did or not?

After several more dances, Laura took a break and appreciated the sight of the beautifully clad people as they whirled about. Her partner for the dance was droning on about his hunting dogs, and she was trying her best to appear as if she was paying attention.

She caught sight of Miss Farris, who was similarly sitting out on the dance and waved her over. Sadly, her partner did not notice her complete lack of attention and continued speaking until Miss Farris reached their side.

"Your come-out appears to be a success," Laura offered as her partner finally realized someone else had joined them. Laura sent him off for a couple of lemonades, which he gladly went to fetch.

"Oh yes, I have been enjoying myself. Mother thinks my ball will be the talk of the town for at least a week," Miss Farris drolly said. They chatted amiably for a short period of time until they were interrupted by Eleanor's arrival.

Eleanor appeared suddenly, surprising the ladies as she stopped in front of them. She first smiled sweetly to Laura and then gave Miss Farris a malicious smirk. A chill descended on Laura, as if a catastrophic event were imminent. She braced herself for what was to come, but prayed she was wrong.

Eleanor loudly coughed, successfully drawing the attention of the surrounding crowd. "Laura, do come away from Miss Farris. She is so very common." She grabbed Laura's arm as if to drag her away.

A loud gasp was audible from the crowd. Laura's ears burned. She should have known Eleanor would not sit by quietly and accept defeat. Eleanor must feel she would somehow win this made-up competition between herself and Miss Farris by ruining Miss Farris's come-out ball.

Miss Farris stood still, as if she were in a panic. Laura, at least, was used to Eleanor's fits of temper and would not sit idly by and watch Eleanor hurt Miss Farris's debut. Laura loudly said with derision, as she pulled her arm away from Eleanor's grasping hands, "You must be mistaken. I have come to consider Miss Farris a personal friend."

Eleanor laughed coldly. "Like that signifies." She turned to the crowd and said loudly, "I believe my maid is more interesting than she."

The crowd laughed, enjoying the scene. Raising an eyebrow, Laura hated to be mean but had to defend Miss Farris. "Perhaps you are mistaken who is common. After all, you apparently enjoy the company of your maid."

Another laugh reverberated among the crowd. Eleanor's eyes widened as she realized her words had been turned against her. She angrily retorted, "At least I know who my father is."

A gasp once again sounded. Every eye around them was glued to Laura to see how she would respond. The barb had been aimed at Miss Farris, but Laura knew she could withstand the gossip better than Miss Farris could. After all, she did have several facial characteristics passed on from her father. "Eleanor, do be serious, I have my paternal grandmother's eyes. Obviously, we do know who my father is."

Alexa gave Laura a grateful look, as Lady Chadwick loudly proclaimed, "Enough. You girls can have your little tiff later. Everyone, as Miss Farris's aunt, I would ask that you help yourself to the champagne the footmen are just now bringing out."

The attention of the crowd slowly left the ladies, and Laura glared at Eleanor, whispering, "What is wrong with you? What could you possibly gain from this behavior?"

Eleanor grinned spitefully in response as Lady Ashford and Mrs. Westfield approached them. "It is time to go, girls," Lady Ashford commanded.

"Oh please, let Lady Laura stay. My aunt will chaperone her, and we will ensure she returns home safe and sound," Miss Farris begged.

She consented readily enough. It was clear Lady Ashford did not care what Laura did at the moment. Lady Ashford and Mrs. Westfield quickly escorted Eleanor from the room. Laura was sure Eleanor's ears would be bleeding soon.

Lady Chadwick reached Laura's and Miss Farris's location. Upon seeing Lady Chadwick, Laura realized the lady was the relation of Lord Farris's she had seen at the Songfeld house party. Lady Chadwick looked quite regal as she gave Laura a nod of approval. "You did well. I would thank you, but I am sure my nephew will do so, more than adequately."

Laura blushed hotly and asked, "What are friends for?"

Lady Chadwick laughed softly. "Do not delude yourself. You may be a friend to Alexa, but not as far as my nephew is concerned. Friends do not make spectacles of themselves, as he has done for you."

Curious, Laura asked, "What are you talking about?"

A look of amusement alighted on Lady Chadwick's countenance. "You do not even know that, on your sickbed, Gavin refused to leave your side? He stayed with you until your fever broke." She laughed, delighted. "Mrs. Westfield was quite put out about the entire affair."

Laura had thought she had dreamt Lord Farris holding her hand when she was sick and delirious. Could it be that he really did wish to marry her?

Lady Chadwick broke through her thoughts. "Oh, there is the boy now. I do believe I had better do something else right now." Then she very obviously turned her back to leave Laura to Lord Farris. Miss Farris, catching the hint, also left Laura's side.

Lord Farris approached with a worried frown marring his face. "Are you all right? I came as soon as I heard what happened." News certainly travelled quickly.

As the adrenaline began to wear off, Laura realized the magnitude of what she had just done. She had openly insulted her cousin in a room full of people. She began to tremble from the sheer excitement of it all. "I doubt your sister will escape all of the gossip. Who knows if what I said helped at all."

"I am sure it will help cast doubts in the minds of the gossips, and the way you dealt with Miss Ashford should discredit her. You did a lot. Thank you."

"Lady Chadwick is supposed to be acting as my chaperone." Laura giggled.

Lord Farris quirked his eyebrow. "She is doing a tremendous job. Would you care to take an unchaperoned walk with me outside?"

She agreed, and he led her out a side door to the

gardens. They followed a secluded path to a gazebo. There were large, fat snowflakes falling slowly down, which made the walk even more secluded from the ballroom full of people. The air was chilly, but she felt warm with Lord Farris there to escort her.

They took a seat in the open gazebo. It was dark, but the light from the ball gave off enough of a glow, allowing them to see around them. Laura shivered again, only this time from the cold. Lord Farris wrapped his arm around her and pulled her snugly to him. He frowned with disapproval.

Laura saw his frown. "Do you like my dress?" She could not help herself.

Lord Farris scowled at her. "I like it too well."

She laughed and said coyly, "I will have to remember that should I need a favor from you."

"You can earn a favor simply by promising to never wear that dress in public again. It is much too distracting."

She smiled brilliantly at him. This must be the charm he was so famous for, finally.

His answering smile quickened her heart. The brilliance of the white snow illuminated his dark looks, drawing her to him as if he were her beacon. Her gaze settled on his lips, and he lowered his head for a kiss. He kissed her as if she were his anchor, and he would be lost without her. Laura responded in earnest and lost all track of herself as a person. She was a slave to the sensations he ignited in her and would not fight it if she wanted.

He pulled her on to his lap, and she let herself get swept away in a dream. A dream that suggested, maybe he really did love her and wanted her to be his. She maneuvered herself until she straddled him with her skirts up around her thighs. She deepened the kiss, feeling very empowered and in control. Thrilling at her boldness, she lightly nibbled his lower lip. An answering growl resonated from Lord Farris. The heat between them was building as Laura wriggled against him. She wanted more of him but did not know what more was.

Lord Farris growled again and fluidly swung Laura up against the gazebo wall without her moving from her straddled position. Her legs were tightly wrapped around his hips, and he firmly pinned her arms above her head. His lips trailed hotly down her neck, but Laura did not approve of the absence of his lips on hers. She had never felt more alive, or more frustrated. "Gavin, please." She moaned, as she writhed, hoping he would kiss her again.

Lord Farris stilled and then stepped back. His sudden absence left Laura bereft and cold. Her nerves were tightly wound in a bundle, just waiting for anything to set them off. Lord Farris cursed and paced, sweeping a hand through his hair.

"Forgive me. I did not intend this to happen."

Setting her skirts to rights, Laura paused. What had he intended then? She was ashamed of her wantonness, but it had at least meant something to her. She asked coldly, "What did you mean to happen?"

He laughed sardonically, "I meant to have a nice chat with you, but I can never seem to keep my hands off you, or say the right thing at the right time. You could have been ruined out here, you know. If we had kept kissing like that…" His voice trailed off.

Laura began to understand. She had been wrong.

He did not want to marry her, after all. She was so stupid. Numbness engulfed her as she gazed at this man that she loved so. "I apologize, my lord. I also had not intended to behave so indecently. Now, if you will excuse me." She began to walk back to the ballroom, the snow falling like pinpricks on her overly sensitive skin. She was so ashamed.

Lord Farris hurried to her side and effectively stopped her by taking hold of her arm. "Please, do not go. You did nothing wrong, and any other time your wantonness would have been very much appreciated."

Keeping her face averted, Laura could not control her expressions and did not want him to see how she felt. Her hopes were shattered, again. "I see no reason to remain. There is nothing here for me."

Lord Farris turned her face to him and exhaled. "Come back to the gazebo."

Laura shook her head, not trusting herself to speak.

Cursing, Gavin glanced at the ground. It was muddy and cold. He placed one knee down and slid his hand down her arm until he was holding her fingertips.

"What are you doing?" Laura asked in a state of shock.

Lord Farris ignored her question and said, "Lady Laura Rosing, from the very first day we met, I fear I have been falling for you. I tried my hardest to forget you, but there is not enough liquor in the kingdom to make me forget you." He paused to draw in a breath. "You have awoken feelings in me I never knew existed. I love you, Laura, with every part of me. The only thing in this world that would make me happy is if you agree to become my wife. Please, Laura darling, will you marry me?"

Laura could not move. She was entrenched in a dream, one where too much movement would destroy it in a puff of smoke. "You do not believe in love or marriage," she managed to squeak out.

Lord Farris smiled at her. "You never can allow things to be simple, can you? I had not wanted to marry and had not believed in love, but then I met you. You have transformed my life in so many ways, I cannot picture a happy existence without you at my side."

"And yet you stayed away for two months," she said accusingly.

"I was not ready for your love then, but I am now." He shifted slightly but his unwavering gaze never left hers.

She breathed in the frigid night air and stated her fears. "I do not believe we will suit. With other gentlemen, I do not care if they have mistresses. With you, I would die to hear you were with another woman."

"I do not have a mistress, nor will I ever be unfaithful to you. I love you, Laura, and only you."

She looked at him. It all sounded perfect. Almost too good…She stopped her train of thought abruptly. What was wrong with her? The love of her life was proclaiming his love for her and asking for her hand in marriage. She had no reason to doubt him and was not about to let her insecurities win. Smiling down at him, her heart soared as she simply said, "Yes."

Lord Farris grinned, regained his footing, and swept her into his arms. "Do me a favor," he asked as he placed her back on the ground, still holding her close.

Laura felt as if she would do anything for him in

this moment. "Of course."

"Dance with me." He pulled her even closer as they swayed to the barely audible music drifting from the ballroom. The snow fell around them, but Laura was no longer cold. Not as long as he was with her.

Their dance came to an end, and she looked into his eyes. "What happens now?"

He laughed. "Again with the obvious questions."

She scowled and then stomped her foot. "I do not ask obvious questions."

"They seem awfully obvious to me," he responded in a matter-of-fact manner.

"I think I shall be the judge of that."

He let go of her and began to lead her away. "We go announce our news to the world."

She gazed at him, the love shining brightly from her. "I do not believe I said so, but I love you, Gavin Farris."

He smirked. "I know. You told me when you were sick."

She wanted so badly to hit him right now, but it would be terribly ill-mannered of her to hit her fiancé right after he proposed. Instead, she said haughtily, "I doubt my father will approve of you."

"And there she is, my prickly princess." He smiled when she swatted his arm. "I do not know why you think he would disapprove of my offer. My stallion is of most excellent stock."

At this, Laura giggled. "You already asked him?" Without waiting for a response, she said, "He always said you can judge a man's character by his horse."

He held out his arm. "Shall we go in then? It is rather chilly out here." He looked down suggestively at her décolletage.

"Yes, could you not have chosen a warmer location for this?"

"I am not the one who refused to return to the gazebo," he pointed out mildly, as he escorted her through a door. He quickly found a linen closet, and they both dried themselves of the melted snow. "Shall we return and share our news? A ball is a great place to announce an engagement."

Laura agreed and placed her arm on his proffered one as they walked to the ballroom. They entered the room just as Lord Dunbar called out loudly from the staircase. He commanded the room's attention, which allowed Gavin and Laura to enter unnoticed.

"I have some most exciting news," Lord Dunbar said loudly as Lady Robbins stepped to his side. "Lady Robbins has just consented to become my wife." He smiled lovingly to her and the crowd cheered.

Laura spoke quietly. "We cannot announce our engagement now. It would be very unkind to steal their moment." She clapped her hands together excitedly. "I am just so glad to see they will marry. Just think if Lady Robbins had not bribed me, I may have been the one announcing my engagement to Lord Dunbar tonight."

"I would have never allowed that," he said flatly.

"Just how do you imagine you could have stopped it?" He was so very sure of himself.

Bringing her hand to his lips, he ran a seductive kiss across her knuckles, which caused an alarming amount of desire to shoot through her. "I would have simply compromised you, darling." As he smiled a catlike smile, Laura knew he would have succeeded if it had come to that. "Speaking of your ruin, when will our wedding be?"

Laura had never cared to have an elaborate society wedding, but she still wanted a quaint, family affair, which took time to prepare. "I think at a minimum I will require six weeks to prepare everything."

"I will give you a choice, either we go to Gretna Green now, or we wed once the banns have been read."

To think she was to experience a lifetime of his overbearing ways. The idea of eloping was appealing, but she did not want that sort of scandal unless absolutely necessary. "Fine," She answered begrudgingly, "Three weeks it is."

Chapter 15

The following weeks were a whirlwind of activity. Laura tried to compile a trousseau in that time, figure out every detail of the wedding, and get fitted for the perfect dress. It was exhausting, but she had help in the form of Miss Farris and Mrs. Westfield.

Eleanor and Lady Ashford were of no use, as they had departed for the country a few days after the Farris ball. While it would have been preferable for Eleanor to confront the gossip about her, it ended up being far more reasonable for her to take a break from the season. She had attended a ball the following evening and managed to offend an earl after making a disparaging comment about his attire. Rather than hope Eleanor would start to behave herself, Lady Ashford instead made her take a break until the gossip abated. Laura hated to admit it, but she would not miss her cousin's presence at the wedding.

Every morning, Gavin accompanied her on her ride in Hyde Park. The groom was soon used to disappearing for short periods of time, which allowed Laura to become more skilled at kissing. She was very much looking forward to her wedding night, as the kissing was not fulfilling and led to many restless nights where she wondered what was in store for her.

Finally her wedding day arrived, which was a sunny, albeit, cold day, the perfect sort of day for a winter wedding. Anna helped her bathe, then elaborately styled Laura's hair.

She had decided to use the amethysts from the gown she wore at the Mansor ball on her wedding dress. Her gown made her look virginal, yet still had a seductive aspect due to the amount of cleavage displayed. She heartily approved of the cleavage, as it would drive Gavin to distraction. Not that she expected his full attention today. He had been showing more and more anxiety as the wedding day had drawn near, although he insisted it was a nervousness of happiness and not of regret.

The carriage pulled away from the house, and Laura gazed wistfully out the window. There were many details of her day that she was missing or she would forget. Everything was happening so quickly, but all that mattered were the words stated at the altar in the church.

Her father helped her down from the carriage, and her throat constricted as a tear formed in his eye.

"I am so proud of you, darling." He smiled reassuringly at her. "You have chosen a fine man."

"Thank you, Father, I quite agree," she responded with conviction.

Extending his arm, he asked, "Well then, shall we? I believe everyone is waiting for you."

Laura agreed and was escorted in to the church. The chapel was demurely decorated in a plethora of roses. The scent reminded Laura of the house party where she had first met Gavin, and she decided that scent would always represent their love. Gavin stood patiently at the altar with a serious member of the clergy. Her soon-to-be husband was dressed in unrelieved black, except for a pristine white waistcoat. He looked utterly handsome, which left Laura spellbound.

The guests were small in number, mostly family, but with a few exceptions. Lord Collins had journeyed back from the country to act as Gavin's best man. Lord Collins had expressed his sincere happiness for Gavin but had vowed to stay away from any marriage-minded ladies at the wedding.

Lord Deering was in attendance, having escorted Allison along with her chaperone. Allison had almost fainted when Laura had told her the news of her impending marriage to Gavin. Allison swore she had seen it coming a mile away.

Laura was transfixed by Gavin as she walked down the aisle. Not a shred of doubt crossed her mind, as she realized this was the single most important choice she had ever made. Soon she stood next to him, and the vicar performed the ceremony. Neither of them heard the words the clergyman said, until it was their turn to recite the vows. Having noticed neither the bride nor the groom were paying attention, the vicar had politely coughed to interrupt their thoughts before continuing. They recited the vows, and Gavin slipped his grandmother's ring onto Laura's finger. It fit perfectly, and Laura was awed by its beauty. A more ideal ring could not have been ordered for her.

The vicar ordered the groom to kiss his bride. Gavin bent over and swept a sweet kiss across Laura's lips. There would be time for a more thorough exploration later on, but she was pleased to have experienced her first kiss as a married woman.

The assembled crowd cheered as Gavin swept her

into his arms and made his way to his carriage. They would attend a customary wedding breakfast at Lord Rosing's townhouse, but once that was complete, Gavin would have unfettered access to his wife.

Laura wanted nothing more than to skip the wedding breakfast and get on with the evening's events. She would never be so wanton as to actually suggest it to Gavin, instead she said dreamily, "This has been such a perfect morning. I never imagined when we first met, that I would someday be married to you."

"I never did either." He laughed ironically. "I never imagined I would marry anyone at all."

She smirked. "Especially the poor relation you pestered at the house party?"

He raised his eyebrow haughtily. "Pester? I do not believe that is how matters progressed." He pulled her onto his lap and eyed her cleavage with delight. "Should I demonstrate what my pestering actually entails?"

Laura gulped at the suggestive look he was giving her. "I think it best you do not. We have to attend this breakfast, and I would prefer to do so with my hair properly assembled."

"I cannot say that your hair will remain intact, which means I must make a choice." He rapped on the roof of the carriage and yelled, "Take us home."

Laura could not believe her ears. "What are you doing?"

"What did I tell you about obvious questions? If I cannot mess up your hair and then take you to the breakfast, I will simply skip the breakfast." He kissed her passionately. "By the time I am through with you, you will forget entirely that a breakfast even existed."

Laura could believe that, based on the one kiss alone. She was not going to argue with him, either. Intertwining her arms around his neck, she smiled. "Very well, my lord, do your worst."

And Gavin did.

A word about the author…

Naomi Boom is an author with a newly-discovered love for writing. Her inspiration struck when she was searching for the perfect historical romance novel to read. Nothing sounded appealing, so she decided she would write her own. That one novel has morphed into a series, and hopefully many, many more.

She currently resides in Kansas with her family but has her eyes firmly planted on an acreage in eastern South Dakota. Once her husband retires from the United States Army, they will return to her home state.

~*~

Visit Naomi Boom at:
www.naomiboom.com
Twitter: @naomimboom
Facebook: Facebook.com/naomimboom

Thank you for purchasing
this publication of The Wild Rose Press, Inc.

If you enjoyed the story, we would appreciate your
letting others know by leaving a review.

For other wonderful stories,
please visit our on-line bookstore at
www.thewildrosepress.com.

For questions or more information
contact us at
info@thewildrosepress.com.

The Wild Rose Press, Inc.
www.thewildrosepress.com

Stay current with The Wild Rose Press, Inc.

Like us on Facebook

https://www.facebook.com/TheWildRosePress

And Follow us on Twitter
https://twitter.com/WildRosePress